33^1/$_3$

Mark Moore

$33^1/_3$

Mark Moore

Cover Design by Julia Midgley

Map by Rosie Collins

Does the silkworm expend her yellow labours
For thee? For thee does she undo herself?
Are lordships sold to maintain ladyships
For the poor benefit of a bewitching minute?...

The Revenger's Tragedy
Thomas Middleton

CHAPTERS

1. LP

It was either the Beatles or the Rolling Stones. You had to choose one or the other. You couldn't like both, Camo explained. 'In the 1960s it was like that.'

'But they're both good,' Rosie said. 'Giants. Legends. Massive.'

'Looking back we can see that now. But it wasn't clear at the time,' Camo went on. 'That's what my grandad says.'

It wasn't the music really, Camo said. 'Nor any real differences in the music. After all, the Beatles were doing I Wanna Hold Your Hand and She Loves You. My grandad said they were tuneful ditties indistinguishable from the crap Cliff Richard was doing. And while the Rolling Stones' songs had a bit more muscle they were just cover versions of Chuck Berry songs. They didn't write anything themselves. So you couldn't say there were any great cultural and creative differences in their music at that time. I'm talking about the early days, when they both first broke onto the scene.'

It wasn't the music, Camo said again, that made them opposites. 'It was what they represented. It was Zoroastrian.'

'What does that mean?' Rosie asked. 'It's a bit over-philosophical. Have you turned French?'

Camo smiled at the idea. 'That was the word grandad Jim used. This was all a while ago, as you know. I used to ask him about those times a lot. I looked it up at the time. He meant you had to choose either the Beatles or the Rolling Stones because essentially it was a universal conflict between Light and Dark.'

Rosie frowned and tilted her head. She looked obliquely at Camo. Her look said you are precariously in danger of being exposed to people talking crap. In a way the tilt was worse than the look. The tilt said explain yourself or else.

'Jim said your mum would like the Beatles,' Camo said. 'Even your gran wouldn't be horrified. Jim said that was all part of Epstein's package. Brian Epstein was their manager.'

'I know that. Everyone knows that.'

'He wanted to make them unthreatening. With their floppy basin haircuts and their quirky but conformist suits they looked like they were *safe*.' Camo stressed the word. 'For Epstein safety meant success. Safety meant money. Sure they looked like scrubbed-up street urchins. But above all they were safe street urchins. Oliver Twist not the Artful Dodger.'

'And the Rolling Stones weren't *safe*?' Rosie's echo of Camo's stress on the word was all ironic.

'Exactly. You could bring the Beatles home. They looked like they'd help your granny cross the road. There's no way you could bring the Rolling Stones home. And that was the point. You either liked a group your parents didn't mind, or you liked a group your parents hated. Zoroastrian. Light and Dark. Remember, it's not me. It's my grandad Jim. He was there. And he always said that very soon it got to the stage where your parents hated them all anyway. Even the Beatles. So then it was no longer Zoroastrian. It was just generational. It wasn't Light and Dark any more. It was New-is-Good and Old-is-Bad. And both sides were happy with that.'

Rosie frowned again, but it was less than before. And the tilt was gone.

'That's what my grandad says. And he was there.'

In fact Camo's grandad was more than there. He was the 60s. And Camo didn't say that his paternal grandad thought his own band, Dr Edge, or the Dredge as aficionados had it, was better than either the Beatles or the Stones. The grandad, Jim Lyly, known later in his solo career as Dredge Lyly, was lead guitarist with Dr Edge.

To be fair, Dredge Lyly wasn't alone in that opinion. Many cultural and music critics thought Dr Edge was not only musically better than both the Beatles and the Stones, but were more culturally important.

Unfortunately the band didn't kick on into the 1970s to leave a series of live and recorded masterworks to prove this contention. All five members of the band bar one were killed in an air crash flying out of Chicago on the band's third American tour.

It was just another in the calamitous series of popular music disasters of the 20th century.

Dredge Lyly was the only survivor.

He survived because he missed the flight.

He missed the flight because he was stoned out of his head on acid. No one knew where he was. Neither did Dredge.

On the plane they talked about sacking Lyly. He was high-maintenance, they all agreed on that, all four of them. This had been coming for a while. It wasn't going to stop. But deep down they also knew they couldn't sack him. He was lead guitarist, one of the best around, that gave the band its distinctive sound – 'like a freight train braking hard on diamond rails but not slowing down' - as one critic described it. He also wrote their best songs. They couldn't sack him. But they sacked him anyway. Then the plane crashed. Dredge following on the next flight two hours behind never knew they sacked him.

It was 1971. Two years after Armstrong and Aldrin landed on the Moon. Two years after the Beatles began to split up. Two years after Hendrix died. Two years after Dr Edge had taken Woodstock by storm.

The year before, in 1970, Dr Edge's live album, Open The Gates, taken from their second US tour, went gold and topped the charts on both sides of the Atlantic.

They were in the university bar smoking roll-ups and drinking lager. Camo Lyly and Rosie Stevin, undergraduates.

For four years after the crash nothing was heard of Jim Lyly. Then in 1975 he came out of retirement and took the music world by storm again as a solo artist. Dredge Lyly he called himself.

After the crash it seemed that Lyly had disappeared. That was as far as the record-buying public was concerned. But he hadn't. He was still very much there in the music business, but behind the scenes. Between the crash in 1971 and his emergence in 1975 as the major blues-rock solo artist Dredge Lyly, Jim Lyly became one of the most highly prized and sought-after sessions-men in the business. There wasn't a significant rock or blues track laid down on both sides of the Atlantic between 1971 and 1975 that didn't have Jim Lyly on it somewhere as lead guitarist or second lead. Many of these tracks were laid down without public acknowledgement of Lyly's input. He wanted it that way. But the men and women, and it was mostly men, who mattered in the industry knew all about him and his inestimable value to a song.

Everyone wanted that sound of 'a locomotive braking hard on diamond rails' that only Lyly could get out of a guitar. That phrase about a locomotive on diamond rails became famous, and the critic who wrote it in an early piece in the NME went on to carve out a career as one of the foremost popular music critics of the day. Others went further – if over the top – in their efforts to write memorable descriptions of Lyly's distinctive style. 'A beam engine raising mercury in titanium pails' wrote one. Another had it: 'A steam hammer forging steel in an underground redoubt.'

'What the hell's a redoubt?' Jim Lyly said in response to that one. And 'Bollocks to titanium pails. What's wrong with buck-ets?' Lyly himself never sought to define the sound he got from a guitar. In a way he believed that the more he analysed it the less distinctive it would become. He left the analysis to the analysts. Either way, nearly all the analyses, similes and metaphors about Lyly's guitar playing style had metal of some kind in the descrip-tion somewhere.

However it was analysed and whoever described it, every-one agreed Jim Lyly was one of the best.

Another reason why Dr Edge were thought to have a sound far ahead of their time was they had two lead guitarists. Jim Lyly was joined very early on in the band's career by Felix Fairfax. They did this way before any other band did it. Even Fleetwood Mac – famous for having three lead guitarists - didn't try it until Dr Edge had led the way. Some critics and observers thought Fairfax better in some ways even than Lyly. Not live, perhaps, but on some of the band's studio work Fairfax seemed to be able to give more to a track than Lyly could, especially when it was a song that Lyly hadn't written himself.

The standard line-up in those days was drums, bass, lead guitar and rhythm guitar – the Beatles were a classic exemplar of that kind of line-up. A five-man band such as the Stones would add a singer. Dr Edge did it differently. They had drums, bass, two lead guitars and a singer.

It created a much deeper and more distinctive sound. Quite soon other bands tried to emulate the Dr Edge line-up and brought in a second lead guitar. But in most cases it wasn't a success. The addition of a second lead guitar seemed to dampen rather than augment the first lead. That was probably because whatever combinations they tried none of them were as good as Jim Lyly and Felix Fairfax.

And another reason why Dr Edge were way ahead of any other band at the time was nothing to do with the distinctive sound they made. It was purely to do with the fact that Felix Fairfax was a woman.

As one critic observed: 'It takes four blokes and a bird to make the best sounds on the planet.'

Camo knew there was something mysterious and tragic about Felix Fairfax. She had disappeared immediately prior to the band's third and last US tour. He'd often been told about the emergency by his mother and father and by his grandmother.

Felix Fairfax had walked out on the band, it seemed just at the height of their success. Some said she was dead. Others were convinced she was hiding out in a remnant hippy commune somewhere. Others said she had joined a cult, a religious sect in the wilds. The wilds in question were always deep in the South American jungle, or in a hidden monastery lurking on the Tibetan plateau, or in some remote oasis in the heart of the Sahara desert.

Wherever she was, it was assumed she'd gone because she couldn't take the pressure anymore. The pressure of maintaining such a high peak of music perfection was always ready to strike at shy and sensitive souls whose talent had thrust them up into the greedy, unforgiving spotlight. They hadn't thought it would be like that and they weren't ready for it or couldn't adapt. Some of them didn't even want to be famous.

'No matter how good you are, the treadmill always gets you in the end,' one journalist wrote. 'And perhaps the better you are, the more likely you are to fall off.'

Camo had been told all about the desperate search for a replacement to join the band on the big US tour. Eventually, just before they were getting ready to cancel all the American gigs, Pram Johnson walked out of his own band and took Felix's place on the tour.

The loss of Fairfax in the line-up seemed to affect Jim Lyly more than the rest.

In some ways it made him a better player; in other ways he was worse. Whatever it was, all critics agreed that Dr Edge, while still the best of the best, weren't quite as good without Felix Fairfax as they'd been with her in the band.

Camo sometimes wondered if Fairfax was still alive? Was it really that possible to just disappear?

'How is he? Your grandad?' Rosie asked.

'Not good,' Camo replied. 'A lot of the time he doesn't know who I am. Other times he doesn't remember in the afternoon that he's seen me in the morning or vice versa.'

'Has it got worse?'

'Yes definitely. The afternoon's better than other times. That's when I go. When he's been playing. Mostly.'

Jim – Dredge – Lyly was in a nursing home. It was an exclusive upmarket nursing home in West Sussex high up on the Downs with a sea view. Lyly after all was a wealthy man. But it was a still a nursing home. He still had to be looked after, because Lyly was not capable of looking after himself. He was only in his late 70s yet the mind-destroying disease had begun to bite when he was fairly young. Some commentators, with more than a hint of I-told-you-so and what-do-you-expect about them wondered whether his lifestyle of decades of drink and drugs had engendered the problem at such an usually early age.

It was possible, certainly; who knew? But it may have been genetic, or completely random, brought on by nothing at all. It could have just happened. But whatever the reasons that Lyly's memory and mental facilities were much impaired, his guitar playing was almost as good as ever. It was still the unstoppable freight train braking hard on diamond rails.

Camo would visit as often as he could. Sometimes he would spend hours there in silence as his grandad finger-picked his way through one of his famous solos. He played both his Fender Stratocaster and his Gibson Les Paul without the amp, the nurses demanded that for the wellbeing of the other residents. It still sounded good to Camo. Often in summer they let him hook up the twin Marshall amps and let him play away under the beech tree at the bottom of the long garden. He connected to one of the modified garden lights for a power source. Everyone noticed that after a session playing the guitar Dredge's mental capabilities seemed to strengthen and even come back for a while. It seemed to bring back some of his memories. Those were the times he knew who Camo was. Sometimes then he even seemed to know who he was himself.

Camo came most often. He was at university in London and could easily take the train out to West Sussex. Other members of the family came to a certain extent. Camo's step-sisters – one by each of Dredge's first and third wives – came when they could. But they were living further away. Dredge's son Vinny – real name Vinyl – Camo's dad - came regularly for a while, but then he died of a heart attack a few months ago.

We are quite a family for strange names, Camo thought.

Camo's dad had been christened Vinyl Strat Lyly by his own dad Jim Lyly. His aunt, Vinny's sister, had been christened Donna Wahwah Lyly. Quite reasonably, Camo thought, his aunt hated her middle name and never used it. While his dad hated all his names.

'Why couldn't Jim and Sylvia call us some normal names, for god's sake?' he'd complained to Camo in the pub once, a while before his last and fatal heart attack. 'They all did it, didn't they, that generation. Thought they were changing the world. And all they ended up doing was changing normal Christian names to bloody stupid ones. At least your name is just a nickname. You don't have to use it if you don't like it.'

Vinyl Strat Lyly had called himself Vin or Vinny for as long as he could remember. So much so people couldn't believe he wasn't Vincent. It never occurred to anybody he'd have such a stupid name as Vinyl.

'At least your aunt's got one name she can reasonably use. I've got none.'

Look on bright side, Camo told his dad. 'Vinny's a pretty good name. You could have ended up being called Moon Unit.'

In fact Camo did like his nickname. His real name was Archer. Not Archibald, nor Archie, but Archer. In the old days he always called himself Arch, because at least that was fairly normal and didn't need correcting or explaining. He got tired of explaining that it was Archer and it wasn't Archie and it wasn't Archibald. It wasn't as bad as Vinyl Strat. But it still wasn't that normal.

They called him Camo at school because he kept hiding. He kept hiding because as a grandson of a famous – and notorious – celebrity, one of the rock giants in music credibility and one of the rock legends in terms of excessive behaviour, he was always being compared favourably and unfavourably to his grandad. He too was assumed to be a libertine and wastrel and the first and last occupant of Edge City and so somehow must have genetic knowledge of all the worst aspects of the human condition. In response he just hid as much as he could. He hid in the school grounds. He hid behind the bike shed. He even hid in the lavatories. So they christened him 'Camo' on account of his ability to camouflage himself and hide and be undiscovered and merge into the background. In many ways he preferred it to his real name. He got used to it.

'Are you seeing him tomorrow?' Rosie slid her empty plastic pint mug across the low table. She stood up. 'Same again?'

'Yes. Not sure when yet. There's something I want to do first. Yes please.'

He delved in his British army Second World War vintage khaki canvas backpack. He brought out a thick leaflet, so thick it was almost a book, and plonked it on the table in front of them.

Samuel Trellis & Daughters it said on the front in large black letters, with *Auctioneers* underneath the name. Then underneath that it said *Auction: Pop, Blues & Rock Memorabilia 1960s & 1970s.*

Rosie sat down and picked up the leaflet

'See page 39.'

She flicked through the pages. Page 39 had a long list of items under various lot numbers. She looked quizzically at Camo without saying anything.

'Page 39. Lot 39. The gold disc. I want to buy it.'

2. LOT 39

The gold disc in question wasn't just any old gold disc. It was The Gold Disc. It was the one and only gold disc Dr Edge had obtained in their short, tragic but stellar career. It was for their album Open The Gates selling over one million copies. It had ended up selling a lot more than a million copies. But the first million was a major landmark.

There were actually two gold discs for Open The Gates. The first, calendar wise, was for sales of over one million in the UK. The second was for one million, well over one million, for sales in the USA. The UK disc was considered the prime disc, the sought-after collector's item. The USA one was considered an also-ran, an afterthought publicity stunt.

Whether there were one or two gold discs depended on the record company. Some had a gold disc, just one, for total sales worldwide of over one million. So one million sales, one gold disc. Others did it differently. One gold disc per major market. A lot of the time it depended on who was running the company and how publicity hungry they were. In this case the American record company couldn't resist issuing a gold disc, especially as sales rapidly ran well over the one million mark in the USA. After the initial frantic take-up in both countries, sales in the USA moved into areas of much bigger totals than they did in the UK. Issuing the gold disc in the USA was done almost certainly against the wishes of the parent company back in London. Their own gold disc, issued four months earlier, was always thought of as the prime one, and the US one considered a spoiler, an uncalled-for also-ran, a kind of fake.

Camo knew that his grandad had the British version, the prime. He took it from the recording company in London after the plane crash when sales had boomed then just as rapidly plummeted. A couple of years after the crash they couldn't give it away fast enough.

It had been hung on the wall in Dredge Lyly's recording studio in the country house in the woods south of Haslemere. It was now in storage somewhere on a nearby industrial estate. It had gone like everything else, and the mansion sold, shortly after everyone close to Dredge Lyly realised he wouldn't be coming out of the nursing home.

The one being auctioned, it seemed, was the USA version. The afterthought, the back-up, and even when it was made, the relatively unwanted gold disc.

Camo knew the disc had no inherent value in itself. It wasn't made of gold. It was a normal vinyl disc with a gold wash on it. A gold-painted disc. Some said you could actually play a gold disc. They weren't valuable, they were for display purposes. And to mark a remarkable event. Sales of over one million copies. It marked the first million.

They were mounted in display cases and put on a wall. Often, and usually at first, this would be on the walls of the recording company's head office. Later they could show up anywhere. They tended to end up in the possession of one or other of the band members. It usually meant something more to them than to anyone else.

The auction of pop memorabilia, focussing on the 1960s and 1970s, would be held in Samuel Trellis & Daughters auction rooms on London's Farringdon Road, north from Blackfriars Bridge, between Fleet Street and the slope where Ludgate Hill rises up to the great grey-white dirty hemispherical blancmange of the dome of St Pauls.

It was the day after Camo had shown Rosie the auction brochure. The first thing he'd done after that was to source the money.

Camo Lyly had a trust fund. This had been established for him at birth by his grandfather Dredge Lyly. In theory he was a very wealthy student, among the most wealthy twenty-two year olds in the country. Trouble was he couldn't access that money without other people's permission until he was thirty.

He'd talked to Laura, his mother, on the phone. She was head trustee of the trust fund. Also on the trustee committee were Sylvia, who was Camo's grandmother and Dredge Lyly's second wife, and Robert Rogers, the son of Dr Edge's first manager Rod Rogers. Dr Edge bandleader (self-styled) Danny Weathervane had sacked Rogers and appointed money-man Lionel 'the Lion' Azmoun as the band's manager as soon as they became famous and the money started rolling in. But Dredge Lyly had broken ties with the Lion after the plane crash and gone back to Rogers, and both Rogers father and son had been Dredge's managers and friends ever since.

As chairperson Laura could authorise withdrawals from the trust fund on Camo's behalf of up to £5,000 without referral to the rest of the committee.

As soon as he explained what he wanted the money for, Laura agreed immediately to withdraw £5,000 and have it transferred to his bank account.

'If it's any more than that you're buggered, I'm afraid,' she said.

Camo said he hoped it wouldn't be. It was after all not the UK one, the sought-after collector's item.

Camo found the address on Farringdon Road, not far from Holborn Viaduct. He took a seat near the back of the large hall. Already most of the seats were full. A quick look round told him he was by far the youngest person there. A man approached and asked him his interest. He explained he was interested in buying one of the items. The man looked down his nose at him over the top of his half-moon reading glasses, as if to say what money have you got to spend here, sonny? This is way out of your league. Nevertheless he registered Camo's name and address and issued him with the latest version of the auction catalogue. He also handed him a kind of wooden paddle like a miniature cricket bat. Lift it, the man said, wave it about, when you want to make a bid. 'Keep waving it until the auctioneer has acknowledged you and your bid. Wouldn't do to miss out would it.' His tone implied the exact opposite. Camo guessed he imagined Camo would cause a scene by making a bid then not have to funds to actually buy the item. He moved away. As he did Camo was sure he was shaking his head.

No that wouldn't do at all, Camo thought. He practised waving the bat around, then felt silly, and stopped.

The hubbub of conversation diminished as the auctioneer emerged from a back room and stood behind the lectern desk on a dais in the middle of the far end of the hall.

The auctioneer smacked his gavel, a wooden disc held in his hand, onto a similar wooden disc fixed on the lectern top. There was a sharp clack sound and the room fell to silence.

'Good morning ladies and gentlemen. Welcome to Samuel Trellis & Daughters auction rooms. Today's business is pop, blues and rock memorabilia from the 1960s and 1970s.' His voice had the smooth assurance of someone used to doing their job. 'Please refer to your catalogues. Let us begin.' He slapped the disc down hard again. 'Page one lot one…'

It took longer than Camo expected.

It was a combination of putting the real items on display allied to a Powerpoint presentation. Functionaries emerged from the store rooms at the back of the hall behind the auctioneer carrying the items as each lot was called and placed them on tables next to the auctioneer's lectern. Heads bent down as the punters studied the item and the description in the catalogue. At the same time the auctioneer ran a Powerpoint presentation of the item on a large screen above and behind him on the wall. He went through the item's description, its provenance, its meaning and importance, and whether it might make a useful addition to any collection. He then named a starting price and called for bids.

Some items attracted intense bidding. Others not so much. A pair of Elton John's outlandish glasses went for what Camo thought was the astonishingly high sum of £9,900. One of Jimmy Page's guitars went even higher. Others failed to meet their starting bids and were withdrawn, presumably to have another go another day Camo thought. A signed copy of John Lennon's *A Spaniard in the Works* failed to attract sufficiently high bids to meet its reserve price and was withdrawn. A piece of Jimi Hendrix's spat out chewing gum – now in a sealed Perspex boxed container complete with signed provenance - raised nothing more than a susurrus of laughter round the room. A large glass stoppered and sealed jar of mud – now dried powdery earth – from the field of Yasgur's farm during the 1969 Woodstock event went for over £1,000.

It was a motley collection. Guitars. Clothes. Shoes and boots. Books. Instruments. Signed autographs. Letters. Photographs. Rare albums. Original artwork for sleeve designs. At one point interested parties were invited to join the auctioneer in the yard behind the hall to inspect a particular lot, a Rolls Royce once owned by Keith Moon and supposedly driven by him into a hotel swimming pool. Back inside the hall the auctioneer brought the car up on screen and bidding began.

Despite his fascination the event became surprisingly dull and repetitious. Camo was falling asleep when eventually the auctioneer suddenly clacked his gavel and announced, 'Page 39. Lot 39. A gold disc.'

Immediately an image of a gold disc reflecting the light brightly behind glass in a black wooden case flashed up on the screen on the wall. At the same time a functionary emerged from the back store room and carried out the disc in its black display case and propped it up on the table.

'Ladies and gentlemen what you see is one of the two gold discs awarded to legendary band Dr Edge for their one and only million-selling album Open The Gates. As many of you here will know, issuing two gold discs for a million sales is a relatively rare event. Dr Edge were one of the seminal groups of the epoch-marking, in music terms, late 1960s and early 1970s. They almost single-handedly defined the sound of early rock music. And are consequently now thought of as one of the most influential bands of all time.' In a rare personal aside the auctioneer added, 'Open The Gates is one of my own personal favourites.'

'Before we start it must be acknowledged that this is the lesser of the two known gold discs awarded to Dr Edge for sales of this album. This is the American version. A curio in itself. The whereabouts of the prime disc, the version cut in Britain, are currently unknown.'

Camo could tell him the whereabouts of that disc, but he kept silent.

The auctioneer clacked his gavel. 'The bidding starts at five hundred pounds.'

Immediately a man on the far left side of the room to Camo flashed his bat.

'Do I have six hundred?'

A number of people in the auditorium simultaneously flashed their paddles. The auctioneer deemed that one had flashed first and aimed his gavel at him. He then looked quizzically at another of the simultaneous bidders, a middle-aged woman.

'The bid stands at six hundred pounds.'

The woman raised her bat.

So the bidding continued. Some bidders stayed in for a while, then dropped away. Meanwhile as the bid level increased new bidders came in.

By the auctioneer's keen but slightly bemused expression the bid, now up to one thousand pounds, had gone well beyond the initial expectation.

'One thousand one hundred,' the auctioneer said, acknowledging a raised bat from the centre of the floor.

'One thousand two hundred,' the auctioneer said looking to the back of the room. Camo turned his head to look obliquely behind him in time to see a young blonde haired woman lower her bat. That was her first bid.

'One thousand three hundred,' the auctioneer pointed to a desk at the right side of the room where a man on the phone had just raised his bat. Camo thought it was the first bid from telephone man too.

'Can I get one thousand four hundred?'

Camo raised his bat, feeling very self-conscious as heads turned to look at him. It was his first bid.

It went on.

The bidding settled down to a battle between the four constant late-entry bidders. The man over on left side of the room dropped out at two thousand two hundred pounds. The young blonde woman standing at the back of the room made her last bid at two thousand nine hundred pounds. The man on the phone trumped that at three thousand pounds; and Camo outbid that at three thousand one hundred.

Finally it was between Camo and telephone man, the anonymous bidder on the phone via the table on his right. They battled and traded bids up to the four thousand pound mark. Camo was silently urging and willing his anonymous opponent to drop out.

The whole room was silent, breathless. The auctioneer couldn't believe what was happening. The disc was not worth this much.

'Four thousand six hundred pounds,' the auctioneer pointed his gavel at the desk on the right. 'On you sir,' he said now looking at Camo. 'Do you give me four thousand seven hundred?'

'Four thousand seven hundred?' he repeated.

There was utter silence and stillness in the room. All heads were turned to Camo He felt cornered and out of his depth. He thought of his grandad, bewildered with his mind gone. Yet he had created this thing whose sales symbol they were bidding for, the album Open The Gates, one of the great works of art of the twentieth century. Feeling desperate with a tightness in his chest but with a new certainty he raised his bat one more time. It was the least he could do.

'Four thousand seven hundred!' The auctioneer triumphed. He actually sounded pleased.

He pointed his gavel in the direction of the table on the right with the man on the phone. 'Over to you sir in New York, the bid stands now at four thousand seven hundred pounds.'

The man whispered rapidly into the phone. He seemed to be urging what was presumably his client to stay in the hunt. There was silence as the man listened intently to the phone. He sucked his teeth. Finally he looked up and across to the auctioneer and shook his head.

'Four thousand seven hundred pounds. Lot 39. Anyone else'

The auctioneer raised his gavel.

'Four thousand seven hundred pounds,' he repeated. 'Last time. Four thousand seven hundred pounds.'

He paused. The wait dragged on. Camo was staring rigidly at the wooden disc held high in the auctioneer's right hand willing it to descend, strike the receiver and end the torture.

Suddenly he brought it down. There was a loud clack. 'Sold. Four thousand seven hundred pounds, to the gentleman in the denim jacket,' and pointed in Camo's direction.

Camo breathed again. His forehead felt it was bursting out of his skull and his chest hurt with tension.

The rest was easy. He gave his bank details to the accountant at Samuel Trellis & Daughters. He arranged the bank transfer by phone. The functionaries wrapped the gold disc in bubble wrap, folded it in old-fashioned brown kraft paper and knotted white string lengthways and breadthways round it in a cross shape. The envelope with the certificate of provenance was placed inside the package and Camo walked out of the auction rooms with his prize under his arm.

He was already planning to dig out the other disc from storage and thinking about the best place on the wall of his grandad's room to place them.

They would make a great pair. The real thing and the US imposter.

3. THE GIG

Camo was thinking about the Lion. When the auctioneer had mentioned the counter bidder had been phoning from New York Camo immediately had a weird and totally unsubstantiated feeling that it was the Lion on the phone.

To tell the truth he didn't know if the Lion was still alive.

The Lion was Lionel Azmoun, an American wheeler-dealer originally from the Lebanon. Well wheeler-dealer was hardly fair, Camo admitted. He had made Dr Edge a lot of money when he'd become their manager. When Danny Weathervane, Dr Edge's lead singer, sacked Rod Rogers as Dr Edge's manager and brought in this strange character from New York via Beirut, the other band members couldn't believe what was happening. They liked Rogers, and he'd done all right for them, they said. He'd found them. He believed in them when no one else did. He got them a recording contract. He got them their first US tour. They shouldn't just discard him now.

But Danny insisted. And when the money started rolling in, the rest of the band changed their minds about the Lion.

Unusually for those times among bands, Camo knew, Dr Edge – or rather Danny Weathervane and Dr Edge - had managed to hold on to most of the money they made in their heyday. The Lion had instantly scrapped the deal which Rogers had negotiated with their recording company. In its place came a new deal in which the band kept the vast majority of the money they made, and only a relatively small percentage went to the recording company. It was in fact almost a complete reversal of the original contract. At the same time the Lion made sure that the band kept most of the huge amounts of money they made during their tours. The band had to admit there was a huge difference in their income between the first and second US tours. And the difference was down to the Lion. Anyone on tour looking to take a cut of the action had to go through the Lion. He always cut them down to size. Again this was unprecedented at the time.

With the Lion in charge it was clear to everyone around and

in the industry at large that what Dr Edge earned was theirs. It wasn't anyone else's.

They all got very rich very rapidly.

Whether they held on to their money was a different story. Camo knew his grandad had. And anyway as Dr Edge's main songwriter he benefitted from a stream of royalties not available to the other members. That income stream was still flowing. He'd also been careful with his money when he rehired Rogers as his manager in the mid-1970s to look after his solo career. Dredge had told Camo many times that Danny was the canniest among them with money.

'Sometimes it felt obsessive. Like he was counting it all the time. That's not natural for someone that young.'

Whether the other three band members had held on to their cash Camo didn't know. Anyway they all apart from Dredge had been killed in the plane crash in 1971. So it was probably too soon to say whether they would have held on to it had they survived.

He went to the nursing home. Grandad Dredge was in the garden setting up his guitar and the two small Marshall amps. It was June, swallows were swooping barely eighteen inches above the ground, the leaves were fully out and the first warm weather of the season was bringing a touch of optimism to the air.

Camo approached the beech tree and the stool on which his grandad sat tuning his guitar. He wore his habitual blue jeans, Texas-cowboy steel-heel-and-toe-tipped snake boots and a faded black denim shirt. He had a blue light down-filled sleeveless vest over the top. He hadn't yet plugged the amp lead in.

'Felix?' Dredge said looking up from his guitar as Camo's shadow fell on him. 'What are you doing here? Are you coming back?'

Presumably that was Felix Fairfax, disappeared, perhaps dead, nearly fifty years, but alive and well under the skirts of the dim swirling avalanche of Dredge's mind where linear time was a non-runner.

'It's not Felix, grandad,' Camo said. 'It's Arch. Your grandson.'

It often went like that. Sometimes his grandad thought he was Danny Weathervane, but more often than not he mistook him for Felix Fairfax. Even though Camo was the wrong sex, Dredge's clear yearning in the tranquil turmoil of his mind to have Fairfax back in the band was that strong it overrode such seemingly obvious things.

'Oh good,' Dredge said. 'Come for the gig?'

'Yes. Of course.'

'You've got the best seats.'

There was only one seat. This was a piece of garden furniture by the bird bath on a piece of hard standing set at an angle to the beech tree.

Dredge began a few chords still unplugged.

Camo looked at him.

His grandad's hair was his best feature, he always said so himself. But Camo wasn't so sure. He still had it hanging in great wavy curtains to his shoulders on either side of his long angular face, just as he had in his heyday. But all the black had gone. It was now all grey with long white streaks. The white streaks looked like he'd been dive-bombed by a flock of seagulls. But regarding Dredge's reputation for extremes, Camo couldn't be sure he hadn't done just that. He resisted an urge to reach out and touch a white streak to make sure it was real hair.

Dredge seemed to be satisfied and now plugged in the amp lead. But he didn't sing this time. He played one of the well-known tracks from an album in his solo career but without the words. He plucked and strummed quite gently, humming the words occasionally, but mostly remained voiceless. Perhaps that was his mood at the moment; a kind of deep but harmonious melancholy that the words didn't suit but the chords did.

Camo doubted Dredge cared what the other residents thought. The nearest neighbours were farms to either side of the nursing home, but both farmhouses were a good half mile away.

Camo was amazed just how good his grandad's playing was. He was amazed too that he remembered all the chords. That was so strange, he thought. Much of the forebrain had gone, except in the occasional lucid moment, but all the deep brain stuff, like these complex and quite exceptional chord sequences, remained. How could that be?

He sat on the stout wooden bench and let the music seep into him like warmth from the sun on bare skin.

Time passed. Dredge ran through a full album's worth, all without singing the words. In just one song, the lovely Take It To Sylvia, his second wife and Camo's grandmother, did he add the words and sang a single verse. That was the verse about when she left for good.

The music stopped. Dredge unplugged the jack. He seemed to sit in thought, the guitar cradled across his thin thighs.

Camo stood up and approached. Dredge looked up.

'Arch-boy. Glad you made it. Didn't see you come.'

'Great playing grandad. I enjoyed the gig.'

'Good. Good. I'm glad. Always glad to know I can still do it.'

'You can grandad.'

Camo told his grandad he'd bought the gold disc, the other one, the American one, and was going to bring it to hang on the wall. That was as soon as he'd had it cleaned and the display case repainted.

'Did you. Shit me. That's good to know. Haven't seen that one in decades. They gave it to us in New York. Danny took it.'

'We'll get the British one out of storage and put them both on your wall. Would you like that?'

'Yes. Yes. Great idea.' Dredge's eyes lit up in excitement at the prospect. 'It'll be good to see them both together. It will be a first. That was a good time. That tour. We were ready to take on the world. We weren't going to change the world. But we were going to change music.' Then he frowned. 'Danny's proceeds all went to Madeline.'

What? Camo thought. Who was she? He asked.

'I kept mine. But the Lion arranged it all for Danny. Then the plane came down. I think Madeline's still got it all.'

Camo asked again about Madeline and who she was, He'd never heard about her before.

But it was too late. The light that shone brightly for a moment in Dredge's brain had faltered, then spluttered out and gone.

4. BACK

'If we're going to clean it we better see if it opens up.' Rosie said. She was standing in the sitting room in the house Camo shared with Sally and Nick and Tyko. It was a three-bedroom house in Richmond. Camo had one room, Tyko had another. Sally and Nick shared the third; they were an item. Rosie lived not far away in another house she shared with a couple of other students.

Camo had temporarily hung the gold disc on a nail in the wall. He thought it looked good. Both the glass case front and the gold disc behind it caught the light in different ways.

'Ok,' Camo called from the kitchen where he was dropping teabags into three mugs.

Rosie reached out and unhooked the display case from the nail. It was light enough. She held it up to read the label in the middle. The silver writing could be read very clearly against the background of the famous black label. Above the spindle hole was the name of the recording company <AQUEDUCT> it said, with the logo of a stylised and silhouetted example of Roman hydraulic engineering alongside. Below the spindle hole it said <OPEN THE GATES> and under that <DR EDGE>. Then below that it said <SIDE 1> and the five tracks on this side were listed. She noted that in brackets after each song it read <Lyly>. She flipped the LP over anchored on her fingertips. The record label and the logo were repeated, under which were the band name again and the name of the album. Below that it read <SIDE 2> and the four tracks on that side were listed. She noted again that they were all written by <Lyly>. She laid it down on the battered trunk with a board on top they used as a coffee table.

'Where did it come from?' Rosie shouted through to Camo in the kitchen. 'Who had it before? Who sold it?'

Camo didn't know.

'There's information about it in the envelope,' he called.

Rosie picked up the A4 envelope from the coffee table and slid out the certificate.

'Says Danny's sister Jane had it. Passed to her after the crash as part of his estate. She's the one who's just sold it.' She replaced the certificate and picked up the disc again.

'Why don't we play it?' This was from Tyko who had just come in. He was looking over Rosie's shoulder at the disk.

Rosie's eyes lit up. 'Wouldn't it be fabulous to actually play a gold disc!'

She passed the case over to Tyko.

Camo came in carrying three mugs of tea. 'Can you play them? Gold discs?'

'Don't see why not,' Tyko was peering intently through the glass to the disc behind. He carried it to the bay window.

'Yes the grooves are quite clear and pronounced. Can't see any reason you can't play it.' He angled the case, trying to throw more light into the grooves. 'Might see better if we took it out.'

'Go ahead,' Camo said handing over a mug.

Tyko turned the case over and laid it face down on the board. They could see four brass screws set into cups at the corners of the case. 'Just needs a Philips screwdriver,' he said. 'I'll get one.' He left the room.

Tyko was an electrical engineering student.

'But what are we going to play it on?' Camo said as Tyko came back into the room carrying the necessary screwdriver. 'We don't have a turntable, a record player.'

'Does anyone have a record player these days?' Rosie said.

'Leave that part to me,' Tyko said. He thought he knew someone who knew someone who had one or could get hold of one from somewhere. His college workshop might even have a few. They were useful bits of kit for electrical engineering practicals. Especially for practicals of old-fashioned pre-digital pre-electronic electrical engineering.

Tyko already had the back of the case off and had removed one of the padded brackets that held the disc in place. He held the disc gently in his fingertips and took it over to the window. He stared intently at the grooves.

'Yes,' he said. 'I think this baby will play,' he said. 'Might not be perfect sound. The paint is clogging the grooves to a degree. You might not like what you hear. But it will play.'

Two days later he brought home a primitive turntable. It had been a quality Bang & Olufsen record-player in its day, he said. But now it was used as a demonstrator of electric motors, wiring systems, field magnets, armatures, polarities and primitive 1960s control valves and codecs and ancient analogue amplification methodologies. It was part of the college collection, as he expected.

Camo and Rosie inspected the record player. Amazing, she thought, this was how people listened to music in the old days.

'It might play. But will it play at thirty-three and a third revolutions a minute?' Rosie said. She beamed and demonstrated a kind of pride in knowing the correct speed for a long-playing record from the old days to revolve at. 'That was the speed for LPs.'

'If it don't, I'll make it,' Tyko said.

In the interim two days Camo and Rosie had fully dismantled all the separate parts of the display case. They cleaned – very gently - the gold disc with a soft toothbrush and soap and water. And Rosie had repainted the wooden case with several coats of black paint.

They plugged in the record player. Then opened the lid, shifted the disc stacker arm to one side, placed the hole in the centre of the disc on the spindle in the centre of the rubber mat on top of the platter turntable, rotated the stacker arm back in place above the disc, selected the revolution option sliding switch of $33^1/_3$ out of a choice of 16, $33^1/_3$, 45, and 78. Then Rosie lifted up the stylus arm. Immediately the turntable began to rotate at the set speed. She lowered the stylus arm back on its rest. The rotation stopped.

'You better do the honours,' she said to Camo.

He came forward. He lifted the stylus arm. The turntable began to revolve again. He moved the arm across to the outside edge of the disc. Very very gently he set it down. There was a constant crackling sound and after a few moments of more crackle scratch and hiss then the music started.

It was awful.

Tyko had been right. The paint was sufficiently clogged into the grooves to distort the sound.

But they listened anyway. It was like some kind of pilgrimage to a holy shrine. It was the action that counted, not the content.

Sometimes the stylus needle bounced and skittered, missing out chunks of songs. There was constant crackling and hiss behind and below the music.

After twenty-three minutes and five songs the music and the crackling stopped – to the unspoken relief of those listening – and the stylus began its run-out following the final spiralling groove towards the hole in the middle of the disc.

Just before it automatically lifted itself off to return to its rest position a number of things happened at once.

A series of ghoulish sounds and noises began coming from the end of the disc, where the needle was still in contact with the surface of the disc and still following the final groove.

At the same time Camo had risen to his feet, collected the empty mugs, and was making his way to the kitchen. As he passed the record player his left heel tangled in the slightly upturned piece of carpet in one of the joins in the floor covering. He stumbled to his left, momentarily catching the record player with his knee and badly jarring it.

For a second the needle running in the gold paint-encumbered final groove in the disc was jolted backwards.

As it did so one of the odd sounds and moans coming from the disc became suddenly clear and made sense. It sounded like a single word.

<gold>

Then the strange noises, moans and groans, whoops, urghs, gloops, and arghs resumed. They went on for what felt like a surprisingly long time before the needle ran to the end, lifted itself off the record and returned automatically to its rest position.

All three were looking at each other with big eyes.

'Did you hear what I heard?' Rosie said.

'It sounded just like 'gold',' Tyko said.

'Or was it 'cold'?' Camo said.

'But what's all that other stuff?' Rosie looked at each of them. 'There was quite a lot of it. It seemed to go on for quite a while. Was it speech?'

'Was it even human?'

'It certainly wasn't music.'

Among them, Tyko the electrical engineer had said the least. He was thinking.

'You know what,' Tyko said. 'What they could be is this. They could be normal words spoken normally but recorded backwards.'

Once you've heard some words played backwards you can't rest until you know what the words really said the right way round. It didn't really matter if it was gold or cold they'd heard, that wasn't important. It was what the rest of it said that mattered. Camo knew he wasn't going to rest until they'd heard what they were.

'We all heard the word 'gold' coming from the end of the record. It was pretty clear wasn't it?' Camo said. 'So--'

'Unless it was 'cold'?' Tyko said.

'--So. Even so. What does the rest of it say?' Rosie finished for him. 'But how do we play something recorded backwards the right way?'

'In other words, how do we play what we've just heard backwards so it sounds forwards?' Tyko said. 'Leave that to me.'

'Can't we just switch it off and push the turntable backwards by hand?' Rosie said. 'It probably rotates freely either way once the power is switched off?'

Tyko said it would. 'But without the power you won't get the benefit of the amp. So it's likely we won't really hear anything. It'll also be bloody difficult to get anywhere near the right rotation speed, and maintain it at a constant rate. But we could try it?' He looked at Camo, implying that pushing the stylus the wrong way could also do an unknown amount of damage to the disc, especially to the gold finish.

'I'm not sure I want to subject the finish to too much needle scratching,' Camo said. 'What else can we do?'

In which case, Tyko said, it would be best to play it clearly just once rather than have repeated cack-handed attempts by hand to rotate it backwards and hear it. What Tyko said he could do was modify the turntable so it rotated the other way.

'At the moment if you look at it from above it's rotating clockwise. I can change that so it revolves anti-clockwise. It's all governed by a simple electric motor. Straightforward really.' He knew if necessary he could replace the motor with one that spun the other way. Or one that had a forward and reverse control.

'Then all we have to do is place the needle down just at the point where the run-off groove almost hits the hole in the middle. It will then start winding outwards, back into the record edge instead of towards the hole,' Tyko said. And if the sounds were anything at all they would hear them.

While Tyko went to bring down his bag of tools from his room Camo and Rosie continued to just sit and stare at the turntable. They each had questions of their own, all of them as yet unanswerable.

Both of them were aware of rumours from the old days of popular music, particularly from the heyday of rock music in the late 1960s, of some kind of odd Satanic ritual which involved groups recording Satanic hymns backwards at the end of some of their long-playing records. The legend was that if the sounds that had been recorded backwards at the end of the LPs were ever played the right way round then all kinds of Satanic hell would be unleashed on the world.

With this in mind, Rosie raised the obvious question, 'Do we actually want to find out what it says? Even if they are real words?'

'You mean, is it dangerous in some way? I hadn't thought of that.' He had, but didn't want to appear scared or worried about that kind of thing in front of Rosie.

'I think if it's true that some of those rock bands did that kind of thing on their records, they'd be the first to run a mile if it did unleash anything Satanic. They weren't serious. They just enjoyed pissing about and creating and being part of the legend,' Rosie said. 'It was probably all down to their managers anyway. Reckoned the rumour and the mystery would make them pots more money.'

Camo was certain she was right. But strangely also felt comforted by her sensible bravado.

Aside from Satanic consequences, for the moment the key questions for both of them were if they were words, what did they say? And then who had put the words there? And when? What for? And did it really say gold?

Tyko came down from his room upstairs with his bag of tools. He set about dismantling the record player. Then when it was all in pieces he set about reconstructing it.

'It might take a while,' he said. 'I'll text you when it's done.'

Both Camo and Rosie had work to do, essays to write. Camo was an English student, and Rosie studied law. Camo wasn't in the mood for essay writing. What he was in the mood for was sex. He asked Rosie if she wanted to come and work in his room. He knew she would be coming over to stay the night later, but it was the here and now that mattered.

She smiled. She knew what he had in mind. 'Perhaps later. I really do have to catch up. I'll come back when Tyko's got it fixed.'

They were all in the same WhatsApp group, so she would receive Tyko's message at the same time Camo did.

It took longer than Tyko expected. He did have to go back to the college workshop and bring back a reversible electric motor with its own DC adapter lead. And even when that was fitted it took time. He wasn't stuck or flummoxed at any time. He knew what he was doing, and he knew how to do it. It was just fiddly and relatively complicated, and some of the screws were tiny, for which he didn't have the right screwdriver, so had to improvise. But he did it.

Two hours and a half later he plugged in the reassembled record player. He lifted the stylus. The turntable rotated. It rotated the other way. He smiled and sat on the floor with his back against the settee. He punched the air. He dug out his phone and sent a message to the others.

The three of them stood round the record player as Camo deftly placed the gold disc on the surface of the turntable. There was no particular reason why it should, but it definitely looked wrong rotating the way it now did.

Another thing Tyko had done was modify the restraining limiter on the stylus arm so that it could now pass the spindle hole in the centre of the turntable. In that position, if placed onto the surface of the disc the stylus would still be a trailing arm as the disc rotated anti-clockwise. He wanted to minimise any damage the needle might do to the surface, and thought that acting as a trailing arm would be better. It was in other words now a mirror image of its original set-up.

Camo lifted the stylus arm. He held it hovering over the end of the last track on the disc. Then he remembered. Now it was rotating backwards he had to drop the stylus right at the end of its line, as far as it would go towards the hole in the middle. It would work its way back to the rim from there. He looked briefly at the other two. They both nodded. Rosie smiled and gave a quick thumbs-up. He travelled the arm past the spindle hole. Then he gently placed the stylus in the groove next to the spindle right at the end of the disc. It started moving outwards.

There was the same crackles scratches squeaks and pops as before, but this time the constant background hiss sounded like some imminent heavy human breathing. Perhaps it was.

Then a man's voice spoke quite clearly with a light Merseyside accent. It said:

Madeline got the gold with her in the hold
Madeline got the gold waiting in the cold
Madeline got the stacks never to pay tax
Madeline over under still more asunder
Madeline under over will mark a trover

This five line refrain was repeated once more. Then there was silence, broken only by the click and hiss of the pickup on the stylus arm as it headed outwards from the centre towards the perimeter and the end of the last track on the album.

In total silence before it reached the track Camo lifted the stylus arm up and returned it to its rest.

5. SENTINEL

'I think I recognise that voice,' Camo said. He thought it was Danny Weathervane. He'd never met him obviously. He died well before Camo was born. But he'd seen him on family videos and old Super 8 cine film; and heard him on recordings, made both by his dad and by Dredge. He'd also seen some of the celebrated films and TV documentaries about the band, including the landmark film where the filmmaker accompanied the band on their first US tour. Danny was usually the band's main spokesman.

'Is it Danny Weathervane?' Rosie asked.

Camo said he thought it was almost definitely Danny Weathervane. The voice had a slight Liverpudlian element to it. He recalled Dredge saying that Danny would always correct anyone who said he had a Liverpudlian accent. 'Birkenhead pal, not Liverpool,' he'd say.

Danny Weathervane was the lead singer of Dr Edge. He thought of himself as the leader of the band. He was after all the only one who had something more than a basic school education. Danny had been to art college, he let that be known to everyone. But Camo knew that wasn't strictly true. Dredge, his grandad had been to art college too. The same art college as Danny. That's where the two of them met and formed the band. But Danny was the one that received most fanmail from teenage girls. More than twice the amount the rest of the band received put together. He thought that must count for something. He said he was the people's favourite therefore he should be the public face of the band. The other three members of the band Grog and Dave and Pram didn't go to any kind of college. Maybe Felix had, but he didn't know. They were ace musicians but not really up for speaking in public or being interviewed anywhere in the public eye. Camo knew that his grandad was quite happy for Danny to take the lead in most situations. It took that kind of weight off his own shoulders and let him concentrate on playing and writing the songs. So Danny was de facto band leader and spokesman. He liked it. Camo also knew from what Dredge had told him that Danny was also the decision maker when it came to anything to do with the band's money.

'Ok. We know who said it,' Tyko said. 'But what does it mean? Who's Madeline?'

'She's got the gold. But have you ever heard of her Camo?' Rosie said.

He hadn't. Yet he knew that just three days ago his grandad had also mentioned Madeline. That was also in the context of this gold disc. The American gold disc. He told the other two what his grandad had said.

'At one point he said 'Danny's proceeds all went to Madeline.' I think – or rather assume – he meant proceeds from the sales of that – this - album.' He pointed to the turntable. 'And shortly after that he said 'I think Madeline's still got it all.' But he didn't reply when I asked him who Madeline was.'

Camo said he could try again, but wasn't hopeful.

'What about your mum? Or your grandmother Sylvia?' Rosie had met both of them. 'Maybe they'd know who Madeline was? Or is. A groupie perhaps?'

That was definitely a possibility he could follow up, Camo said.

'But was Sylvia actually there then?' Tyko asked, pointing to the turntable where the gold disc still lay.

'No. That's true,' Camo said. 'She came on the scene much later. She was the reason Dredge and his first wife Maggie split up. Probably you don't know that Maggie's dead so I can't ask her.'

'There must be someone, many people surely, around from those days who might know something. We should be able to track them down.' Rosie insisted. 'What about roadies, fixers, drivers, publicists, record company people, recording engineers, all those kinds of people?'

'She might even be one of them,' Tyko said. 'Or know who she is if she's not.'

That was true. Camo wondered where to start. He knew

his grandmother was still in touch with some of the people from those days. Maybe she could point him in the right direction. But then he had an idea.

'I have an idea,' he said.

He was going to talk to the man who had come up with the description of Dr Edge's sound as like a freight train braking hard on diamond rails but not slowing down. They all thought that would be a good place to start.

He was going to talk to Chris Sentinel.

Later that night Rosie woke Camo up. It was near three in the morning.

'I know what Madeline is,' she said, barely containing her excitement. 'I'm almost certain of it. She's not a who, she's a what.' She was sitting up in bed leaning against the wall.

Camo pulled himself up and sat up alongside her.

'She's a ship. Or a boat. One or the other,' Rosie said.

'How come? Why do you reckon?'

'He says *Madeline got the gold with her in the hold.* Right?'

Immediately he understood where she was going. It sounded good to Camo.

'Yeah could be. Ships have holds.'

But did boats? He didn't know. But owning a boat, a yacht, a launch, a gin-palace cruiser, a rowing-boat, a narrowboat, even a pedalo were all more likely than Weathervane owning a ship. Or was it? He had no idea. Maybe the Lion got Danny investing in ships?

'Or maybe 'hold' is just a metaphor for a strong place?' he said. He always seemed to be the one pouring cold water on the adventure, or possible adventure. But he supposed that someone had to do that, and then it would be down to Rosie and the other two to fight back and undermine his scepticism. That might always be the best way forward.

'So I think we should try to find out if Danny Weathervane ever owned a boat called Madeline,' Rosie continued, ignoring his hesitation for the moment. 'And what happened to it.'

'And if it's no longer around. Sunk maybe. Who knows. Then the gold may still be lying on the bottom of the sea somewhere.'

'Sunken treasure,' Rosie clapped her hands lightly. 'Wow, Blackbeard.'

'In which case it might be a bit out of our league.' Neither of them, nor the other two to his knowledge, had ever done any diving.

'Good point,' she agreed. 'In which case we may have to bring some of that kind of expertise in.'

'I think we should still talk to Chris Sentinel first.'

There were many journalists and reporters working for the music press in the 1960s and 1970s who made names for themselves. The two main weekly music papers of the day were New Musical Express and Melody Maker. It was the job of those two papers to keep the public informed about the music and the groups. Some writers felt the priority was the music. Others were convinced the priority was the bands. Some tried to do both. But what all were agreed on was there was a seemingly insatiable demand among the readers for information about both the bands and their music. Increasingly the band's real private lives became much more relevant to the readers than the mundane publicity stories put out by the public relations companies about their clients, the groups. And increasingly reporters from the big two weeklies became intent on finding the real stories behind the press releases and the marketing. In doing so some members of the music press became quite close to members of the groups, some were trusted outlets for insider leaks and snippets, and some were even considered part of a group's inner circle.

One of the earliest and the best among the crop of reporters for the two weeklies in the 1960s and 1970s was Chris Sentinel. He worked in that early part of his career for the New Musical Express. From unearthing stories about the private lives of group members he went on to become a respected music and cultural critic. From the music press he moved on to the daily papers as columnist, reviewer and music critic. He later became an author of books on music and social history and a TV commentator on the arts and cultural affairs.

Chris Sentinel was the one who wrote that the sound Dr Edge made, and especially Jim Lyly's guitar playing, was like 'a freight train braking hard on diamond rails, but not slowing down.'

One of his most recent and best works was a book about Dr Edge and their whole music and cultural legacy. It was during the writing of that book three years ago that he had interviewed and got to know Camo Lyly quite well.

Camo thought if there was anyone who knew about who-was-who and who-wasn't-who in the music world in the late 1960s and early 1970s, it would be Chris Sentinel. He had after all accompanied Dr Edge on both their second and third tours of America. The second tour was the one out of which their classic album Open The Gates had emerged. The third tour was cut short halfway through by the tragic air crash.

For that interview he'd been out to Sentinel's house up north near Newmarket on the fringes of East Anglia, not far from the big RAF and US air bases at Mildenhall.

He contacted Sentinel, who was delighted to hear him. Camo explained he'd like to tap Chris's brain about the late 1960s and all things to do with Dr Edge, especially as his grandad couldn't be such a valuable source any more, but wasn't more specific than that. He asked if he and Rosie could come up to see him the following weekend.

They could. Sentinel said he'd crack open a barrel of beer in readiness and get 'the other stuff' ready for them. By other stuff Camo assumed he meant various drugs. It seemed you could take the man out of the 60s, but you couldn't take the 60s out of the man.

Camo had a second or third-hand Land Rover. It was all the trust fund would stretch to for a vehicle for him. But he didn't mind. It went. It was solid. And hadn't yet broken down. It had once been owned by a farmer. It even still had the power winch on the back. Camo couldn't believe he was driving a car which had a winch on the back.

It took two hours that Saturday for Camo and Rosie to drive up from London to Chris Sentinel's place near Mildenhall.

Chris Sentinel owned a row of cottages in a village near Mildenhall. They were once workers cottages for a big estate. Over the years he'd bought the whole row of six cottages. He had them modified, all knocked into one, and extended at the back with a large courtyard and outbuildings embracing the entire length of the six-cottage frontage. The courtyard occupied the whole area where the cottage backs and gardens had been. But that didn't matter too much since Sentinel owned the field beyond too. The courtyard housed games rooms, mainly and stables. In his late middle-age (Sentinel was 72) he had discovered the joys of fast cars. The stables weren't for horses. It was where Chris Sentinel housed his collection of fast cars.

Camo drove the car through the open gates between the matching brick pillars into the courtyard and parked there at the back of the house.

Isobel Sentinel, Chris's wife since the far-off heady NME days where she had been a sub-editor, opened the back door to them. She for her part hated fast cars. She welcomed them in, hugged Rosie and shook Camo's hand.

Chris was in the kitchen making coffee. He came over to them, a mug of coffee in one hand, which he put down on the worktop to shake Camo's hand, and a cannabis roll-up joint in the other hand, which he didn't put down while he hugged Rosie.

'Arch good to see you again,' Chris said. 'How's it going? Can I get you a spliff?'

Camo laughed. 'No thanks, A coffee would be great.'

'Rosie? One or both for you? Or neither?'

Rosie went for a coffee too.

On the way up Camo and Rosie had talked through how they wanted to play the meeting with Chris Sentinel. They agreed they'd keep quiet about the secret message on the gold disc. There didn't seem any need for anyone else to know about that apart from the three of them. They would be looking, they'd tell Chris, for anything he could tell them about the gold disc, the US one, the origins of the album Open The Gates, and as much as he could about that tour of the USA. That was Dr Edge's second US tour, their big one, the one where they'd played stadiums not just cinemas and indoor halls. Sentinel had been with the band on the whole of that tour.

They would be particularly interested in Danny Weathervane during that time and what Chris could tell them about him and what he did.

'Shall we mention Madeline?' Rosie had wondered.

'I think only as a last resort. See if she comes up naturally in the course of events. If not, we'll ask him directly at the end if there was anyone around at that time with that name.'

'Before that, before the stuff about the US tour and Danny, how about we lead in by asking what he knows about the Lion? From what you've told me he sounds a key element in their environment. And a slightly mysterious figure. He was close to Danny too wasn't he? He made all their financial decisions didn't he? Maybe he has some connection to this gold we're wondering about?'

If it is real gold, Camo thought. Not some weird metaphor for something. A wild gold chase.

They agreed that's what they'd do.

'So you want to pick my brains?' Chris Sentinel said. 'What there is left of it,' he said waving his joint around.

'Why don't the three of you go into the study to talk about all this?' Isobel said. 'Then we can all sit down and have some lunch afterwards.'

Camo said he was trying to find out as much as he could about those times, now his grandad wasn't able to do it as much.

'Yes. So sorry to hear about Dredge,' Sentinel said. As an ex-journalist he kept himself well informed. 'He was one of the best. This country would be a smaller, slighter, meaner and a far less significant place now if it wasn't for people like him. The only reason Britain is on the world cultural map nowadays is because of him and that music generation. They did change the world.'

It was quite a speech. Camo smiled his thanks.

'He still plays. He's still amazingly good. Considering.'

'Does he? That's so good to hear.'

They followed Sentinel out of the kitchen, down a corridor, past some other rooms and several staircases to a large room at the end of the row of former cottages.

The room was lined with books on three walls, floor to ceiling. The other wall was covered in framed photographs. Photographs of groups and gigs. A big leather topped desk was set at ninety degrees to the large sash window. Sentinel sat on an office chair behind the desk with bookshelves behind him and waved them to the other chairs in the room, two armchairs and a long settee. Camo and Rosie took each of the armchairs. Chris leaned back in his chair, dug out the equipment from a desk drawer, hunched forward over the desk, and began to roll another joint. His long grey hair framed the sides of his head as his hands worked away.

They all had that hairstyle, Camo thought, in those days. Parted in the middle and hanging in drapes either side of their face. Chris Sentinel's hair was the same style as his grandad's but neater and with no white streaks.

Before Camo could begin asking Chris Sentinel about the old days when his grandad's band had been the biggest cultural thing on the planet, Sentinel started talking himself.

'Funny you should come just now as a matter of fact. I'm just starting a new project but based on those heady days of Dr Edge and their US tours. It might make a book. I don't know yet.' He waved his spliff around for emphasis.

Camo asked what the project was.

'I want to once and for all find out what on earth happened to Felix Fairfax.'

'Is she dead or alive, you mean?'

'Oh she's dead all right.'

Camo let him talk and didn't interrupt. It wasn't what they had come here to talk about, but he guessed it would be a good move to keep Sentinel talking about those times.

'Why so?' Rosie asked.

'It really isn't that easy to disappear. It really isn't. Or disappear and still be alive, at any rate.'

No I guess not, Rosie thought. Even if you have no internet footprint, you were almost bound to know people who did. Even if you pretended to be the new Simeon Stylites and live on a pillar ten metres in the air in the middle of nowhere, people would notice and they'd get it on the internet. These days your very absence would get you noticed and searched for.

'Are you going to tell me that in the fifty years since she's been gone, Felix Fairfax hasn't needed a doctor or a dentist or an accountant or a lawyer? At least once?' Sentinel said with self-convincing logic. 'And the taxman, though she may not have wanted to see him, he'll have wanted to know all about her. If she really did become a nun or is hiding out in a commune somewhere, then the people she knows are keeping amazingly quiet about her and her whereabouts.'

'Maybe that depends on what country she ran off to?' Camo said.

Sentinel pulled a face and nodded.

'Sure, that's true.' He paused. 'But I think she died very early on after she walked out. If she walked out at all.'

They were staring silent but wide-eyed at him.

'What are you suggesting?' Rosie thought she knew what Sentinel was saying.

'I have a suspicion that all wasn't well with Dr Edge in those days. I'm suggesting that Felix may have killed herself—'

'And the band hushed it up?' Camo let his scorn and concern show.

'Not the band, no. Not the whole band at any rate. But Danny Weathervane knew a lot more than he let on at the time. I was sure of that even then. In fact the police had reopened the case just before the aircrash. They were treating it as a missing persons case. And they were keen to talk to Danny again.'

Sentinel explained that Danny and Felix had been an item.

'A very much on-off item. The public never knew of course. It was kept quiet for publicity reasons. Managers and PR people in those days thought it would put the screaming fans off if they understood that their idols were sleeping with each other and so wouldn't be available for them to fantasise about. Although that wouldn't have worried Danny. We all knew what was going on. But there was a kind of unspoken agreement that we wouldn't mention it. She was exasperated at his rampant shagging. He would even bring groupies back to their place when they were living together. She walked out a lot. And the last time just looked like she decided to do it properly and leave no trace. But I was never convinced then, and I'm even less convinced now. I think Danny knew a lot more than he ever let on.'

Sentinel said it was a common feeling among the music writers at the time that Dr Edge were never quite the same without Felix.

'It was highly unusual to have two lead guitars. That was even more revolutionary than having a woman guitarist. They were the first. They did it before Fleetwood Mac. Pram Johnson was good. But he wasn't Felix.'

She had style too, Sentinel said. His voice had taken on a dreamy quality and Rosie wondered if there was more here than just the cannabis speaking. Did Chris Sentinel in those days have a crush on Felix Fairfax? And did that lead to this insistence that she hadn't walked out on the band, but she had died, maybe killed herself or was Sentinel implying murder?

She was an aristocratic rebel, Sentinel said. 'Her real name was Felicity of course. But she preferred Felix. It means the same thing. and she thought the two Xs went well together. Her family has a country seat in Cheshire, near Chester or somewhere round there where she hobnobbed as a kid with the assorted offspring of Delamere, Cholmondeley and Grosvenor.'

'Did they think she was dead?' Rosie asked.

'They didn't care. To them she was an embarrassment. At one point they completely disowned her. It was bad enough that kids were playing this awful music. Rebelling all the time and not showing any respect to their elders and not doing what they were supposed to do. It wasn't so bad when it was other people's kids. Though that was bad enough and showed how much the country was going to the dogs. But when it was your own kid, it was the pits. So they kicked her out. You had to set an example.

'Perhaps because of that unsavoury distancing by the family she never signed her name – always used FFF. Her triple F initials. She almost patented that triple F. It's what she always signed herself as and if you asked for an autograph that's what you got.

'Her family just didn't get her. She was far ahead of them. In fact she was far ahead of most people at the time. She always wore DMs and black jeans and a black wrangler jacket. Everyone wore blue jeans in those days. But she wore black. She had the stitching redone in green thread. Eventually the company brought out a triple F signature jacket and jeans in black with green stitching.

'Under the denim she always wore a white tee-shirt. Sometimes it'd be just plain white. Other times it would have the image of a famous woman on it. Florence Nightingale. Jane Austen. Marie Curie. She'd never identify them or tell you who they were. She expected you to know. Just like if you saw an unlabelled picture of Albert Einstein you'd know who it was. She expected the same. Class.

'She had real style. Way beyond all of us then. When everyone else was fixated on Zippos she always used an IMCO lighter. IMCO were an Austrian outfit that Zippos were based on. She went for the original, the real thing. Sod the rip off. She was always ahead of the game.

'And do you know why she was such a good guitarist? Almost as good as Dredge? Because she had six fingers on her left hand.'

It was some kind of genetic throwback that expressed itself every couple of generations, Sentinel said.

'But the publicity people always had that fact hidden from the public. As much as they could, especially when the band was starting out. They even tried to get TV shots of her hand blanked out, or demanded they only showed her right hand when playing on telly. Or only show her face. How could they imagine you could have one of the world's best guitarists on telly and not show how she played? Total absurdity. Fucking idiots.

'It was ludicrous the lengths they thought they needed to go to. In the early days of a band's rise record company people were so scared of anything that might conceivably scare off fans or diminish sales. But Felix herself didn't give a damn. And Dredge always called her the six-fingered wizard.'

6. SHAGFEST

Now before Sentinel could carry on eulogising Felix Fairfax any further Camo asked him, 'What can you tell us about the Lion?'

'Ah yes. The Lion. Danny brought him in. No one quite knew where Danny found him, New York maybe,' Sentinel said. 'In a lot of ways Danny had a very different lifestyle to the other members of Dr Edge. Different in many ways to any band member at that time. He didn't do drugs – poor sod – nor booze really which is amazing. He kept himself honed and really fit. On their second tour, the first one I was on, Danny would go on a two mile run before breakfast every day. Jogging in those days was unheard of. But Danny told me once that he'd met the Lion on their first US tour in 1967 when they were not much more than a support band. But if Danny didn't do drugs and booze he certainly did women.' He nodded a kind of apology towards Rosie. 'I've never seen anything like it before or since. The rumour was he'd got over a dozen illegitimate kids across Europe and the US by the time of the crash.'

She shrugged as if to say she didn't care, nothing to do with her. It was all a case of: 'but it was in another country and besides the wench is dead.' Camo had told her that one once, it was a quote from Marlowe. She liked it. It was such a non-sequitur and slightly disconcerting.

'But apart from women, the really really big thing in Danny's life was money. Bands in those days didn't make any money. We all know that. Some of them even knew it at the time. But Dr Edge did. And that was all Danny's doing.

'He was the one that sacked their manager Rod Rogers. I always liked Rod. And hired Lionel – the Lion – Azmoun. I always reckoned the attraction of the Lion for Danny was that he knew how Danny could keep his money.

'And the Lion was the one that persuaded them all to go into that stupid tax exile in 1970, between the second and third US tours, when they lived in some godforsaken castle up a

French mountain for over six months, longer maybe. That was the Lion's doing.

'I think only Danny liked it. I was told Danny had bought the place some time before and done it up, or part of it up. He'd spend time there on his own before that, or with a bunch of groupies in some kind of isolated non-stop shagfest.

'We in the press referred to it as Chateau Shagfest. But he persuaded the rest of the band to join him there for tax reasons. All the others hated it. It nearly broke the band. A rock band at the top of their game lost and stuck up a mountainside in the middle of nowhere with just the eagles and wild goats for company is no way to carry on. With the band leader acting the sex-starved priapic goat. I remember some people in those days often referred to him as Danny Leathercock, not Danny Weathervane.

'It was absurd. They only survived as a band by forcing Danny out of the castle eventually and going on their last US tour together. They gave him some kind of ultimatum and that shook him.'

This is easier than I expected, Camo thought. He likes to talk. And he likes to talk about those times.

'But back to the Lion,' Sentinel was saying. 'His real name was Lionel, pronounced the French way 'Lee-o-nel' because he was brought up in the Lebanon speaking French. Naturally in England he was known as 'Lion-el' and he hated that. But then somehow it got shortened to 'Lion' and he loved that. He especially liked it with a definite article – the Lion. And he responded to that and used it himself all the time he was associated with the band. Afterwards too, I'd imagine.

'When anyone interviewed him we had to call him 'Lion' to his face and refer to him as 'the Lion' in the piece. He was a prime pain in the arse. Maybe bands needed people like that in those days. And Danny Weathervane liked him.'

'What happened to him?' Rosie asked.

'Oh I think he retired with his gotten and ill-gotten gains to a fancy apartment in New York overlooking Central Park. He may have made the band wealthy, but they made him wealthy too. Extremely I shouldn't wonder.'

'Is he still alive?' Camo asked. He was thinking about the anonymous bidder on the phone from New York.

'Not sure. He kind of fell through the cracks and dropped out of circulation. I got a feeling he might be dead. I think I saw an obit recently. Not sure. I'll take a look if you like. But I do know he was educated at Robert College in Istanbul. Danny told me that. Apparently it's an American foundation, a real topnotch academy, like the Eton of Turkey, or something, but English-speaking, so he speaks perfect English, American English. I guess that's where he first learned about how to manage money.

'Then after that he went to Harvard Business School. He told me that himself in one interview. 'I am the Lion from Harvard' he said. It was ridiculous. There was always such a strange contrast between the total lack of ridiculousness in what he did for the band, and the total ridiculousness in how he talked about himself. Danny always said he didn't manage the band so much as manage their money.

'That may well be true, because he didn't come on the band's second and third US tours, the ones I was on, in 70 and 71. He managed and arranged everything remotely from London or New York, operating mainly on the road through his teenage daughter Bayb. I suspect that side of managing a group bored him.

'But the daughter was a sight to see. You should have seen this sixteen year old kid, Lion's daughter, ordering everyone around on behalf of her dad. They took it too. They knew if they didn't, if they disrespected his daughter, they'd have to answer to the Lion at some point. And he would find a way for it to cost them. The kid was at some top US college at the time.'

'Was she in the plane crash too?' Rosie asked.

'No she wasn't on the flight. She had some business back in Chicago. I guess something for her dad, and stayed there a couple of days longer. She was going to catch up later.'

'How was Danny on that third US tour?' Camo asked.

'Oh fine, fine. Always prepared to talk to me and the other

journos.' Sentinel paused. 'Maybe a little preoccupied. Seemed like something was on his mind. He was remoter than he had been.'

'Do you know why?' Rosie asked.

'No. No. not really. I got a feeling, don't know where from, that Danny was getting ready to split from the band. That the band somehow had taken him as far as they could and no further. I never wrote that up anywhere. I couldn't prove it. I think he always felt he'd be better off money wise and career wise as a solo artist. I think he saw himself as the new Elvis. I think if they hadn't crashed, that would have been Danny's last tour with the band anyway.'

Dunno about that, thought Camo. Without Jim Lyly's songs Danny Weathervane might have been nothing special at all.

Camo informed Sentinel at that point that he had just bought the Open The Gates gold disc, the other one, the American one.

'That's interesting. It's turned up over here, has it? Danny had it on the last tour. Even went in to the recording studio with it on his own for some reason. Treated it like a talisman. The company gave it to the band as soon as they arrived in New York. I was there when they handed it over. I sometimes wondered what happened to it. Was it in Danny's luggage when they crashed? Or did it go on another flight with all the other baggage? I guess Dredge has the UK one?'

'Yes.' Camo told him he planned to put them both on the wall of Dredge's room in the nursing home.

'Good plan. Oh that reminds me. Maybe it's the talk about gold. There was a rumour going round shortly after the crash, funnily enough in the French press but not in the English press, that Danny had got hold of a stash of Krugerrands – you know those gold coins, I think they were the only gold coins you could buy at the time. The rumour said Danny had splashed out £300,000 on a stack of Krugerrands and hidden them or buried them somewhere so the taxman couldn't get his hands on them.

'If true, I'd be surprised if the Lion didn't have a hand in arranging that. He'd have organised it through a French bank, hence the rumour in France.

'I know, everyone did, that Danny was paranoid about the taxman. And remember at the time the tax rate for big money earners like Dr Edge was ninety-eight or ninety-nine pence in the pound. Ninety-nine percent of your income would be filched by the taxman. Even if you earned a fortune you couldn't hold on to it. It's no wonder they hid from the taxman in France, really. Surprising in a way they didn't hide longer.

'I tried to follow that Krugerrand rumour up. Would have made a good story. But it didn't seem to hold water. I reckoned there must have been a French bank involved, as I said. I talked to Credit this and Credit that and Societe the other, but no one seemed to know anything or weren't talking. I even went to France to try to track it down but couldn't find anything. Then after the crash no one was interested in talking about money and that kind of story disappeared for good.

'It's probably not relevant but I know Danny was scared stiff of flying. Maybe he went into the recording studio on his own to lay down some tracks as a kind of legacy if he didn't make it. But if he did those tracks have never emerged.'

'He was right to be scared,' Rosie said. 'Weren't you lucky too? Shouldn't you have been on the plane that crashed?'

'No not really. We sometimes travelled with the band on the same plane. We'd get some good stories then. Straight from the horse's mouth. But as often as not there'd be no room for us on their plane because Danny had filled it up it with girls and groupies. Talk about the Six Mile High Club. Danny was a founder member. Took his mind off where he was, I guess. So we'd have to travel separately with the baggage and all the Marshalls and other stuff. So I wasn't on that flight. Funnily enough I was on the same later flight with Dredge.'

Camo was intrigued at the idea of a bunch of English musicians idling their time away in a castle halfway up a French mountain. What exactly did they do all day? Maybe Danny took a bunch of groupies with him. He thought his grandad would have hated it.

'What was this French castle? Was it a chateau?' he asked. 'Chateau Shagfest. Do you know where it was?'

Sentinel stood up from the desk and moved in front of a bookshelf.

'Can't really remember now,' he said, scanning the shelves, clearly looking for a title. 'No. It wasn't a chateau. Shagfest we all called it, but not to Danny's face. It was much more barebones than that. Much more military, I think, more of a fortress. I never went. Even as a way of hiding from the taxman it was an absurd thing for a top band to do. Not a good idea to take a top band like themselves out of circulation for eight months.

'One good thing that did emerge from that self-inflicted purdah was the bootlegs. So maybe not all their time there was wasted. Track after track emerged in the years after the crash. Pure gold. All produced in the makeshift recording studio they built in a basement there. Or maybe it was an old dungeon.' He laughed a kind of wheezing whistle at the idea.

Chris Sentinel turned and looked out of the window. It seemed he was lost in memories of a time when the world changed and was being changed and he had been an observer on it all, a witness and a recorder.

'I do remember it was in the Pyrenees. Sodding miles from anywhere. I wrote about it in one of my early books.' He turned back to the shelf and pulled out a book. 'The one I did about that last tour and the crash and the time leading up to it. They were a great band. Perhaps the best,' he sighed. 'Here have a copy. I'll sign it if you like.'

He handed the book to Rosie who was nearest to him.

'You'll find all the details in there.'

'Did Danny ever own a boat?' This was Rosie, looking up from Sentinel's book she was flicking through. Camo looked across at her and nodded.

'No. No. Not that I ever heard,' Sentinel responded, frowning slightly as though the idea was odd. 'I don't think he had any interest in sailing or the sea. Or the entire oceans of the world for that matter. He was much more interested in dry land and castles. Castles in the air even, but not on the water.'

He stopped to take a long drag on the third joint he'd rolled while they were talking. He was looking out of the window again, and spoke over his shoulder.

'I do remember one thing. The castle. Chateau Shagfest. It was called Madeline, Fort Madeline.'

7. PLAN

'So not a ship then?' Camo said, pulling Rosie's leg.

Rosie laughed. The others smiled. They'd heard Rosie's idea that Madeline might be a ship or a boat. It was a pity; they'd liked it too.

'So what do we know?' Rosie said.

They were back in Richmond. She, Camo and Tyko and Tyko's girlfriend Rox were in the pizza joint.

Tyko and Rox made a very interesting couple, Rosie thought. For a start they were both strikingly good-looking. And secondly they both studied subjects so far removed from the orbit of her own knowledge as to be almost magical. While Tyko was an electrical engineering student, Rox was a student of structural engineering.

'What I do is engineering,' Tyko said. 'What Roxy does is enginerring. The only way they can go forward is by learning from their mistakes.'

Rox thumped him lightly on the shoulder. She smiled though.

They'd filled her in on the whole back story. And she had heard for herself the message on the gold disc. Only four people had heard it now. They would keep it at that.

'It made the back of my neck shiver,' she said. 'It's so weird.'

Rosie knew what she meant.

Camo started checking off his fingers with his other hand.

'So what do we know? Well what have we got? One, we have a message definitely left by Danny Weathervane on the gold disc. Two, the message talks about gold. Three, the gold appears to have been hidden in a place called Madeline. Four, we now know Madeline is Fort Madeline in the Pyrenees. Sentinel's book tells us how to locate it. Five, Sentinel told us of a rumour that Danny Weathervane spent £300,000 on Krugerrand gold coins. Six, we can imagine, guess or infer that the gold referred to in the message are these Krugerrands. Seven, it is likely that a stash of gold coins was hidden somewhere in this Fort Madeline in the

French Pyrenees by Danny Weathervane, who died soon after. Eight, It is possible they are still there.'

He held both hands with the fingers pointing upwards in front of him like a screen. He dropped his hands and looked round the table.

'Nine,' Rox said. 'I did some calculations. £300,000 worth of Krugerrands in 1970 would be worth £12 million today.'

There was a collective gasp round the table.

'And ten,' Rox carried on. '£300,000 in 1970 would buy ten thousand gold Krugerrands. It was £30 for one then. Does ten thousand coins sound right Camo?'

'I don't know really. I don't know anything. But if the £300,000 figure is right, then let's assume we're talking about ten thousand coins.'

'And they were one ounce each,' Rox continued. 'That was the idea. You were buying the weight in gold rather than the value of the coin. Ten thousand one-ounce gold coins would weigh a total of 284 kilograms. Or 625 pounds if you prefer. Roughly just over a quarter of a tonne. Imagine it as five or six bags of cement. Closer to five and a half bags. A car or van can carry that easy. Then I would guess for portability and ease of transport, and for carrying, the coins would be packed in quite a few boxes or strong leather or canvas bags. If you said ten boxes then each box would weigh 62.5 lbs or 28.5 kg without counting the packaging. If you said twenty boxes then each box would weigh 31.25 lbs or 14.25 kg. Both are manageable but I fancy the smaller boxes would be more practical.'

She sat back, pleased with the look of utter admiration on their faces at her expertise with numbers.

'If there were twenty boxes,' Rosie said, 'How many coins in a box?'

'That's an easy one,' Rox said with the slight disdain for people to whom arithmetic didn't come easy. Or were lazy, her look said. 'Five hundred coins to a box, if they are in boxes. Same number to a stout bag. I don't know how these things are done. And each coin is now worth £1,200. A single box of five hundred coins would be worth £600,000.'

'Twelve million quid,' Tyko said. 'Jesus Christ.'

'Amazing what time can do to money,' Rosie said with a dreamy look.

'£600,000 to a relatively small box,' Camo said, holding both hands in front of him about a foot apart. He whistled, a wheezy kind of hoosh sound, almost silent.

'Ok,' Rosie said. 'That's what we know. The question now is, what do we do about it?'

What can we do? Camo thought. We are just students after all.

'We go and find it,' Rox said. 'What else?'

There was a stunned silence round the table. Until now it had been a fascinating mystery, a pleasant fantasy they had enjoyed chasing. But now it was the real thing. What did they do about what they knew?

'We could,' Camo said hesitantly. 'We could just go and find this castle and have a look?'

'At least it won't involve diving,' Tyko said with a grin at Rosie. She pricked his arm gently with her fork.

'Who owns it?' Rosie's legal training was beginning to assert itself. 'Didn't Chris Sentinel say Danny Weathervane owned it? He'd bought it at some point and done it up?'

'That's right. Maybe it was mentioned in his will.'

'If he made one,' Rosie insisted.

'What happens if he didn't make a will?' Tyko said. They were all looking at Rosie for knowledge of this kind of thing.

'His assets pass to his family, his nearest relations.'

'Either way,' Tyko said. 'Either someone, one of Danny's heirs, owns this castle or they don't. Or maybe his heirs sold it off as quick as they could. But, more importantly for us, either someone's living in it or they're not.'

'And if they're not, and it's empty we can easily sneak in and have a look round?' Rox said.

'Exactly.'

'Anyone speak French?' Camo asked.

Rosie put her hand up. 'I do. Used to be not bad. I went on a French exchange a couple of years ago. Summer holiday.'

Camo looked at her, surprised. 'I never knew that.'

Rosie shrugged. 'I know what you're thinking.'

'Exactly. If we find out where this place is, we should be able to find out a certain amount of information about it on the net.'

'Just Google it?' Tyko said.

'Why not? Even if the website information about it is in French, we can Google Translate it, or better still–' he gestured to Rosie '-translate it ourselves.'

In the twenty-first century nothing stays hidden, nothing stays unknown, they knew.

They all looked round the table at each other. Each willing the others to assent to the idea, to say yes.

It was Rox who put it into words.

'What's stopping us going exactly?'

They were all in their second year of their various courses The summer term was coming to an end. If they had exams they weren't course defining nor affected the level of their degrees. They had a car. They had the time. They had the motive.

They agreed they would find out what they could as soon as possible. One of them would read Sentinel's book. Camo volunteered to do that. Depending on what the book said, the others would research the place as much as they could on the net.

They would go in two weeks' time at the end of June. They would drive down through France to the Pyrenees in Camo's Land Rover, find Fort Madeline, or Chateau Shagfest as they all now called it, and see what they could see.

And if they found nothing worthwhile, or Chateau Shagfest appeared to have permanent residents and there was no way they could explore it, then they would go and have a fortnight's holiday on a beach somewhere down in the south of France or over the mountains in Spain.

8. OTHERS

Things returned to normal over the next two weeks. There were lectures and seminars to attend. Essays to write for Camo and Rosie, and for Tyko practical electrical tasks and tests to perform. He took the record player and the borrowed electric motor back to the department workshops.

Before he did they played the message back one more time so they could record it on their phones. Camo also made a written transcription on his phone.

Madeline got the gold with her in the hold. That first line stayed in his mind. It was a metaphor then. Not a ship's hold, but some kind of strong place, a stronghold.

Rox went on an Engineering Faculty coach tour to Ironbridge in Shropshire to see the world's first iron bridge.

She came back full of its praises.

'We must go there again,' she said. 'All of us. It's unbelievable it's still standing after all this time, nearly two hundred and fifty years.'

The most amazing thing about it, she said, was they built it as though it was made of wood.

'It's got mortise and tenon joints, and dovetails, just like it would if you were making it in wood. Yet it's completely iron, there's no wood in it all.'

They said they'd all go on a day trip to see it with her before they headed off to France.

Rosie was the one that suggested they camped rather then went in hotels. It would be a lot cheaper. As a regular and frequent family camper from her childhood days onwards she laughed at the look of horror on the others' faces at the prospect of tents, sleeping on hard ground and cold water showers.

'It's not like that at all,' she said. 'It's so much better than hotelling. Modern campsites have everything you need. They're great. We can take camp beds too if you like. We've got some. And sleeping bags. And we've got two two-person tents. Don't worry, I'll get everything from home.'

Reluctantly and still extremely worried, they agreed.

A few days later she reported back that she'd found out some more information about Danny Weathervane's will from information and references on the net.

'He wasn't married apparently. And no direct heirs. But he had a sister. She's the one that sold the gold disc. So almost certainly still alive. According to various news sites I found all his assets went to his sister Jane. Known as Janey it seems. Danny and Janey. I guess Chateau Shagfest went to her as well. Camo do you know her? Does your mum?'

Camo said he didn't know her, but his mum and grandmother would probably know a lot more. He said he'd find out.

'Jane Shadwell?'

A woman's voice on the phone said it was. The voice was thin and suspicious and tentative.

'This is Arch Lyly. I'm Jim Lyly's grandson.'

'Sylvia's grandson?' Her tone of voice changed to warmth and interest. 'What was your mother's name? Laura?'

'Yes. That's right.'

They talked of families and times past.

When he'd asked her a few days after Rosie suggested it, Camo's mother had told him her mother Sylvia had kept in touch for a while with everyone after the crash. Everyone who was left. Then they had drifted apart, meeting up only for weddings, occasional reunions, and gatherings brought together by filmmakers and TV companies and documentary makers; and then later on it was just funerals. Then it was only the Christmas card stage. But they'd all kept each other's addresses and made sure they were up to date. It seemed important. They'd even moved onto exchanging email addresses and later on mobile phone numbers. Each one of the prime and minor players from the old days needed to know where each of them was, it seemed, without it being verbally expressed. It was the least they could do. They owed it to the past they'd shared.

Camo moved the conversation on to the reason for his

call. He explained that he and some other student friends were wondering about the castle they'd heard of that Danny owned in France?

'Castle?' Jane Shadwell laughed down the phone.

'Chateau, I mean,' he said, apologising.

She laughed even more. 'Fortress actually. Well, prison, more like,' she said.

As they talked Camo learned that yes it had been left to her and she did indeed still own it.

'Don't know why I held on to it. I hated it. But the kids enjoyed it. And it seemed important to keep it.'

Camo understood it was a link to her brother.

'Danny loved it. Thought it made him some kind of medieval monarch or bandit king in his hideout. It was his crusader castle. He called himself the Young Man of the Mountains. That's why I kept it I suppose. In his memory. But I know the only kind of crusading or knight-erranting he did there was of a different sort. More mounting than mountain. He said it was an amazingly sexually stimulating place. Love among the crags. Never seemed like that when I went there. Cold stone and dark.'

He was surprised at her candour. So everyone knew what Danny got up to there, Camo thought. It really was Chateau Shagfest.

Camo explained that he and some friends would love to go down and see it, perhaps spend a holiday there if that was possible? It was after all a place where his grandfather had spent some time too, writing songs and producing bootleg recordings if nothing else.

'Of course you can. Of course,' she said. 'But do you really want to? It's pretty isolated. I haven't been for years myself. Decades probably. I don't know how habitable it is. You might have to camp out in the courtyard. Good thing is it's not too far away from a town.'

A thought seemed to strike her.

'Actually in fact you could do me a favour. We pay a local farmer to keep an eye on it. But I've not heard from him for ages.

Which may be a good thing or a bad thing, I don't know. If you do go down there, could you look them up and see if they're still monitoring the place? Also it would be good to find out what sort of state it's in. Let me know if it's a wreck, if any reasonable work might need doing. That kind of thing? And if you could get me the name of a local estate agent too who might be interested in selling it for me? It's time.' Then she added more quietly, more to herself than Camo. 'Yes. It was time a long time ago.'

Camo said he would be very glad to do that.

'So why not come over and get the keys? I can give you directions and the name and address of the farmer. And I'll write a letter of authorisation you can show to the farmer so he knows you're legit.'

Camo spent an interesting afternoon in the house in Tunbridge Wells where Jane Shadwell lived. She seemed really glad to meet him. They talked of the old days, or she did at least, but it was all interesting to Camo. She had known his grandad well, and liked him. So warm was she and wistful about him, and so sad to hear about his current condition, that Camo wondered if there wasn't an unrequited romance there. Well, could be requited for all he knew. The 60s wasn't a time for much unrequiting.

She was Danny's younger sister and that would put her a few years younger than Dredge, so maybe 70 or 72.

A thought struck him. And he offered to take her to the nursing home when he came back from holiday. There was a possibility that Dredge might remember her, especially after one of his garden gigs.

'That would be good,' she said simply. 'I'd like to do that.'

Camo came away from Tunbridge Wells with a large set of keys all hung on a carabiner, a thick ring binder with instructions about how to do various things about the place, such as turn the water and power on and off, and the heating ('Better than you'd think,' she said), and the name and address of the local farmer, plus the letter of authorisation signed by Jane which would identify Camo to the farmer or anyone else who might need to know. Inside the folder was a leaflet in French with a short précis of its history, and a local detailed map and directions to the fortress as Camo now tried to call it. Realising now it was some kind of 17th century fortress didn't stop him mentally still referring to it as Chateau Shagfest. That title was now stuck fast.

Jane Shadwell had told him she had been to the fort a few times with her family. After the first time they'd taken a small inflatable dinghy with oars and a small outboard motor.

'There's a lake there,' she said. 'That was the best thing about it. That's what the kids liked.'

But you had to be careful she said if you went on the lake.

'You have to watch out for the run-off, if you go swimming, where the lake drains down the mountain by the side of the fort in the mill race, before the waterfall. The flow's quite strong and can suck you down. That's what happened to the previous owner before Danny. Went swimming and got sucked down the mill race and went right over the cliff in the waterfall.' She shuddered. 'It is really dangerous. Especially in the spring with the snow melting and the lake level high. The race then is ferocious. Fortunately there was an iron grating there across it in those days after that when we were there. Danny had it put in. But it may have gone. You must check that before you do anything.'

Camo said he would be sure to do that.

Another thing that Camo came away from Tunbridge Wells was the knowledge that if they did find anything in the castle, any gold, then they would be obliged to share it with the owner Jane Shadwell. Or would they? He was aware of the first stirrings of a moral dilemma.

According to the map in the ring binder and Google Maps and the Michelin map of France, Fort Madeline was perched high up in the Pyrenean mountains south of Toulouse, south of Foix, south of Ax-les-Thermes.

Before they left, one thing Camo wanted to do was retrieve the other gold disc from storage and hang them both on his grandad's wall in his room at the nursing home.

First he went to the storage depot where all his grandad's

belongings were kept. It was quite easy to find what he was look-ing for. Early on his mother had recognised that there had to be some kind of order to the storage, and she'd instructed the removal people to do that. So everything was ordered, labelled and classified on industrial shelving and in large storage boxes. He found the disc in one of the boxes in the 'Dr Edge' section.

He went over to the nursing home. He borrowed a hammer and nails from the home's gardener and oddjob man.

The discs looked a treat when they were mounted side by side on his grandad's wall.

Dredge didn't seem to recognise them or know what they were. It was morning and he hadn't yet played any music that day. But as Camo left he turned one last time to say goodbye. Dredge was standing in front of the two framed discs on the wall.

'Yes,' he said with a smile.

Camo's heart lifted.

Rosie came back from her family home with all the camping equipment. Her old red Renault van was crammed full. Among the things she brought back from home was a large box of water purification tablets. She insisted they would be necessary. She knew they had permission to access and stay in the fortress. 'But what's it got for fresh water? Is it just a well? God knows what's fallen down there over the centuries. And even if they're not nec-essary, it's better to have them just in case.' Since Rosie was the only one among them who had done any sort of camping, they followed her lead.

They would travel in Camo's Land Rover. They knew from the detailed map that they would have to travel a few miles along a mule track. The Land Rover would be best for that. In any case it was the only vehicle they had that had room for all four of them and their bags and the camping equipment. That would go on the roof rack along with a couple of spades and shovels. They didn't know what to expect and wanted to be prepared.

Camo loaded a strange bag of tools up there too. The bag was a maroon coloured heavy jute plumber's bass. It contained all sorts of tools including crowbars, hammers and chisels, two bolsters, a pair of different sized pipe wrenches and much else. He didn't really know what it contained. He just called in to his mother's house and raided the bass from his dad Vinny's old tool shed.

Vinny didn't actually do any work with the tools. He just liked tools. He collected them. His favourites were pipe wrenches – known also according to Vinny as 'a pair of dogs'. Vinny kept many of the tools in his plumber's bass. This was a large heavy-duty oval shaped bag made from jute with two handles. It had no closures: it just opened out and you could see everything that was in it at one glance. It was folded closed by holding the two handles. Surprisingly to Camo a tool hardly ever fell out. He didn't check what was in the bass when he grabbed it out of the shed. He just assumed there'd be a bunch of useful tools in it. They might not need them anyway.

Rox added a twenty metre spool of wind-up steel measuring tape.

'You never go anywhere without the ability to measure,' she said. She didn't say but she'd also packed her state of the art tools, her engineer's digital instrument for measuring lengths, heights, angles and levels, a laser rangefinder plus its stabilising tripod. They all went in what she called her engineer's backpack. You never knew when you might need them. You could get apps that did that kind of thing, but they weren't as good as the real thing. She also took a large pad of drawing paper, her precision pencil, her scale rule and a small adjustable set-square. She knew they'd need to make a plan at some point, probably. It was the only way. She didn't tell the others. It was her secret weapon.

Tyko and Rosie brought their cameras. Both were good quality and both had a series of lens options.

They were ready to go.

They were going to take the Channel Tunnel. Then make their way south across France. They'd go east of Paris, heading south all the time.

The day before they set off for France a text message from

Chris Sentinel pinged into Camo's phone. It read:

<Funnily enough I had someone else over last night, asking about the old days like you did. Just turned up on the doorstep at night, out of the blue. Almost barged her way in. Isobel didn't take to her at all. Strange thing is, she asked who Madeline was too. Sorry but I told her it wasn't a person it was a place, then re-gretted it and decided not to tell her anything more. She said she was the Lion's daughter Bayb. Lionel Azmoun's daughter. Maybe seven or eight years younger than me. I thought I recognised her. And she said he knew me. So she could be. Chris>

Camo called him back.

'Yes she could well be the Lion's daughter for all I know,' Sentinel said. 'I did recognise her a bit. Mind you Bayb was a kid when I last saw her in 1971, a teenager. A bit slight, sure, but this women was stick-thin with a big dark almost black eyes. And jet black hair – odd for her age. She never stopped moving. The eyes looked like they were used to getting their own way. There was also a muscly-looking younger bloke in a dark suit standing by the car all the time. Looked like protection, I've seen quite a lot of those sorts over the years. It was a sodding-great Mercedes SUV with blacked out windows. I definitely didn't tell her anything about you, or that you'd been to see me with similar questions. So don't worry she doesn't know anything about you. But I got a bad feeling about her, Arch. She looked mean. She was impatient and unfriendly. May be unnecessary, but watch yourself.'

9. MADELINE

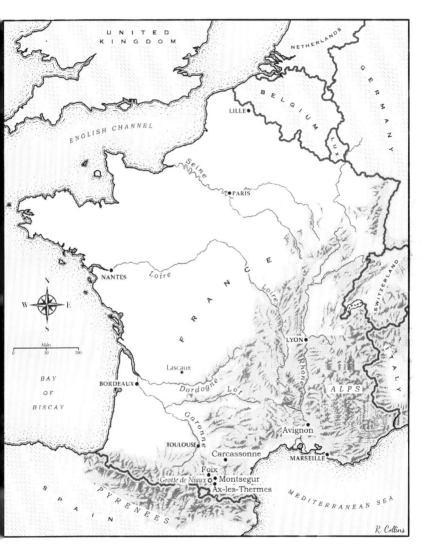

If you drive south out of the ancient town of Foix in the Pyrenean foothills heading for Andorra you will eventually come to the little spa town of Ax-les-Thermes.

Foix itself is forty-five miles south of the great aerospace city of Toulouse. The mountains begin beyond Foix shortly after the fabulous Grotte de Niaux, where our ancestors lived before the Stone Age and after, painting animals on the walls and spitting pigment on the backs of their hands spread against the walls to show their silhouetted handprints. Still heading south, with the mountain foothills growing round you all the time, you come to the hot springs of Ax-les-Thermes where the road levels out for a while.

If you headed east out of Foix instead of south you'd shortly come to the isolated *pog* on top of which stands the small castle and redoubt of Montsegur. This is the scene of the last act of the Albigensian Crusade, where the heretic Cathars made their last stand and were all burnt alive by the victorious crusaders, their fellow Christians and countrymen. This is still Cathar country.

After Ax the real climbing begins and the boulder-strewn Ariege river is a torrent between exposed rock banks. This road, the N20, leads eventually to the high hidden valley of Andorra la Vella, another country.

Before Andorra, still in France, south of Ax a small road, a former mule track and packhorse trail, turns off the N20. Tarmacked at first, then covered in gravel, it eventually peters out above and past the successive hamlets of the three Bazerques, Premiere, Deuxieme and Troisieme Bazerques. Before it does it runs past and alongside a high stretch of water to the big archway and double doors of an old stone fortress.

On a small plateau above Troisieme Bazerques, and below the modern ski resort of Ax 3 Domaines higher up the mountain sits a small lake. Beside the lake on an exposed rocky bluff stands the Vauban fortress of Fort Madeline, overlooking lake Madeline before the land drops away steeply on the other side to the proximal Ariege river far below.

Military engineer Sebastien Vauban designed and built Fort Madeline for king Louis XIV in the last years of the 17th century to protect France from an invasion route over the mountains from the south. It dominates the upper Ariege river valley and blocks an easy descent into France by an invading army.

The Land Rover seemed in its element as they trundled along the old packhorse trail.

They'd enjoyed the trip. Even the novice campers had enjoyed it. They found it surprisingly sexy. It was weird to be situated on one of the fixed and demarcated aisles of a campsite with only the thin textile sheet shielding you from the prying eyes of your neighbours. You could get up to all sorts of mischief and they couldn't see you. It was exposed but thoroughly private. Tyko and Rox were particularly exhilarated by the sexual possibilities. They both knew they would be doing this again.

You felt the weather so much more in a tent too. And that was good. Camo was astonished to be warm and dry and snug inside the tent he shared with Rosie as a thunderstorm hit them in the campsite on the first night out of the Tunnel.

One thing Rox had been worried about was how would they eat when they were camping? She was delighted to discover that all the campsites they stayed in on the three-and-a-half day journey south all had mini-supermarkets and restaurants. There was hot water too! And proper lavatories!

Sometimes they ate in the camp restaurants; other times if they were staying in a town in a municipal campsite, they'd wander into town and find an eating place there.

They'd come out of the Tunnel and headed east and south. Rosie said the roads were better east of Paris and the countryside was nicer, so they followed her advice. From Reims they'd curved in a big sweep south-west, heading for Orleans, and from there they went due south to Chateauroux and Limoges. They were making for the Massif Central, the roof of France. They passed through the Dordogne, and the Lot. They stopped in a campsite beyond Brive and took a detour to see the wall paintings in the exact replica of the Lascaux cave. They talked excitedly about what they'd seen. And then they were silent for a while, each of them thinking about time and art and the deep past and the silent unknown but reachable future.

All the way they kept off the autoroutes. They were in no

hurry and anyway felt that travelling on toll motorways was not only a waste of money it wasn't really applicable to them. They had time and space and they wanted to feel the journey. Passing through France at their own speed was an adventure in itself. They passed through old towns embedded in the landscape linked by old straight roads.

It was as though the topography of the country existed in various layers, like design and layout software or a photo-editing program. The top layer was ultra-modern and was made up of the motorways linking the city ring-roads, the transport intermodal hubs and fast rail stations and the airports, and the modern business parks and retail outlets. This was the metal machine level. Then underneath that there was an older layer made up of old towns and straight narrow roads. Here there might be an industrial estate or a canal basin or a high street. Here there were people walking. This was the stone and brick level. Then underneath that there was an even older more rural layer made up of villages and concrete-paved farm entrances and war-of-the-worlds irrigation conveyances and plastic covered hay bales and the odd stretch of cobblestones. Here there were no people and the landscape seemed deserted. This was the earth level.

They ignored the top ultra-modern machine metal layer of France and made their way across country with their movement existing only in the underlying layers.

On the last leg they went through Cahors and then they came to Toulouse. They stayed in a campsite just south of the city. Next day they knew they were on the last lap. They passed through Foix. They came to Ax-les-Thermes.

Finally south of Ax, around midday, they took the minor turn-off from the Andorra road to the three Bazerques hamlets. And after Troisieme Bazerques as the road turned to a track they found the packhorse trail that led directly up the mountain.

At first the trail headed through thick waves of birch and hazel, then pine trees and stunted gnarly oaks. The oaks died away and they were left with the conifers, gradually diminishing in height a little as they gained altitude and the ground became steeper.

The track twisted and turned, but always maintained a constant slope through the trees. Camo could keep in the same gear and same speed and didn't have to constantly change down to maintain momentum, The constant gradient made it easy. It was made that way. The packhorse trail was originally made by the military as a supply route to the fortress. It was made to be as easy and gentle for the mules and packhorses as possible to take the grade, loaded as they would be.

Rox marvelled at the masterful engineering of the packhorse trail.

'Just because it's not a road doesn't mean it wasn't built by engineers. It was. And they knew what they were doing.' She clapped her hands in delight. This was good, she thought.

Up and up and up they went.

After three miles the Land Rover crested an elevation and the track levelled out. Camo stopped the car. The trees opened up.

Ahead of them stretched a broad flat lake surrounded by trees on all sides except one. Beyond the lake and on its banks on a bluff on the opposite side stood a low broad strong massive-looking grey stone building with a long grey roof. The fort itself and a long high grey stone wall in front of it ran along much of the far side of the lake. At the far left hand end of the wall, as they looked, the lake seemed to fall away from sight through a narrow gap between the wall and the rocky bank. Perhaps there was a waterfall there. Set into the right hand side of the front wall as they looked at it across the lake was an archway over a pair of stout double doors. The packhorse trail ran into a wide large rectangular shaped parking area in front of the doors. The trail then emerged from the far end of the parking area and followed the side of the fortress before turning aside and passing over a rocky shoulder and disappearing from sight into the trees, destination unknown.

'Da-dah,' said Rosie, in the back seat with Rox, looking up from the detailed map from the ring binder she had on her lap. 'Welcome to Lac Madeline. And that, ladies and gentlemen, beyond is Fort Madeline.'

'Chateau Shagfest awaits,' Tyko said. 'Anyone up for a bit of midnight skinny-dipping?'

'It'll be bloody freezing,' Camo said. 'We're not far below the treeline here.'

'We're around five thousand feet,' Rosie said. 'Maybe even more.'

'It probably gets snowed up in winter?' Rox said. Yet she was thinking that the old military engineers had probably designed the packhorse trail to be fully passable even in winter. The fort needed this supply route kept open. She hadn't noticed – and she would like to check – if the trail deliberately followed sheltered areas where less snow would fall. They would have thought of that.

'Ice-skating then,' Tyko said.

'Skinny ice-skating?' Rox said. 'Not sure about that.'

But there was an obstruction. Ahead of them on the right by the lakeside the trail rose sharply up to pass over a stone bridge structure. The bridge abutments were high up and looked completely unnecessary. A wide but relatively shallow stream passed under it from the conifer-covered high ground on the right and discharged into the lake. The whole bridge structure looked unnatural, artificial and unnecessary.

Camo drove on along the flat land by the lake, then with much more caution slowed down to a crawl when the track began to tilt up and elevate to reach the bridge.

He was right to be cautious. When the track levelled out again on top of the bridge parapet there was a section of about five metres of thick steel panels on the bridge top, coloured a deep red with rust. They looked solid enough and he crawled forward. Then he stopped dead. There were more thick steel panels which after dropping down a small lip carried on over the five metre gap between the abutments, making a drivable steel deck to the bridge.

He wasn't sure he trusted them, whether they would take

the weight of the car.

'Looks like we have to go forward on foot from here,' he said. 'Looks like the old military didn't want vehicles approaching too close to the fort.'

He looked around just in case he could drive off the track and ford the stream in the Land Rover. But the approach to the stream was blocked on both sides by a series of tetrahedron-shaped concrete structures, each about three feet high. Between them there were large steel tank traps. These were four-spiked welded pieces of thick steel. They were designed that no matter which way they lay on the ground as any of three legs stood on the ground the fourth thick spike extended forward. The bridge was the only way forward. It looked like they would definitely have to walk from here or risk the steel deck bridge. That was a pain but they had no choice.

Rox wasn't so sure this was the end of the trail. She could see that the track carried on over the other side of the bridge the same width as it did on this side. It looked very much as if the track was designed to be used by vehicles and had been used by vehicles all the way to the fort. If it wasn't for these steel plates bridging between the bridge abutments they could drive right up to the parking area in front of the fort's perimeter wall. And what was the parking area for if vehicles were prevented from going no further than this point?

'Hold on,' she said. 'I think it's designed to take vehicles. But I'll check.'

She opened her door and got out of the car. She went forward. At the top of the parapet by the side of the steel decking was a large iron vertically positioned wheel raised on large solid rusty gearing. There was a similar wheel and gear combination on top of the other parapet on the far side of the gap.

The steel decking looked solid enough. She went to one side, knelt down and peered under the deck. The plating was at least twenty millimetres thick, perhaps threequarters of an inch. Plenty strong enough. Not only that, it was supported all the way across the five metre span of the bridge by heavy steel girders. She counted six of them, about a metre apart.

She bent her head lower and inspected the underside more closely. The underside of the plates had a series of toothed rollers set at intervals attached to the underside. The tops of the girders were all set with a solid row of teeth. So the teeth on the rollers on the underside of the steel plates meshed into teeth running along the top surface of the girders. She was reminded immediately of the rack railway which took the narrow gauge trains up mount Snowdon.

Also as she looked across the five metre gap to the far parapet and approach on the other side, she could see there was a thin dark space above the steel road deck stretching the full width of the steel plates. She looked down at this side. There was a dark hole on this side too.

She knelt down at the edge and peered over the top and looked back. The steel plates seemed to run back in the darkness into a compartment under the deck on which she was kneeling and on which the Land Rover behind her was standing. She looked again at the big iron wheel. Then she got it.

'It's a retractable road surface!'

The others had joined her on the edge of the parapet. She went across to the wheel. There was a large iron pin in a hole between the wheel and the gearing below which seemed to act as a locking mechanism.

'This wheel and the one on the other side rotate,' she said excitedly. 'They wind the steel plates back into a narrow compartment on both sides under the decking we're now on.' That was how vehicle access to the fort was allowed or prevented.

She took out the locking pin and let it dangle free on its chain. She tried to rotate the wheel. It refused to budge. She tried it the other way, clockwise. It moved, but very reluctantly.

'I'm sure if we dripped oil in the wheel and the gear teeth below we could shift it. But we need oil,' she said.

Camo raised his hand in acknowledgement. You couldn't own a Land Rover without having a can of oil to hand. Especially a Land Rover with a power winch on the back.

'We've got oil,' he said. 'An oilcan and a tin of oil.'

'Ok. We don't need it now. But if we did get these wheels rotating I'm sure the steel plates would retract and all you'd have over this gap would be six girders and a lot of air.'

'No way any vehicles could cross those,' Camo said.

'Exactly. It's a vehicle trap. You wind the steel deck back, take away the winding wheels – I'm sure they're removable - and no vehicles can go past this point. It's a kind of modern draw-bridge.'

She returned the dangling pin to its hole. Now Rox walked ahead out on to the steel decking over the steel beams.

'Solid as a bloody rock,' she said, standing in the middle of the bridge. She jumped up and down. Nothing moved. It was solid underfoot. 'I think this is designed to take some seriously heavy ordnance. Field guns and limbers, maybe, that kind of thing. Might even take a tank, or a tank transporter. So we're definitely all right in ours.'

They went back to the car. They moved forward with re-newed confidence. As they drove over the bridge they could see the drop to the stream below, running between the deep stone parapets, was about twenty feet. Clearly the only reason it was built the way it was was to act as a barrier in the trail. A modern drawbridge as Rox had said.

As they continued along the track, back on the flat down at lake level, Rox looked back through the window. The whole bridge area and the parapets had been artificially raised above the natural ground level. It was designed as a vehicle trap, just as she thought. It was a drawbridge. She wondered if they should wind the steel decking back, so no one could cross after them, but there seemed no point. They would be driving back and to across it quite a few times in the coming days and they'd need the decking in place. Probably. And if not, they could wind the steel plates back once they had left for good. Which might be straightaway if they couldn't get in to the fort or find some lights or power. Or they could leave it as they found it. She'd ask Camo at some point what he wanted to do.

A few minutes later they came to a stop in the broad flat parking area in front of the large double wooden outer doors set in the high perimeter wall of Fort Madeline. The doors were closed and padlocked.

It was warm and sunny and there was no chill in the light breeze. But they knew it would be chilly when the sun went down. It would be cold at night.

They all emerged from the car. Camo carried the carabiner of keys to Madeline.

The other three gazed across the lake as Camo found the right key for the padlock. He called them over to help when he'd removed it. He and Tyko pushed the heavy right hand door inwards, walking it backwards as far as it would go. It creaked and protested, but moved quite easily. It was well balanced on its three huge sets of bolt-hinges and it also ran on two iron rollers between the ground and the underside of the doorsill. The rollers ran on curving iron tracks set in the stone paved ground surface. They pushed the door all the way back until it was resting against the same wall in which it was set. The door had rotated almost one hundred and eighty degrees and the two iron roller tracks curved round in a full semi-circle. Camo secured the door with a thick L-shaped iron bar hanging on the interior wall which slotted into a ring on the back of the door. As the two women walked forward through the doorway, Camo and Tyko repeated the action with the other door.

The archway was now fully opened and clear and the two doors were secured back against the wall. He returned to the car and brought it forward through the archway and parked it.

'Shall we shut the doors?' Camo said.

'Maybe not yet. We've got to go down and find a supermarket and get supplies. Later today probably,' Rosie said.

This was really a look-see. They hadn't known if they would find the fort, nor whether they would be able to get in. Once they had achieved that they would set about securing all the things they needed for an extended stay.

Ahead and around them was a broad wide courtyard open

to the sky, paved with stone flags underfoot and perfectly level. Ahead of them was the main body of the fort. Over to their far left set against the outer wall of the fort was a series of three large single doors letting on to what might be old stables and workshops, Rox guessed. The one on the far left as they looked across was split into an upper and lower half. So almost certainly a stable, Rox thought. On the right and behind them was the massive bare wall, four metres high, of the fort's outer perimeter wall. The main body of the fort straight ahead of them had a repeat of the arch and double doors they had just passed through in the perimeter wall. That presumably was a cart or vehicle entrance. This was confirmed by groove marks in the stone flags below their feet that showed the long-time passage of steel shod wheels leading from the arched double doorway behind them to the arched double doorway ahead. Further away over to the left in the main fort wall was a single door. That could be the one for pedestrians.

Just behind them now, on their left, further on past the leaf of the double doors on the back of the front wall, were two large 5,000 litre steel tanks raised up on matching pairs of low concrete walls.

Rox was looking at the tanks with great interest.

'That's good. That's really good. I think these are oil tanks,' she said. 'Let's hope one of them at least is full.'

Above ground, at first floor level in the fort a row of small windows set deeply in the thick wall ran along the full length of the facade.

'Amazingly, the windows are all glazed,' Rox said. 'None of them are broken either.'

That was a good sign, she thought. Firstly because it meant there'd be no howling gales blowing through the fort through any unglazed casements. It also meant the building was weathertight. And it meant no birds, bats and their droppings would have been able to come and go at will. And also it might suggest that the fort was looked after to some degree. Or at least checked and monitored.

'So it's got two floors,' Camo said. 'Ground and first.'

'Might have an underground basement level as well,' Tyko said.

'Or more than one,' Rox said.'

'I guess that's the front door,' Rosie said pointing to the single door over to the far left of them. 'Shall we ring the bell.'

'Actually I think this is the back door,' Rox said. 'The front overlooks the drop down to the valley below.' She did a kind of bouncing and hooping gesture to indicate the far side of the fort from where they now stood. 'And we're now standing at the back. Though it's probably the only way in.'

'Let's try those big doors,' Tyko said. 'Then we can try the small one if we can't get in here.'

They agreed.

Camo found the right key as they approached the doors. Each key was labelled. There were two locks, both hefty mortise locks set into the thick wood of the right hand door of the pair. The same key fitted both locks.

Tyko dug out a torch from the backpack he was carrying. 'I got this,' he said.

'We need to find some sort of utility room,' Rox said. 'Boiler room, electricity switch board, control panel, anything like that.'

They all knew that if they couldn't get the power and the lights going they wouldn't be able to stay. They'd have to drop down to the valley and find a campsite. Then travel up each day. It was doable, but tiresome.

Tyko turned the locks and pushed the right hand door open. It creaked but moved smoothly enough. He pushed it against the right hand wall and noticed there was some sort of retaining mechanism set in the floor as the door swept towards the wall. The doorsill passed over a balanced iron wedge in the mechanism which pressed down as the door moved over it, then flipped back up behind the door, so holding it open and preventing it closing. Camo saw that you could take it out of operation by flicking a catch which kept the wedge in its housing to stop it popping up. But for the moment he thought it a good idea to leave the door open. It let in a lot of light. He let the door stay open. They let the other leaf of the double doors stay closed.

They were in a roofed and enclosed unloading bay, walled on all sides. On the left hand wall was another door. Camo found the key for that one. He unlocked it and pushed it open. It too had the same retaining mechanism set in the floor as the outer door. He pushed the door over the wedge and it locked open.

Straight ahead of them was a broad whitewashed corridor. It was following the line of the fort's back façade facing on to the courtyard outside. There were no windows on this ground floor level. The light from the open door and the light reflected off the whitened walls made the entire corridor light enough, if a little gloomy. Now immediately to their right was another door.

'Let's try this door,' Rox said, pointing to the door to their right. 'It would make sense for any control room to be as close as possible to the way in.'

Not for the first time, Rosie was thankful Rox was with them. She understood buildings and how they worked.

The stout door on the right had a sturdy latch handle but no obvious lock. Tyko lifted the latch which in turn raised a large iron bar out of its seat in a catch on the door frame. He pulled the door towards him. A set of steps disappeared down into the darkness.

'I'll check it out,' he said, switching on his torch.

They could hear his feet and see the torch beam disappearing as he descended the flight of steps. There was silence for a while. Then he called up.

'Yes. I think this is it. Come on down.'

He moved back to the bottom of the stairs and pointed the torch upwards so they could see the way.

All three came down to join Tyko. He flashed the beam around the large room. It appeared to be full of machinery of various kinds, all hulking and mysterious in the gloom.

'What's that over there,' Tyko pointed the beam to a control panel on the wall by the bottom step. In the middle of the panel was a large H-shaped metal frame with a handle.

'Ah, that's it, I think,' Rox said.

While Tyko held the beam highlighting the panel Rox went over to it. Without hesitating she grasped the big switch by its handle and threw and rotated it upwards and pushed it home into a sprung housing.

Immediately bright strip lights flickered and then came on strongly in the ceiling above them. What appeared to be a big generator set on concrete footings started up in front of them with a smooth and powerful hum, and various lights flashed on and off in a series of control panels along the near wall.

'Well, we've got light and power,' Rox said. 'Now how about some heat.' She turned to inspect the various control panels.

'Tell you what,' she said. 'While I'm doing this, why don't you lot go and explore upstairs. All the lights should be working.'

They were in Fort Madeline and it was up and running.

10. ASSESS

Rox was right. The lights were working everywhere they tried. Some, it seemed, had been left on, switched off only by the main power switch.

Once they realised the fort was operational they decided they should descend the mountain and stock up at a local supermarket.

Tyko offered to go and Rosie said she would go with him. She didn't trust the men's abilities to buy the right amount of the right things.

'Let's unload all the gear first,' Camo said. 'We'll definitely need the camp beds and sleeping bags, if not the tents.'

The three of them unloaded the Land Rover into a pile in the courtyard. Then Tyko and Rosie set off down the mountain. They knew they'd passed several supermarkets in the outskirts of Ax, maybe less than ten miles away.

Camo went back into the main body of the fort. He could hear Rox muttering and swearing in the control room in the basement. He continued along the broad corridor. There were iron pipes of all sizes and gauges and electrical conduit fixed in the angle of the wall and ceiling overhead. The wall through which they had entered the building, and the courtyard beyond it, was on his left. The bulk of the rest of the building was on his right.

The ground floor appeared to be set out in a series of rectilinear blocks like a new town. The broad corridor he was in stretched the full length of the building. It was broken regularly by equally broad corridors that came in at right angles from the right. Spaced along the length of the building were two narrow stone staircases and a third central much wider staircase rising from the broad ground floor corridor. Sunlight from the glazed windows was streaming down the staircases from the first floor.

He noticed two things at the staircase wells. Firstly the steps came up from the lower depths below the ground floor before carrying on upwards, which meant there was at least one basement level down there underground; and secondly set next to the big central staircase was a set of concertina doors indicating there might be a lift behind.

He pushed the lift door open sideways. It folded back on itself. There was a large lift standing behind the door. Was this a goods lift? He thought. He'd ask Rox. She'd know.

Realising they had all the time in the world to explore the place, he now prioritised his search. The immediate requirement was for some kind of sitting room, a kitchen, a bathroom, and somewhere to sleep. And reasoning that all of these requirements might probably be rooms with windows, he backtracked and ascended one of the two smaller staircases to the first floor. For the time being he didn't trust the lift.

The first floor mirrored the layout of the ground floor: it had a broad corridor along the outside wall, but with a row of windows unlike the corridor below it, and subsidiary corridors joining it at right angles.

Camo heard footsteps below.

'Up here Rox,' he called.

She joined him on the first floor landing at the top of the main stairs.

'I got the boiler working. It's a big old oil-fired beast. I put it on a timer. We've got hot water and we can get heat if and when we need it. There was some sort of room diagram down there and I think you have to specify which room you want the heat to go in. But it works.'

'You're the one.'

'As long as the oil doesn't run out. I'll check that tomorrow.'

Camo explained his search for bedrooms and somewhere like a sitting room which they could use as a base or day room.

They had a pleasant surprise the third room they looked in. There was a large bedstead in it and a bare mattress. The next room was the same. In fact all six rooms along this section had bed frames with mattresses. Between each room was a large washroom with six showers and four baths and a series of basins. Some but not all had a lavatory and bidet as well. Those items looked recent. Possibly Danny's doing, Camo thought. They also found rooms with basins and rows of urinals and lines of privies in cubicles in them – the kind that are just ceramic footstands and a hole in the floor. So it looked like Danny hadn't fancied the holes in the floor either and had installed the modern WCs.

'The technical name for those scary toilets is Asiatic closet,' Rox said. 'If you're writing a specification.' She knew they were usually specified in places where the only cleaning available might be the occasional hosing down. The military used to like them, and she bet Rosie had seen plenty of them on European campsites. They were designed to be low maintenance, easy to clean.

'So far, so good,' Camo said.

They turned through ninety degrees and followed a cross-corridor running to the front of the building. At the front there was the mirror-image broad corridor running the full length of the building as there had been at the back where they entered. They turned left and followed the front corridor.

They were still on the first floor and were progressing along the front corridor towards the far end of the building, checking the rooms as they went. But unlike the floorplan on the ground floor below where the front and back wall corridors were unobstructed, the first floor front corridor ended at a large door.

Camo lifted the latch and pushed the door open. It was a broad big brightly lit corner room with windows on two sides. Through the two front windows they could see the river Ariege far below. Through the one side window they could see the mountain rising then falling away in that direction. But also by craning their necks back to the left they could just catch sight of the edge of the lake.

Inside the room was a large number of heavy wooden chairs and tables. Over by the side wall under the window was a broad sideboard with six drawers.

'Well this'll do,' Camo said.

They realised why this room had been chosen as the main sitting room, and the furniture brought there. Though there were four large corner rooms on each floor, this one had the most light and the best view.

Later, after the other two had come back with supplies, they were all assembled in the far left corner room on the first floor, which they agreed made the obvious place for a day-room. Rox had worked out the heating options and had directed the hot water to the big cast-iron radiators along the outer walls of this room. She'd also directed the heat to a couple of the bedrooms and bathrooms. And to the huge kitchen they'd found downstairs. The kitchen had a vast heavy wooden table and twelve wooden chairs. It also had some machinery. There was a heavy cast iron cooker and range, and a washing machine, dishwasher and fridge. The fridge was unplugged. There was nothing in the cupboards.

Surprisingly the cooker worked. The gas hissed through and they lit it to test it with a match they'd found in a large box in a drawer. A propane gas bottle lurked in a corner next to the cooker and a gas pipe connected the two. It meant, Rox said, that there might be a store of gas bottles somewhere. Possibly in one of the outhouses.

In the corner room they were all sitting or looking out of the windows as the sun went down.

Another surprise was there was a good mobile signal. They hadn't expected that. For some reason they'd assumed that being in the mountains would make mobile phone signals weak and problematic. But the opposite seemed to be the case. They all had maxed-out signal strength. Depended where the mast was, Tyko guessed. There must be one on a ridge nearby.

'This is garden furniture isn't it? It's teak or something.' Rosie said, banging the arm of the chair she was sitting in. She was reading the French leaflet about the history of the fort.

'Yeah, looks like at one time they threw out anything that would rot, like the bedding, but kept the mattresses, and just kept the hardwearing basics,' Camo said. He thought Jane Shadwell may have organised that at some point. Perhaps when she knew she wouldn't be coming back. That reminded him. He would go and introduce himself to the farmer in the next couple of days.

Tyko rose up from the teak garden chair he was lounging in and went to the sideboard under the window.

'We've not looked in here, yet,' he said. He started at the top, pulling the drawers out.

The top five drawers were empty. He pulled open the bottom drawer.

'This is interesting,' he said. He reached in and brought out a series of large sheets of paper. They were yellowing and looked old. He laid them out on the top surface of the sideboard.

'I think they're plans,' he said.

The others came over to look.

'Well that's good,' Camo said.

It was two sets of identical plans. The second set was obviously a copy of some kind of the first. All the plans had a name, an address in Ax, and a scale in a box at the bottom right hand corner. There was a date: 1958.

'That name's probably the architect or the surveyor who did the plans,' Rox said. 'And the date he did them.' She was thinking: you usually had plans made when you were thinking of making big changes to a building. You needed to see what was what so you could see where and what you wanted to do. Accurate plans were the start.

They were good, she thought, but it wouldn't be enough.

Rosie said the leaflet was interesting.

'It was built between 1695 and 1699, as we thought, by a guy called Vauban who was some kind of fortification genius apparently. Took four years. Says Wellington didn't come this way when he invaded from Spain against Napoleon precisely because this fort blocked the route. And that's a hundred years after it was built. So it was still functioning then.

'Then after that it was abandoned and reoccupied repeatedly. Looks like it was so useful because it was so close to the frontier. I guess in Europe until the EU got going you could never trust your neighbours.

'The last and latest period of military occupation was in the late 1930s. Before Danny Weathervane that is. It underwent a big modernisation by the military then. They were worried about Franco and his fascists to the south.'

'Falangists, not fascists,' Tyko said.

'Is there a difference?' Rosie responded.

Tyko shrugged.

'But also, listen to this, just before Danny bought it, it was owned by a French aristocrat. In fact he bought it off this Duc de, the Duc de Montbarrey.' She read more from the leaflet. 'The military got rid of it after the Second World War. Obviously felt they didn't need it anymore. Either that, or felt it was a doll's house deathtrap against modern munitions. Sold it to this Duc. And he had it from 1956 up to when Danny bought it. Though it doesn't mention Danny by name. And it doesn't mention the date. But we know that's when Danny bought it? In the mid-1960s?' She looked across to Camo for corroboration. He nodded.

This Duc must be the previous owner that drowned, Camo thought, that Jane Shadwell mentioned. Danny must have bought it off the estate.

'So everything we see now dates either from the big military refurb in the 1930s or from the duck of Monwhatsit, or from Danny's time?' Rox said.

Rosie tossed the leaflet on to a nearby large teak garden table.

'Yes,' Rosie said. 'So that's why it's in such relatively good nick,' she said. 'The French army was here not so long ago, before the Second World War. Then this aristocrat. Then Danny came in the 1960s with his own army – of girls if nothing else – and did it up again.'

'So it had more-or-less continuous occupation in the first half of the twentieth century – just when it needed it?' Tyko said.

'Then Danny's sister Jane Shadwell and her family came a few times,' Camo said. 'She said the only good thing, the only thing they liked, was a boat on the lake.' He pointed with his thumb over his shoulder towards the back wall. 'You have to be careful of the run off where the lake outlet is, though, she said. It can suck you down, whatever that means. That's what she said. Apparently the previous owner to Danny, which must be the duck de Montbarrey, got sucked down.' He didn't know if he drowned or just fell two hundred feet down the mountain.

Camo told them what Jane Shadwell said about there being a grating across the entrance to the mill race. 'It's really dangerous if it's not there, she said.'

'Definitely dangerous if the duck died that way,' Rosie said. 'So no swimming unless the grating's in place.'

'And not only if it's still there, but it's still sturdy too,' Tyko added.

'Water's too bloody cold for swimming,' Rox said.

Rox picked up the leaflet where Rosie had tossed it on the table. She flicked through the pages, then stopped. 'Says this Duc de Montbarrey was some sort of well-known bibliophile, a rare book collector.' She looked around.

Tyko said, 'Must have made a packet flogging rare books then came to chill out here in a reading retreat for his later years.'

Before they went down to the kitchen to put a meal together Rox had a good look at both sets of plans. She was thinking.

They would look at the outside and all around the rest of the fort in the morning.

'We got pizzas we can heat up,' Tyko said. 'And bread and a whole bunch of weird cheeses. Let's go down to the kitchen.'

11. LOOK

Next day the search began.

Of course they weren't looking for 'Madeline's hold', not yet. They were just exploring the fort and seeing what was what.

Now they unlocked, opened and used the single door in the fort wall, which was nearer the courtyard wall with all the stable blocks and outhouses.

The first thing Rox did was check the level in the oil tanks. She noted that they were connected by a copper pipe with a brass stopcock on it. So it appeared that the second tank drained into the first. Both tanks had level gauges on the front. She pressed the buttons on the front of the tanks and the pink fuel oil ran threequarters of the way up the clear plastic gauge tube in the first one and all the way up to the top of the gauge tube in the reserve tank. Plenty of fuel, then, she thought.

The next thing she wanted to do was make a survey of the entire building. She knew that if you wanted to locate hidden rooms, then the best way to do that was make an accurate plan. She would not trust the Duc de Montbarrey's plans until she had corroborated them with her own. For that you first needed to survey it. But that could wait. First they'd explore.

With corner rooms on all four corners of the first floor, the floor plan was the same upstairs and downstairs. A wide corridor ran the whole perimeter of the building, round all four sides except where the corner rooms blocked it. But each corner room had two doors so you could move between a front or back perimeter corridor to a side corridor by going through a corner room. Cross-corridors ran between the front and back corridors. Rooms opened off the perimeter corridors and the connecting corridors. All the corridors and the rooms were numbered. The big black numbers stood out on the whitewashed walls.

It was simple, neat, repetitious and straightforward. You might say to a soldier to go to a certain room and all you had to say was three numbers, X,Y,Z; level X, corridor Y, room Z.

'I guess it has to be as simple and repetitious as possible, so soldiers can make their way round it without getting lost,' Rosie said.

'Might have to get round quickly in the dark too,' Tyko said. 'Especially if they might have to repel a break-in.'

All the rooms were empty apart from the kitchen, the rooms with beds and the front left corner room full of garden furniture on the first floor. There was a deep basement which followed the same plan as the floors above – a perimeter corridor, connecting cross-corridors and rooms off. They realised however that the basement covered a smaller footprint than the floors above. The basement area didn't stretch to the far left side of the fort. Nearly but not all the way. They wondered why, but had no answer.

The basement walls were different in that they were bare unplastered and unpainted stone. Another difference was the basement rooms were anything up to twice as big as the rooms above. One of them was lined with plywood panels throughout over the bare stone blocks behind, with the big sheets of plywood fixed screwed and plugged securely to the walls behind. The ceiling too was lined with plywood sheets. The clue to what the room had been used for was the large numbers of socket multipliers and extension leads that were still hanging on hooks on the wall.

'This is the studio, the sound dungeon,' Camo said. 'Where they laid down the bootleg recordings.'

He tried to imagine Jim Lyly and the rest of them jamming away in here. The recording equipment, the mixing desk, and the master tape recorders might be over that side, he thought, looking across to the back wall. The stack of Marshall amps over there. And old Dredge might have sat on a stool on this very spot, very pissed off to be cooped up here, but still getting out of his guitar the sound of a freight train braking hard on diamond rails.

He guessed that making good music was the only thing they could do stuck up here in Danny's splendid goat-fuelled fortified isolation. Apart from taking the sun and maybe walking round the lake and the mountains above. But somehow he didn't think people like Dredge and the band did much walking.

Before they left the room and closed the door, Camo took a bunch of photos on his phone. He knew they were unlikely to be coming back in this room again.

Camo asked Rox to have a look at the lift. They all went over to the large middle stairwell on the ground floor. Camo pulled the folding door open.

'Yes,' Rox said. 'It's not a personnel lift. It's a goods lift.'

It was much larger and deeper than a personnel lift. It moved slower than a personnel lift and could take more weight too, Rox said. The interior was lined with bare metal sheeting. The metal appeared to be a series of thick aluminium panels, riveted into place. There was a ribbed treaded pattern on the surface, as though the panels had been flooring in a former life. They were much scratched and dented in places.

The lift would have been used to lug heavy items between the floors, Rox said. 'It's a lot easier than carting it up the stairs.' She drew the lift door back into its closed position. 'It probably dates from the big renovation by the military in the 1930s.'

Once they had thoroughly explored the inside they moved outside.

First thing they did was to see if they could walk all the way round the outside. They couldn't. There was a narrow track running out of the rectangular parking area outside the arched double doors in the courtyard wall. This wasn't the access packhorse trail, which veered away to the right and disappeared over a rise into the trees. This path was smaller and hugged the perimeter wall. They followed it towards the front of the fort with the fort wall on their left.

It came to an abrupt end flush with the front wall of the fort. The ground dropped away steeply. It was almost a cliff. The two-storey fort stood on the edge of this cliff and looked down into the valley of the Ariege far below. It wasn't cliff all the way. The fall levelled out into thick conifers after perhaps a two hundred foot drop. The stretches of conifer forest went down and down, seeming to bounce over the landscape, before giving way deciduous trees lower down and then to wide cultivated fields and farmland below that reaching all of the rest of the way down to the main road and the river.

The other side of the fort was less spectacular but more interesting. A wider path exited the parking area in the other direction and ran along the exterior of the courtyard outer wall. The path was wide enough to take vehicles. The path continued along the outer wall of the complex and came to an end in a smaller parking area at the end of the wall, by the lake.

Here was the outlet fall from the lake. The outlet stream had been canalised into a straight open box-like section dug out of the rock with straight sides and a flat bottom that ran all the way along the side of the courtyard perimeter wall and then along the side of the fort itself. The water spluttered and chattered all the way along the canalised section until it dropped out of sight down a fall at the far end of the fort – down the two hundred foot cliff there in a series of step breaks in a noisy, stupendous and slightly unexpected waterfall.

At this point there were two raised steel walkways. One carried on over the outfall which could be crossed by the steel walkway that was part of a raised sluice gate that could be lowered in place to block the entire stream and stop up the flow completely. They wondered why you would want to do that. The water level surely would just rise up, fed by the incoming stream over by the barrier bridge on the far edge, until it just topped over the sluice gate.

Rox noticed that though there was a thick heavily greased helical threaded worm rising from the top of the sluice gate in a retaining frame, there was no way of turning it to raise or lower it. The handle – or wheel mechanism more like - must have been removed. The threaded worm had a deep and broad square bolt on top where the turning handle must have sat. But the handle was gone.

They all noticed the thick wrought iron grating that was placed in the water across the outfall just in front of the sluice gate.

'Still there,' Tyko said. 'And still pretty strong by the looks of it. The skinny dip is still on.'

The other steel walkway hugged, was attached to, and followed the wall of the fort. It was at least ten feet above the water level.

Ahead and away from them, a low bluff rose on the other side of the outfall stream. They crossed the sluice gate walkway to this grassy knoll on other side, and immediately things became clearer. There was another sluice gate on the other side of the knoll. This one was wound down, blocking this exit. This was the old original river bed, now dry, which ran past the bluff on its former natural course until it joined the canalised section at the falls.

They stood on the low bluff and looked across to the fort wall and realised immediately that the canalised section of the stream was in fact a mill race. The proof lay in two massive wrought iron water wheels that were clearly visible. The lake outlet had been engineered into a rectilinear stone box channel to create a straight stream with a drop rapid and forceful enough to turn two mill wheels. The wheels were not working. That was because they were not in the stream. They were set back from the water in special open recess housings built into the thick wall of the fort.

They could also now see that the steel walkway attached to the fort wall above the mill race actually ran between and above the two water wheels.

They could also see from this vantage point there was another heavy wrought iron grating fixed across the mill race at the far end, just short of where the water and land dropped away in the waterfall and cliff face.

Rox was fascinated by all this engineering. It looked to her like the two big wheels were movable. On the other side of the fort wall, in the courtyard, there must be access to the wheel housings. And there, she was sure, they would find some complicated and sophisticated machinery that would be capable of moving the wheels in and out of the water.

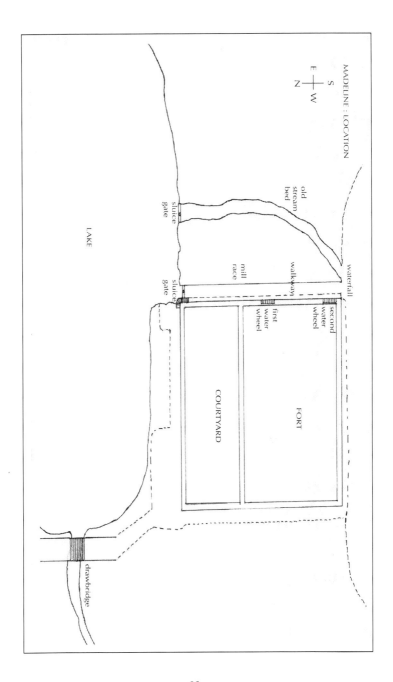

MADELINE : LOCATION

N
W — E
S

old
stream
bed

sluice
gate

LAKE

sluice
gate

mill
race

walkway

waterfall

first
water
wheel

second
water
wheel

COURTYARD

FORT

drawbridge

'These sluice gates must be for maintenance,' she said. She thought the two water wheels would have been there to provide power of some kind for the fort in the early days. She knew that once you had turning and working water wheels you could create a lot of working things with them by means of belts and gearing and pulleys and power take-offs. They probably turned lathes and lifted hammers, and opened and closed bellows for the forge, and moved all sorts of magnificently complex eighteenth century machinery. Judging by their size it also meant they had been carried up here in pieces by mule train or packhorse and assembled in place.

'I don't get it,' Camo said. 'How would it work?'

'Well the mill race will get clogged with weeds and dirt and mud and stones will get in it. Stones can jam and damage the wheels. That's inevitable. And you'll need access to the race when it does, and you'll need to clean it out every now and then regularly too. And those monstrous wrought iron water wheels won't look after themselves either. So you need to stop the flow. You need to stop the water entering the mill race. How do you do that?'

She turned to the sluice gate which was closing off the lake's original natural outfall.

'You open this one. And you close that one.' She pointed to the one by the fort wall. 'They're both at the same level. The water flows through here instead of over there. You let the mill race run dry and then you can get men down into the dry bed of the mill race and clean it out.'

'The wheels too?' Tyko said.

'Not sure. I don't think so. I think they can be moved out of the water - as we see them now – by some mechanism and you can work on them inside, through some kind of access on the other side of the wall.'

She didn't add but she was sure that being lifted and raised out of the water and lodged in their maintenance housings would have been the default position as soon as generators and electrical power came in, when the fort was reoccupied and refitted in the

1930s. Perhaps before. Perhaps as soon as electrical power came in some time in the early 1900s. It was probable too that the original long-gone wooden water wheels would not have been retractable.

Even so, she thought, I bet they made sure the wheels could still be moved back into place if they needed them. Whatever the old mechanism was that moved the wheels in and out of the stream, they would have kept it in good working order. Just in case. She knew there were a lot of things about the military, especially military engineering, that were just in case, with back-ups and multiple redundancies. You never banked on anything.

'And I think that steel walkway–' she pointed towards the fort wall '-on the other side of that wall allowed access to the wheels for inspection or for minor maintenance when you didn't have to retract the wheels.'

She couldn't wait to see what there was on the other side of that wall

'So it looks like it's relatively easy to access the back of the fort, where we are now,' Tyko said. 'But very limited access options at the front. If any.'

They agreed that was the case. It was obviously designed to have supply routes and access from the rear but present an inaccessible, intimidating and unfriendly face from the front.

'It is a fort, after all,' Rosie said.

Finally they went back inside through the double doors in the perimeter wall and walked across to the line of outbuildings on the far side of the courtyard on the mill race side.

Though there were three doors facing on to the open courtyard, there were actually only two rooms.

The first, with the split doors, was a large stable as Rox had thought. There were still the wrought iron horse mangers attached to the walls in the corners at convenient eating height. Horseshoes had been hung on hooks in one wall in such a way to spell out *Madeline*. On another wall the horseshoes and hooks had been rearranged so the words now read *Danny is a bas----*. The rest of the word seemed to be missing, and they could see empty hooks on the wall and horseshoes on the floor under the hooks.

They laughed at that and Camo took a photo.

The second room was larger and had two doors. The doors led to a large smithy and workshop. Heavy metal anvils still stood next to a forge and a water trough. Various heavy iron tools and tongs still hung on hooks on the wall. A big sledge hammer lay abandoned on the floor. A heavy work bench ran the length of the far wall.

Also hanging on the wall in the workshop, Rox noted, were two large wrought iron wheels like car steering wheels, but bigger and far heftier, each with four broad spokes. Each one had a large square hole set in the stout iron square or diamond-shaped hub where the spokes met at the centre of the wheel.

A square hole for a square nut, she thought, and realised these were the wheels to wind the threaded worms to lower and raise the two sluice gates.

Also in the workshop, leading through the wall it shared with the fort itself, was another door. This was an interior door that led back into the fort. It led to a room that was long and deep and on two levels.

Camo switched on the overhead strip lights as they entered. This room contained the access to the water wheel maintenance recesses. For the first time they could hear the rush and flow of water behind the far wall where the mill race lay. The first section of the room was on the ground floor, level with the courtyard outside.

There was a small iron or steel hatch set in the wall on the left of the door they entered. The hatch was set in brickwork one and a half bricks thick, the first brickwork they had seen in the entire fort.

Camo approached the hatch and lifted up the catch. He pulled the door towards him. Immediately extra light and noise flooded into the room. Just beyond was the massive iron water wheel housed in its circular recess. They looked past the broad paddles through the iron structure to the water below and the open air beyond. Camo shut the small door again.

Next to the bricked section of wall was a large circular wooden framework of some kind, with cross-boards all along the circumference, about a metre deep and almost as high as the room, over four metres in diameter, like a giant hamster wheel. It wasn't resting on the floor but was suspended off the ground by a thick wooden frame.

In the corner stood a compact ancient steam engine. Next to it was what looked to Tyko like a generator and next to that an electric motor. He went over to it. A small brass plate was riveted to the curved top surface of the generator. *Siemens 1898*, it said.

'State-of-the-art in its day,' Tyko said.

Alongside the steam engine and generator was a large stack of iron gear wheels and lengths of iron and steel beams and rods. Four massive cast iron weights half the height of the room stood there too, surrounded by loops of serious-looking chain in circles on the floor.

To Rox all these bits of machinery and equipment looked like all the lifting mechanics for moving the wheel. The power, the gearing, the levers, the counterweights. Archimedes would have been impressed, she thought.

'What on earth's that?' Rosie said, pointing to the circular wooden structure. 'Is it a wheel? A wooden wheel. Did they use that before they put the iron ones in instead?'

Rox frowned. She tried to summon fragments of knowledge from textbooks and fleeting illusory half-learnt images. Of men inside a large wheel, walking.

'It's a treadmill!' she said, excited. 'Two men at a time could work it. They just entered here,' she showed the place, and went into the wheel herself and stood on the boards, 'and started walking,' she mimed walking in an exaggerated up and down sort of way, stamping on the boards. 'And the wheel rotates. It works like a rotating block and pulley, a kind of crane. It's how they powered the levers and counter-weights in some kind of windlass affair, I guess, to lift the water wheel in place and lower it back into the water in the early days.' Must have been a hard slog, she thought, even with huge gearing.

'Then later all the hard work was done by a steam engine and then after that by a generator and electric motor.' She pointed to the two pieces of machinery by the end wall.'

And shortly after that, she thought, they realised they didn't need the water wheels at all. And they were raised out of the water one last time and left in their stone homes.

'Maybe that was when they bricked up the hole?' Tyko said. 'When they didn't need the wheels any more?'

'Yes. Originally all this area would have been open and the wheel exposed.'

A wide set of steps ran down to the lower level of the long room. They descended four metres down the steps. The lower section was a mirror image of the upper level, complete with brickwork and steel hatch, treadmill, cogs, beams and counterweights, steam engine and generator.

They now realised why the basement floorplan was smaller than both the ground and first floors. This lower section of the water wheel control room stretched the full width of the fort's underground level.

A difference in the lower section was that the steel hatch on the wall was set much higher up, near the ceiling. There was a set of iron stairs leading up to it.

On the off chance there might be something different, and because there was an unspoken agreement among them that they should never make assumptions, Tyko went over and ascended the iron stairs and opened the steel hatch in the brickwork to look at the water wheel and the mill race below.

He held the door open. The hatch was above the water level. Which meant, Rox realised that the chamber they were in was actually below water level. Poking his head through the hatch Tyko could see the water outside dropped away vertically. They were right at the edge of the falls. Camo nodded.

As Tyko was closing the door Rox noticed this water wheel had deep iron troughs at the ends of the blades instead of paddles. She thought it was presumably a later and better, more efficient, design.

They retreated back into the brightly lit courtyard in the sunshine.

They had been in every room in the fort now, as far as they knew.

'Ok. What now?' Rosie said. 'The message doesn't really give us any clues, does it?'

'I guess we look all over again, but more slowly and carefully,' Tyko said. 'But let's have some lunch first.'

'Well I don't know about you lot,' Rox said. 'But I'm going to do a survey and then make a scale drawing. It's the only way.'

12. SURVEY

But why did she want to make more plans when they already had some? Rosie wanted to know.

Rox explained that if you wanted to conceal something, such as a hidden room, one of the things you could do was not draw it on the plans. Anyone looking at the plans would assume they were accurate and there was no hidden room anywhere. They were in danger of doing exactly that.

'That's why we have to make our own.' She would then compare the 1958 plans with hers.

Rox thought it would take her one-and-half to two days to do it.

First she had to measure the outside of the fort. Then go inside and measure the length of the rooms one by one. The difference between the two measurements would be the sum total of the interior walls, plus the two end walls. A window reveal would give her the thickness of the exterior walls. She would subtract the two exterior wall dimensions from the exterior total. Then subtract the smaller number of what was left from the larger, then divide what remained by the number of interior walls. That would give the width of each wall. Adding it all back up together, room dimensions plus wall thicknesses, the interior and exterior numbers should be the same.

She would repeat the manoeuvre with the two side walls. She would be unable to measure the length of the exterior façade on the front because of the cliff, but would assume it matched exactly the dimensions of the rear façade. She could still measure the room dimensions along the front, though she suspected it would be an exact match to the back.

She would repeat all this measuring on the first floor and the basement.

Then she would take all the measurements she had made and convert them to a scale drawing.

She had the necessary tools. She'd brought a steel tape and her modern laser rangefinder and her drawing pad.

She thought she'd start by measuring the outside back wall the old-fashioned way, with the twenty metre steel tape. She'd do the interior dimensions with the laser rangefinder. She retrieved the steel tape from the Land Rover and rummaged in Camo's dad's bass and took one of the block hammers. What she didn't have was a supply of steel pegs, but she found a stack of various lengths of thin steel reinforcing bar in the workshop, which would do

Tyko asked her if he could help but she said he'd just get under her feet. She could see he preferred to kick a football around with Camo in any case.

'But shouldn't we do something?' Camo said, putting the ball away in the car. 'While you're doing the survey.'

Rox told them the best thing they could do was go over all the rooms on the fort again, slowly and carefully, inch by inch.

Camo agreed. He imagined that just finding the secret room – if that's what it was – would be a good deal easier to find by accident and by good hard searching, than deciphering Danny's code on the gold disc would be.

'Look for anything that doesn't feel right,' Rox said. 'Anything out of the square and straight, for a start.'

She added they should even tap the walls looking for anywhere that sounded hollow. 'Use a wooden mallet.' She'd spotted a couple in the workshop. 'Anything suspicious, make a note of the room number and I'll come and check it out.'

She told them to also look for cracks in the whitewashed plastered walls that were too straight and might show the beginnings of the shape of a door. They should also check the floors carefully too, looking for trapdoors. They should do that throughout but particularly in the basement.

She knew that when she finished the survey and had made the scale drawing, if nothing showed up, she would be tapping the walls with them too.

She told them it might be worth trying just using the torch to highlight the walls of a room. The beam might show up the telltale microscopic shadow that indicated a hidden door much more readily than if they switched the lights on overhead and flooded the room with light.

Another thing she knew they could do in the basement was take a couple of the galvanised steel buckets they'd found in the kitchen, fill them with water and throw the water about liberally in the basement rooms and watch where it flowed. If there were any near-invisible cracks that indicated a hidden access trap set in the floor, the water seeping into them would show up and reveal a void beneath.

Rosie was delegated to drive back down into Ax and bring back more supplies. One thing she was especially tasked with finding was more torches, powerful ones if possible, and plenty of batteries.

Rox also asked her if she could keep an eye open for an artist's supplies shop, and if there was one to buy a roll of high-quality ultra-smooth drawing paper. Rox suspected her A3 pad might not be large enough for the kind of scale, one to fifty, that she had in mind. If Rosie couldn't find a roll of paper then Rox knew she would have to make her scale drawing at one to a hundred purely to fit it on a sheet of A3. Even then the long dimension would be 600 millimetres across. And she had a feeling that with such a big building, a scale of one to a hundred might not be large enough to show up any dimensional anomalies. If Rosie didn't find any paper rolls, then Rox thought she may have to run the drawing across two sheets.

While the boys disappeared inside and Rosie drove out of the courtyard's double doors, Rox took her tape and the hammer and steel pins outside to measure the full length of the front of the courtyard wall on the outside. That was because the stable, workshop and the split-level wheel maintenance room prevented her from measuring the full length of the back wall of the fort directly.

At the far left corner of the courtyard's outer wall, just where the ground dropped into the mill race, she hammered her first pin into the ground. Once satisfied it was firmly held in the ground, she dropped the looped end of her tape over it. Then she walked along the face of the wall, paying out the tape all the time. When it ran to the limit of its twenty metres she pulled it tight, read the distance and made a small white mark on the wall with a sharp piece of limestone she'd found lying on the ground in the exterior parking area. Next to the white scratch she also scratched a single vertical stroke, indicating one full length of twenty metres.

Holding the tape she rapidly waved her arm up and down, creating a wave in the steel tape. When the upwards surge of the wave reached the steel pin it flipped up the brass loop and unhooked the end of the tape from the pin. She hammered a second pin into the ground exactly below her white mark on the wall. She wound in her tape. And when the end loop which came skittering and bouncing along the stony ground reached her she placed it over the second pin.

She played out a second length of twenty metres. Again she marked the wall with her limestone shard. This time she scratched two vertical lines next to it, indicating a second twenty metre run in Roman numerals.

She repeated the action a third time. And, playing out the tape as she past the open double doors of the archway, she came finally to the far right hand corner of the wall.

She noted the length and made a note of the exact figure on her phone. The wall was almost exactly sixty metres long. Just under. For a moment she wondered at that. Why wasn't the wall exactly sixty metres? That would make perfect sense. It would be modular and be easily sub-dividable, especially as the wall appeared to be a metre and a half thick. Then she realised the wall had been built before the French Revolution. The Metric System had been invented and adopted during the Revolution. Before that France had been on a different ancient and traditional system, just like Britain. She didn't know what it was. The French foot and divisors and multiples of that, possibly, but she had no idea. The wall length was probably then a round figure in pre-Revolutionary units. Maybe 180 French feet. But it didn't matter. It was a passing professional interest. What mattered was that she had measured the length of the wall correctly. She knew she'd done that. Accurate, probably, to half a centimetre, five millimetres.

She knew that her laser rangefinder could have done the whole measuring job she'd just done in an instant, but she enjoyed the traditional tape and pin method, and the intermediate wall marking. Knocking in pins with a well-balanced block hammer made it feel she was cracking open the measurements, breaking them and capturing them, however reluctant they were to reveal themselves. The old-fashioned physical method felt much more that it was a way to unlock the secrets of dimensions than pointing a laser did and reading a readout. It got her in the mood.

Then just to be sure she dug out her laser rangefinder from her small backpack, levelled it on its tripod and repeated the measurement. It gave a more accurate figure. She erased her original note in the phone and replaced it with the new measurement. Her tape measuring had been out by two millimetres. Not bad, she thought, over sixty metres.

Next she measured the length of the courtyard side wall, on the outside, to the point where it joined the back wall of the fort. She carried on the measuring until she reached the front right hand corner of the fort.

She now had the full size of the main body of the fort: the length of its front and back walls, and its two side walls. Very roughly, it appeared that the dimensions of the main fort building were 60 metres long by 30 metres wide. She also had the length and breadth of the courtyard. That was roughly 50 metres long by 20 metres wide. All these numbers were recorded on her phone. The stable, smithy and workshop rooms at the far left end of the courtyard took up the remaining 10 metres of width. The size of the full footprint of the entire fort including the courtyard was 60 metres by 50 metres.

Now it was the inside's turn.

She took a break. She sat at the kitchen table with a cup of instant coffee in an old-fashioned white enamelled steel camp mug. Rosie had brought a set. It appeared she'd thought of everything when it came to camping. Each mug had a large initial letter on it. The one Rox was drinking from had the letter E on it. Rox kept opening her phone and looking at the list of numbers she'd just entered.

When Rosie came back from shopping she emerged from the car proudly waving a cardboard tube. It was the roll of drawing paper that Rox had hoped for.

By the end of the day she had completed the interior dimensions of the first and ground floors. She had only the basement to do.

By midday on the second day of the survey, the third day of their stay, she had completed those measurements too. They were all listed and identified on her phone. There was also a back-up list of dimension numbers stored on the rangefinder.

Now all she had to do was make a plan of the building. A scale drawing.

Twice during her survey the boys had come and said they'd like her to check out something suspicious they'd noticed in one room or another.

But they were false alarms, in her opinion. The first one was a hollow sounding area on a wall on the first floor. Camo showed her where he tapped with the mallet on the wall. It did indeed sound hollow. She took the mallet and tapped gently, trying to work round the edge of the hollow area. Rox reckoned it was only a foot by six inches where the wall didn't sound solid. She would have expected a larger hollow area for a doorway, or even for a small trap. She dismissed it as a weak point in the wall, where a stone may have slipped back from the plaster for some reason and created a void. She suspected that the walls would be rubble infill behind the neat dressed stone surface.

'Keep looking,' she said handing the mallet back to Camo.

The other alarm was at first sight more promising. Camo and Tyko took her down into a room in the basement, across from the sound dungeon down a connecting corridor.

Camo took a bucket and poured a litre of water on a section of the floor. The water held up over a crack in the stone flags for a moment, then seeped away inside it. Rox knelt down and tapped the area with a mallet. It sounded hollow.

'Pour some more,' she instructed.

Camo poured another litre. It pooled and then disappeared down the crack.

'Twice that. Try to swamp it.'

Camo poured the rest of the bucket, about half full. The water pooled over the crack, but now did not seep down and disappear. The crack it seemed was full.

'Sorry guys. It's probably just a bit of uneven footing below these floor slabs. A small void. But not big enough for what we're looking for.'

She asked them to keep looking while she went back to taking room dimensions. But after those two times they didn't seek her out again.

Madeline was keeping her secrets.

When she had completed all the measurements, Rox returned to the workshop. She was looking for a straight edge. She was hoping to find a piece of aluminium or steel that would do. She found a length of steel that might do, but it was heavily eaten and encrusted with rust. Would it clean up? She wondered. But then rejected it. The rust had bitten the edge away and made it too uneven. Then in a dark corner she found something. It looked like an old builder's straight edge. It was over two metres long, made of some dark red hardwood. It may have been longer when new, perhaps three metres, but the end had been snapped off at some point leaving a jagged break at that end. A real bonus was there was a fine brass fillet set into the wood running all the way along one edge from the square unbroken end as far as the break. The brass fillet still had its fine sharp smooth edge. It was dented in a couple of places, but they were all up towards the broken end. She reckoned she had about two metres of reliable straight edge.

Now Rox made a base in the kitchen on the ground floor to do the scale drawing. She sat at one end of the large table under a pair of bright strip lights.

She took the roll of smooth high quality paper and un-rolled a long section from the cardboard tube. She unrolled what she thought was about two metres before holding it down with her straight edge and running Rosie's sharp camping utility knife along the edge. She pinned the four corners down with cartons of milk and orange juice from their supplies. She dug out her Staedtler mechanical drawing pencil from her backpack. She laid out the straight edge along the bottom of the sheet of paper. She nested her plastic adjustable set-square against the brass fillet of the straight edge and ran it back and to a couple of times. It moved smoothly enough. It would do. She had a drawing board.

Then she set to work.

The piece of paper was over two metres wide by three-quar-ters of a metre high. That meant she was able to make her scale drawing at a scale of one to fifty. Even so the long sides of the fort and perimeter courtyard wall ran to 1.2 metres long. And the short sides were 600 millimetres wide.

For the time being she ignored the courtyard and made a plan of the fort alone.

She finished the first drawing by the end of the day. That was the ground floor.

That was the end of her second day of work, but the third day of their stay at Chateau Shagfest.

She had finished all three drawings, one for reach floor, by midday the next day. That was the fourth day of their stay.

By the end of that day she had added a fourth drawing: the courtyard, its perimeter wall, and the three outbuildings at its far end.

Each floor of the fort and the outside wall, courtyard and outbuildings was represented on a separate sheet. There were four large sheets in all.

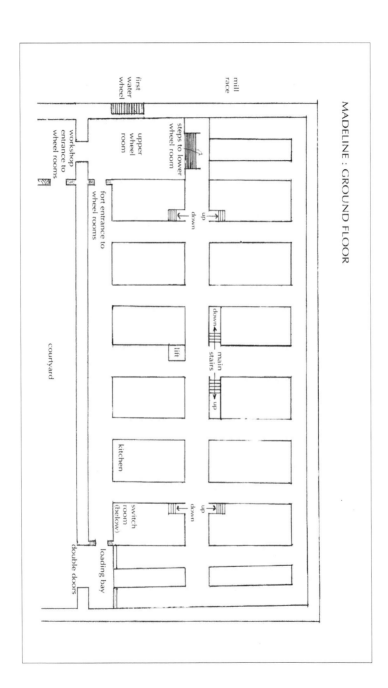

MADELINE : GROUND FLOOR

mill race

first water wheel

steps to lower wheel room

upper wheel room

workshop
entrance to wheel rooms

fort entrance to wheel rooms

down
up

lift

down
main stairs
up

courtyard

kitchen

switch room (below)

down
up

double doors

loading bay

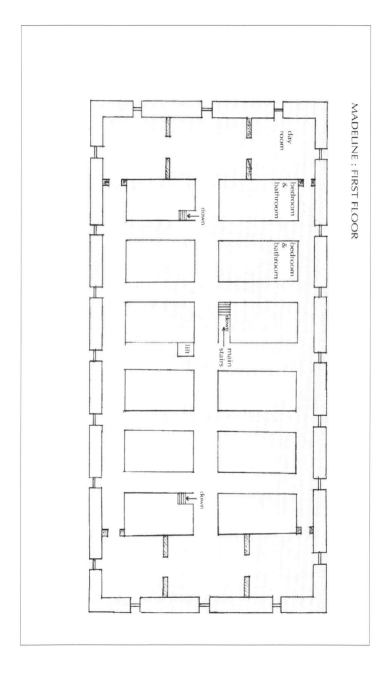

MADELINE : FIRST FLOOR

day room

bedroom & bathroom

bedroom & bathroom

down

down

lift

down

main stairs

111

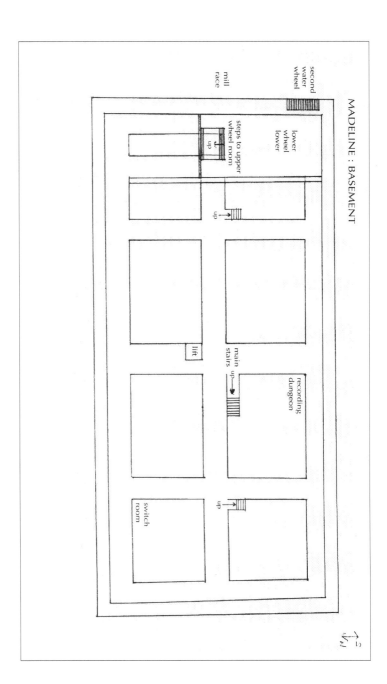

MADELINE : BASEMENT

second
water
wheel

mill
race

lower
wheel
lower

steps to upper
wheel room

up

up

lift

main
stairs

up

recording
dungeon

up

switch
room

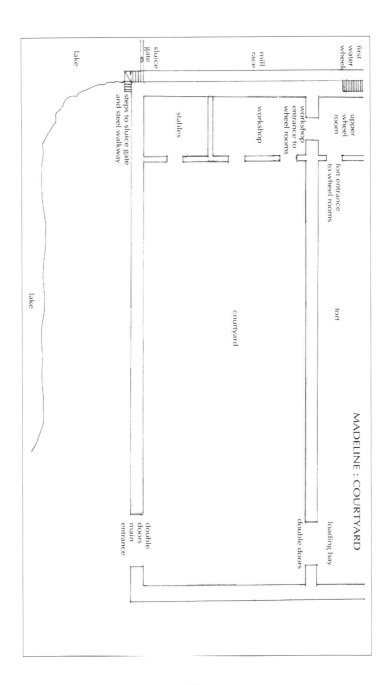

MADELINE : COURTYARD

first water wheel

upper wheel room

sluice gate

mill race

workshop entrance to wheel rooms

fort entrance to wheel rooms

steps to sluice gate and steel walkway

stables

workshop

lake

lake

courtyard

fort

loading bay

double doors

double doors main entrance

113

While Rox had been measuring and drawing, Camo and Tyko had been tapping the walls and floor, feeling the walls with their fingers, shining torches on to the walls, and pouring water into cracks in the floors. They had gone over the whole fort room by room, twice. Rosie had assisted with that. But she'd also at times just wandered about the rooms. She was looking, she admitted, for something that didn't look right or feel right. Camo suspected she imagined the right room would somehow announce itself to her and leap out in her imagination saying This Is It! I'm The One! Look No Further! But he didn't criticise. For all he knew, it might work.

Camo and Rosie took the opportunity of a break in their search to follow Jane Shadwell's address and directions and go and find the farmer who was paid a small retainer to monitor the fort. His name was Lagrange apparently. His farm was lower down, between Premiere Bazerques and Ax-les-Thermes.

Though obviously Lagrange hadn't been to the fort in the four days they had been there, he – or someone – did come to inspect it regularly, clearly. The fort was in relatively good condition and had not suffered from any kind of trespass, theft or vandalism.

Camo found Lagrange's farm. It was a series of old but well kept buildings and barns in the shape of a series of connected buildings round an open courtyard.

He drove into the courtyard and parked. Two sheepdogs ran up to him to investigate. One barked. The other didn't and had an expression on its face that said why should I waste energy barking when he's barking enough for two?

Camo bent down and patted both dogs while they wagged their tails. Rosie waited by the side of the Land Rover.

A woman came out of the front door of the main building. Rosie greeted her and they both went across to the door to say hello. The dogs followed.

Rapidly Rosie explained their presence. The woman, Madame Lagrange, in her fifties, smiled and nodded. She asked various questions. Rosie did all the explaining. At one point Camo showed her the letter from Jane Shadwell. Looking at it now, Camo realised it was in both French and English. Good move, he thought.

Satisfied, Madame Lagrange asked them in to the farmhouse and offered them a little of the local alcohol – the *alcool du pays* as she put it. Christ, thought Camo, it'll be some kind of rotgut home brew. It'll be deadly stuff. Madame Lagrange brought out two former white wine bottles from a dresser in the kitchen that contained a clear liquid, like schnapps or gin or vodka. There was no label on the bottles, and the only difference between them was that one bottle had an entire dead snake in it. The tail end was at the bottom of the bottle, and the head, with open mouth and pointed teeth was up at the top end.

Camo couldn't believe what he was seeing. Rosie seemed to take it all in her stride. Perhaps she was used to all this from her camping days, he thought. She'd never told him she'd been out and about on her camping holidays swigging from snake-filled local brew bottles.

'*Un peu du viper?*' Madame Lagrange offered them. Camo couldn't face the snake, but accepted the version without the snake. Rosie went the whole way and took a small glass with a tot of the viper in it.

They slugged it back. Not as bad as he feared as it burnt its way down his throat. Astonishingly to him, Rosie accepted a second tot of the viper.

They exchanged news. Camo told her all he knew about Jane Shadwell – who seemed very fondly remembered by Madame Lagrange. And he explained their presence up at the fort.

This was all fine with Madame Lagrange. She told Rosie that her husband regularly went up there on his quad bike with the dogs to check on the fort and monitor it. It had been ten years now since they had had to organise any repairs. There'd been a burst pipe and a water leak apparently in a particularly cold winter, after a visitor hadn't drained the pipes when they left. They had sent the bill to Jane Shadwell.

They were happy to keep monitoring the place on her behalf. And it seemed that her son in a neighbouring farm was happy to take on the monitoring duties as well.

'I liked the snake,' Rosie said as they drove away from the farm to go back up the mountain. 'Before we go I'd like to buy a bottle off her and take it home.'

It was dark and at the end of their fourth day in the fort they sat round the kitchen table eating tinned cassoulet and drinking beer. Rox's scale drawings were laid out at the far end of the table, weighed down at the corners and sides by stones from the parking area. One set of the Duc de Montbarrey's 1958 plans was stacked up next to them.

Rox as yet had not studied her plans. She wanted a break from them.

'If Rox's plans don't help us,' Rosie said, digging out her phone as they sat round the kitchen table. 'Then we're just left with trying to crack this awful code.' It sounded so simple, but really didn't mean much, or anything at all. She didn't add, if that didn't work they would be leaving empty-handed.

She read from her phone.

'*Under over…*I was wondering something…' The thought had struck her as she was wandering, apparently aimlessly, round the rooms of the fort. 'Under and over. Over and under. Does that mean the ground floor? I mean if you're between the over, which might be the first floor, and the under, which might be the basement, then you're on the ground floor?'

They all instinctively thought Rosie was on to something. It wasn't a breakthrough, really. But suddenly it seemed they had somewhere, something, to focus on.

'It's only a clue once you're here,' Tyko said. 'And that's how it's likely to be. You wouldn't know until you got here the place just had three floors.'

That was when they heard the sound of an engine coming from outside in the courtyard. It was followed by the sharp tinny insistent and impatient blarting sound of a car horn.

13. VISIT

There was a black Mercedes SUV with darkly smoked windows all round (isn't that illegal? Rosie thought) parked in the courtyard.

A man and a woman in black were standing by the car's two front doors. The man had the driver's door open and was leaning in blowing the horn.

Both of them had black suits. White shirts. Black ties. Shiny black shoes. Christ it's the Blues Brothers, Camo thought, except one is female. The only things missing were the black hats and black shades, and the fact that one of them was wearing bright red socks.

At the sound of the engine, followed by the horn, they'd all rushed out of the kitchen down the corridor and through the unloading bay through the double doors into the courtyard.

Rox was behind the other three. She didn't really know why she did it, but as the others left the room she immediately grabbed her plans and rolled them up and inserted them inside the cardboard tube. She left that on the kitchen table with the stones. She thought it looked fairly innocuous. She hoped so. She left the 1958 plans out on the table in plain view. Then as she left the loading bay after the other three she stopped to flick the switches on the four huge floodlights that now bathed the entire courtyard with sharp bright light.

Christ, thought Camo again as the yard lights came on and in response the two people in black reached in to jacket pockets and snapped on identical pairs of heavy black plastic sunglasses against the glare of the penetrating beams.

'This is a hard place to find,' the woman standing on the passenger side of the car said. She was shorter much thinner and older than the man. She had a quiet clear confident voice with an American accent. She was stick thin. The black suit hung off her like a shroud on the sheeted dead. The cuffs of the jacket were folded back. She was possibly in her mid-sixties Rosie thought. But her age was made more indeterminate by the mass of jet black curly hair that covered her head like a football.

'Why would you want to find it?' Tyko said. He'd taken an instant dislike to the aggressive horn blowing.

'Cool it son,' the tall younger fit looking man said, standing by the driver's door. This was red socks. He looked to be in his forties.

'Say what? It never occurred to us there might be anyone here,' the stick thin woman said.

'Why come at all?' Tyko said, not cooling it. He didn't like the way red socks was casting disdainful but hungry eyes over the women. Tyko had seen that look before. The man was a predator. Women were just sex-meat.

Camo thought he better act the pacifist and defuse the situation a little. Stepping forward he said, 'Can we help? Are you looking for something? Are you lost?'

The woman came forward. She extended her arm, expecting Camo to shake her hand.

'Bayb Azmoun,' she said as Camo shook her hand. 'My father spent some time here a long while ago.' She rotated her upper body a little, looking round. 'We were just passing through – on our way to Spain as a matter of fact – and I remembered my old pa spent some time round here. So we asked around,' she did a kind of including hand gesture back towards the trees and the lake, seeming to indicate the valley below and behind. 'And thought we'd check it out.'

A bit late and a bit dark to be checking things out, Rosie thought.

'Old times sake,' red socks said with a stony face, staring at Tyko. 'That's how it is,' he added unconvincingly.

Camo didn't like it, and judging by his face Tyko liked it even less so, but he felt it would be suspicious and strange if they weren't a little more hospitable.

'Are you any relation to Lion Azmoun?' he said. He knew she was from what Sentinel had said, but didn't want to advertise his knowledge. He tried to put some warmth and interest in his voice.

The stick thin woman with the big ball of black hair round her head tilted it over to one side in surprise.

'I am yeah,' she said. 'My father. But how would you know the Lion?'

'I don't. But I know of him. He managed the Dr Edge band. I'm Dredge Lyly's grandson Arch.'

Rosie looked at Camo. It always surprised her when Camo used his real name instead of his lifelong nickname.

Red socks turned his head slowly but powerfully, as though it was moved by a hydraulic ram, away from the stare battle he'd been having with Tyko and now looked at Camo instead, silent.

'Well. What do you know,' Azmoun said. 'Oo-de-do. Well isn't that interesting. The world is smaller than I thought. I knew your grandfather, once. How's the old cock-rocker doing?'

Camo took a breath. 'Oh he's fine,' he said, not wanting to tell them anything or admit that his grandad wasn't good. 'Still going strong. In his own way. Look, how about coming in for a beer? Or a coffee,' he added indicating the vehicle.

'Sure. Why not. That's good. We will. Thanks,' Azmoun said, clearly making the decision for both of them. She was in charge.

The two visitors followed the students inside. Rox left the courtyard floodlights on. Camo led them to the kitchen. Both visitors were casting rapid glances in all directions, taking it in. Christ, Camo thought again: they'd still kept their sunglasses on.

Camo introduced Tyko to the two black suits. In turn the big man with red socks said his name was Jem.

In the kitchen both visitors finally took off their glasses and folded them away inside jacket pockets.

Before Camo could introduce Rosie and Rox, Jem said, 'Now who are you two fine ladies?'

Tyko was convinced his hungry animal look at them was even hungrier for Rox than it was for Rosie. He tightened his hands into fists by his sides. The red socks man was big and tall, but so were him and Camo. And they were twenty years younger. He and Camo would have greater speed and energy on their side if it came to it. But the man might have more ruthlessness. And if he was a professional bodyguard of some kind he might be far more used to a melee too. Which was not good. He'd watch and wait.

Camo introduced them. As Rox shook Jem's hand he tried to pull it up to his lips to kiss the back of it. She pulled it away firmly before he could. Then she moved to the far end of the table where Rosie was standing. She gently touched Rosie's upper arm. Rosie got the message and the two girls left the room together.

Jem kept staring at the door where they'd left. 'Aw, shame,' he said.

Azmoun was not impressed. She glared at her companion.

'So why come all the way up here in the dark?' Tyko said. He still wasn't happy but had recognised that Camo was making the right moves. They wanted no friction. No surprises. They'd do the minimal hospitality and get rid of red socks and stick thin as soon as they could.

'Well as it turns out,' the thin woman said slowly. 'My old pa left something of his here. A long whiles ago, like I said. And we just wondered if it was still here. We'd like to take a look,' she hesitated. 'If that's all the same to you?'

Though her voice was superficially polite, Camo was convinced he heard an element in it which said we're going to look around whether you like it or not.

They'd both accepted a beer. The older woman, Azmoun, cracked hers open and took a sip. Jem, the younger man didn't even open his.

'What was it your old man left?' Camo asked. 'Maybe we've seen it?'

Azmoun didn't answer for a while. Eventually she said, 'Something personal.'

Camo said 'Ok, sure, by all means you can have a look round. How about in the morning? Come back up when it's light?'

That would give them all a chance to be ready for them

next time. To tidy up. Hide things. Get a story straight. He'd spotted that Rox's plans had disappeared. The cardboard tube on the table top didn't look like anything special. She was bloody sharp, he thought. The stones looked strange though. Too bad, he thought, can't do anything about that now. He noticed Bayb Azmoun's eyes resting on the spare set of 1958 plans.

As soon as she had received and accepted the invitation to return in the morning, Azmoun was clearly satisfied. The two black suits stood up and took their leave. Camo and Tyko escorted them back out to the courtyard. The black SUV glowed sleekly like a feasting black hole in the bright light.

They said goodbye. Jem sat in the driver's seat and started the engine.

'How about midday tomorrow?' Camo said.

'Good with us,' Azmoun said.

Before opening her car door, Bayb Azmoun looked around slowly like a cobra sure of its control over its surroundings. Did he imagine it, Camo wondered, or did her gaze stop momentarily as she spotted the spade and shovel leaning against the second oil tank?

Shit, he thought.

They stood watching as the big car turned round and drove out of the courtyard under the archway. It took off at speed across the parking area, scattering small stones. It didn't even slow down as it rose up, over and down the barrier bridge. Old red socks Jem was showing off, Tyko knew. Maybe they should have wound the steel decking on the bridge back after all. See how fast you drive over six bare beams then, pal.

The headlights lit the trees on the far side of the lake. Then the red rear lights disappeared into the trees like an afterthought.

We do not need this, Camo thought.

14. OUT 1

Early next morning Camo removed the spade and shovel from the courtyard and placed them in the workshop among some other ones there. The others were French-style long handled ones with no crosspiece at the end, but he thought his spade and shovel fitted in well enough.

Rox hid the cardboard tube with her plans inside her sleeping bag on the bed in the room she shared with Tyko. She left the duplicate set of 1958 plans open on the kitchen table. Camo had said he thought that Azmoun had spotted them. But she went upstairs to the corner room and retrieved the master set of the 1958 plans from the sideboard. She rolled them up and hid them in her sleeping bag too.

They knew their own search, and any analysis of Rox's plans and comparison with the Duc's 1958 ones, were now on hold until they'd got rid of Azmoun and Jem.

It was shortly after that, at least two hours before the agreed time of midday, that they heard a vehicle approaching along the trail by the lake shore.

They had decided not to do any more exploring or searching until they had seen the back of their unwelcome guests. It was the fifth day of their stay.

They reasoned it was essential they should all look as if they were having an exotic holiday. They should not under any circumstances give any impression that they were looking for hidden rooms or stashes of gold coins. It was too bad that Azmoun had probably seen the spare 1958 plans on the kitchen table. But that could be explained away. They'd found them. Had looked at them idly. Hadn't bothered to put them away. Likewise with the spade and shovel. They'd found them here and had intended to use them to mark the posts of a goal against the courtyard wall, but hadn't got round to playing yard football yet.

Now mid-morning, Camo and Tyko were playing football in the courtyard. They'd scratched the outline of a half-width goal with a piece of limestone on the courtyard wall beyond the oil tanks. One of them was shooting, the other saving. They reckoned that a full size goal would be totally unfair to the one keeping goal because neither of them was going to be diving around with stone flags underfoot. But half size could be defendable without diving. Yet at the same time it was also wide enough to give the attacker a good chance of scoring.

They called it Twenty Questions. Each person had twenty shots at goal. Then they changed places and the other person would try to beat the score achieved by the first person.

Rox and Rosie were out on the lakeside by the ingress stream and the barrier bridge. Rox really was interested in seeing if they could move and wind back the decking. The arrival of a vehicle at a late hour had given them all a nasty shock. She would prefer it if that didn't happen again. But superficially it looked as if they were just out on a pleasant walk round the lake. They were both wearing their walking boots.

The Mercedes roared into view up the mule track by the lake. Without slowing down it ascended the ramp to the bridge and swept on over the steel deck. Jem in the driving seat blew the horn annoyingly as he spotted Rosie and Rox as it hurtled past them.

The two women followed the path after the car towards the open gates of the courtyard.

When they passed through the double doors, Azmoun and Jem were being shown into the fort by Camo and Tyko. The football was left by the wall.

'I think I'd rather stay out here,' Rox said. Rosie didn't blame her. She too had recognised that the vile Jem had cast a lascivious eye at them both, but especially in Rox's direction.

Rosie thought she'd stay outside too till the Mercedes left.

In the kitchen Camo and Tyko offered the two visitors, still wearing black suits, a cup of coffee. They declined.

'We'd just like to take that look round,' Azmoun said.

'Of course,' Camo said. 'Go ahead. Use those if you want,' indicating the plans. 'We found them. Not really looked at them yet. No need really.' He was trying to imply they were on holiday and what need would they have for old plans?

'Sure. Maybe we'll have a look at those later.'

Azmoun and Jem left through the kitchen door into the interior of the fort. Their crisp footsteps diminished away down the stone corridor.

'What do you think they know?' Tyko whispered to Camo.

Hopefully not much, Camo replied. It all depended on what Azmoun had been told by her pa. How much information did Azmoun have? Certainly, she didn't appear to know about the gold disc? Or did she? Was Azmoun the mystery buyer on the phone from New York? But even if she had wanted the disc for some reason there was no way she could know there was a secret message on it. And definitely no way she could know what the secret message said. Camo wondered how private and secret Danny had been with it once the gold arrived. If they were lucky, Danny had waited till the Lion had left for London or New York before moving and hiding the gold.

It all seemed to depend now on how far Danny had trusted the Lion. Or how much the Lion had withheld from his daughter.

It took over an hour for Azmoun and sidekick Jem to investigate all the rooms in the fort. Sometimes in the kitchen Camo and Tyko could hear footsteps and doors opening and closing. More than once there was a sound they thought was the goods lift moving. Maybe they don't fancy the stairs, Tyko thought.

All the time Rosie and Rox stayed outside in the courtyard. Eventually they went and sat inside the front seats of Camo's Land Rover.

Eventually after an hour Camo and Tyko heard heavy footsteps approaching down the corridor beyond.

The kitchen door was pushed open and both black suits entered the room.

Azmoun and Jem stood just inside the doorway. They stopped and stood still.

They both had guns in their hands.

'Playtime's over,' Jem said.

Tyko leapt to his feet. Camo pushed his chair back.

'Sit down son,' Jem said.

Tyko stayed standing. Covered by his partner, Jem approached Tyko, twisted his gun round slightly, lifted it up and brought the sights on the end of the barrel down in an arc, raking across Tyko's face and opening a vicious cut in his left cheek.

'Sit down.'

Tyko gasped and sat down. He held his cheek. The blood flowed a little, but the cut was shallow. It was a blow designed to shock rather than harm.

The most worrying thing to Camo was that Jem seemed to know exactly what he was doing.

'What's all this?' he said.

'I'm afraid you're leaving,' Bayb Azmoun said. She was waving her gun around like she was painting a fence. In a way that absence of precision and airy lack of control made it even more scary, Camo thought.

'Your time here is over,' Azmoun carried on. She used her hands to accentuate her words and structure her sentences, seemingly oblivious to the fact that one of her hands held a gun in it. 'The place is ours now. It seems we need longer to find what we're looking for than I thought.'

Jem told Camo to go outside and bring the two women into the kitchen. Tyko would stay at gunpoint waiting their immediate return.

Camo didn't see he could do anything but follow the order. This was all way out of his experience.

Two minutes later the four of them were sitting at the kitchen table. Azmoun talked while Jem covered them with his firearm.

'You're checking out,' Azmoun said. She told them they were leaving immediately and wouldn't be coming back. 'I reckon you can take your personal belongings and the crapheap outside. But we'll be keeping those,' she said, pointing her gun towards the 1958 plans at the end of the table. 'I also need to know the whereabouts of the gold disc?' Azmoun finished.

'What gold disc?'

'Do not try my patience. The one you outbid my hitherto dependable associate for. The Dr Edge's inestimable gold disc. The one sex machine Danny kept.'

Camo's heart rate leapt. But he tried to keep his face still and his voice steady. At the same time a wild thought wormed into his head. Did the bitter venom with which Azmoun said 'sex machine' mean something? Had Danny seduced the 16-year-old Bayb on that last tour? Danny's reputation succeeded him. Camo wouldn't be surprised if he had.

'It's, er, it's on the wall of my grandad's nursing home. Why?'

'Maybe we don't need it,' Jem said to Azmoun. 'We got your—'

'Silence,' Azmoun hissed her voice rising into a shrill command. 'But maybe. Maybe not. Good to know where it is.'

Camo knew he had to make out this was all baffling to him.

'I bid fair and square for that disc. It's now the property of my grandad.' He tried to insert a kind of righteous outrage at the idea they might be thinking of stealing it.

'Cool it boy,' Jem said.

'The information is sufficient for the time being,' Azmoun said. 'We shall see. But in the meantime you all are leaving with immediate effect. Time to go back to college.'

Each of them in turn, followed, guarded and watched by Jem, was allowed to make their way to the rooms they were using as bedrooms and collect their belongings. Jem followed as one by one they piled their things into the back of the Land Rover. Rox was the last one to come down from the first floor back to the kitchen.

'You can stay,' Jem said, pointing his gun idly at Rox, who stopped by the table with a pile of clothes and her sleeping bag in her arms. 'Have a seat darlin'. We're goin' to get better acquainted.'

'Stop it,' Azmoun said sharply. 'I won't allow this. Focus. Enough.'

Jem looked at Azmoun for a long moment. It looked as if he

was prepared to ignore his paymaster. But suddenly he laughed and flicked his gun towards the door.

'Go on,' he said. 'Get. Join your boyfriend,' he stressed the 'boy'. 'I'll be seein' you.'

Rox went out of the kitchen, along the corridor, out into the loading bay and joined the others in the Land Rover in the courtyard.

'Ok?' Camo asked.

'Ok,' Rox said. She was breathing heavily. Rosie put her arm round her.

Camo started the Land Rover and slowly they made their way along the packhorse trial over the barrier bridge and down into the trees.

No one spoke.

At the bottom of the trail where it joined the road, Rosie was the first to speak.

'Let's go to Ax,' she said. 'I need a drink.'

On the way down to Ax Rox found a plaster in the vehicle's first aid kit and stuck it over the cut on Tyko's cheek.

They parked in the town square and sat outside in the sun at a bar table.

They had a lot to talk about.

'Is that it?' Camo said. 'Do we give up?' He was serious. They'd just been kicked out of their home at gunpoint. That was very serious. He knew they were outclassed.

'No!' Tyko said. 'We don't give up.'

'Well,' Camo responded, 'What exactly can we do about it?' He wanted Tyko to calm down. 'Within reason,' he added.

'We sneak back at night and surprise them,' Tyko said. 'You and me.'

Camo looked coolly at Tyko. 'That won't work. It won't,' he insisted.

'They'll expect that,' Rox said.

They were silent again. They were all well out of their depth. Even Tyko knew that.

'We go to the police,' Rosie said.

They all looked at her. For some reason that hadn't seemed an option.

'Of course we do,' Rosie said. 'We've been ejected from our rightful abode by armed robbers. By people with guns.' The police will just love that, she thought. 'That's home invasion. It's a kind of armed robbery. Assault. That's a crime. It's a serious crime.' She had a feeling that anywhere in Europe the mention of people doing aggressive things with guns would bring an immediate and overwhelming response from the police. 'We're not talking about a bit of trespass here and stealing the farmer's apples to make scrumpy.'

Camo drained his beer. He could see the police station was on the other side of the road behind the Office de Tourisme.

'I agree. I say that's what we do,' he said.

Rox raised her hand in agreement. She didn't yet want to admit it but she was scared.

'Look,' Rosie said to Tyko, who hadn't yet agreed. 'They think we won't go to the police because we're looking for the same thing they are. They think we're just kids and they've successfully scared us off. Scared us all the way back to England maybe. Certainly scared us off sufficient to give them two or three uninterrupted days at the fort. Well, they have and they haven't. If we go to the police right now, the police will do our work for us. Today if we're lucky. Certainly as soon as they can. They'll get arrested. You can't go waving guns around and frightening people. You really can't.'

Tyko nodded.

But they all felt they needed a break instead of immediately going to the police. They needed time to talk about what had happened. What it meant. And how it might affect their own search. What, for example, did Azmoun know? Why did she want to know about the disc?

They agreed they would talk about it. Sleep on it. Then go to the police in the morning.

They booked into a hotel in a street back from the main square.

Over dinner they assessed the situation.

They agreed that Azmoun had come to Madeline with intent. It appeared she knew there was something of worth hidden there.

'She said her 'pa left something there', so she definitely knows there's something there,' Rosie said.

'It's possible that the Lion knew something about what Danny was up to,' Camo said. 'We think he sorted the buying of the coins, and probably the delivery to the fort too. And has told his daughter.'

'So she may know exactly where the coins are hidden? And we don't?'

None of them knew the answer to that.

Camo tried a logical approach. 'Don't you think if either Bayb Azmoun or the Lion knew anything about Danny hiding something at Madeline they'd have been here before?'

'Yes true enough,' Rox said. 'I think she's been told the gold disc is suspicious but doesn't know in what way. I reckon she thinks it's not that vital because she let you outbid her for it.'

'Maybe she knew she could easily steal it later.' Camo said.

Rox shrugged in acknowledgment.

Rox carried on, 'Perhaps. But I think she's been told something else by her 'pa'. I think she might want the disc to confirm a snippet she already knows. And that must be something the old Lion has told her.'

'Actually it might be something else entirely,' Rosie said. 'What if the Lion is dead? Kept schtum all his life, never told the lion cub anything? Maybe he didn't know anything, or out of loyalty to Danny – he may not have needed any extra cash himself, who knows. Then recently he's died and the cub's found something among her pa's papers?'

That seemed to fit what they knew so much better than anything other solution they'd come up with that they adopted it as their working surmise.

'That's why Bayb Azmoun was never here before now. Her pa has only just died and she's only just come across the information – a document, a dairy, a statement lodged with a lawyer, a deathbed confession, whatever - that's led her here,' Tyko said.

Essentially it meant, Camo said, that Bayb Azmoun knew something, or thought she did.

'And hopefully she actually knows less than she thinks she does,' Rox said.

They all agreed to that.

It was only Camo among them that wondered what Bayb Azmoun would do if what she thought she knew turned out to be not enough. Would she then come looking for them?

They were all tired after the stressful events of the day. You have no idea what it's like having a gun pointed at you till it happens, Rox said. 'Whatever else it is, it's exhausting.' That was true too, they agreed.

They had an early night. They would cross the square to the police station in the morning.

It was the start of their sixth day in the Pyrenees. They finished their breakfast and headed straight over to the police station.

Rosie was right.

The police initially treated their complaint politely and seriously. But as soon as Rosie mentioned guns they treated it very seriously.

Not only that, they swung into action immediately.

They also looked closely at the cut on Tyko's cheek and learned how he had received it.

At one point Camo was asked to show the letter of authorisation from Jane Shadwell. A brief flurry of computer work confirmed that Jane Shadwell was the owner of the old military building. Camo noted, looking at the screen as the policeman tapped the keys, that monsieur Antoine Lagrange was also registered as the local contact and representative for Jane Shadwell.

That was all the evidence the police needed. They asked for Rosie's mobile number. The *capitaine de police* said he would contact her with any news. Meanwhile, he suggested they go back and have a beer. He did however indicate it would be unlikely that they would be able to return to the fort that day. The following day was more likely. They should therefore book into the hotel for another night. He would keep her informed.

Shortly after they reported the incident to the police, they were back at the outside table at the bar in the square, for a coffee this time. And shortly after that there was a flurry of activity at the police station behind the building opposite. Two large blue vans and a blue car with a flashing light on top appeared from the backyard access entrance at the side of the building and headed off out of town in a hurry.

An hour and a half later an ambulance estate car with its siren screaming hurtled through the square and headed out of town on the Bazerques road.

Shortly after that a local company's breakdown truck came through the square at speed and headed in the same direction as the other vehicles.

They waited.

They were back in the bar three hours later when one blue van, the blue car and the breakdown truck which was towing a large black Mercedes SUV drove back into the square and disappeared into the entry down the side of the police station.

Later still, the blue car turned out of the police station and headed back up the road where it had recently come from.

They returned to the hotel to rest up for the remainder of the afternoon. They'd had a relatively dull day, but it was electric with potential.

After a nap Rox went out to look for the artist's supplies shop that Rosie had found. She had an idea. She came back with a roll of tracing paper.

In the evening they went out to eat in a restaurant.

'Yesterday and today are the first good meal for days,' Tyko said.

Later that evening during dinner Rosie received a phone call from the police captain.

The fort was clear, she said. They could return to it if they wished in the morning.

Rosie asked if there had been any problems?

'They resisted apparently,' she informed the others round the dinner table. 'A policeman got shot in the arm—'

'Shit,' Tyko said.

'—And they're now under arrest.'

'Idiots,' Camo said. It was good news for them, they could now go back to the fort. But it was worrying, he thought, that they were prepared to offer armed resistance to the authorities to maintain their position in the fort. They're really really serious. They must think there's something there that makes the risk worthwhile.

'So let's get back there first thing,' Rox said. 'And get the job done.'

Later, in the hotel room with Tyko, Rox had a quick look at both sets of plans, hers and the ones from 1958. She had smuggled them out of the fort the previous day hidden in her sleeping bag under the nose of the hideous Jem. This was the first opportunity to compare her plans with the ones that had been done in 1958.

Good, she thought, as she looked at them. It was as she hoped. They were both drawn at the same scale, one to fifty. That made it a lot easier, she thought.

She worked away while Tyko slept.

She laid her own plan of the ground floor on the table. She spread a sheet of tracing paper over it. Taking her drawing pencil she delicately traced the lines of the walls from her plan onto the tracing paper above. Then she inked in the pencil lines on the tracing paper with a fine-nibbed drawing pen from her backpack.

It was half past two in the morning when she completed the fourth and last tracing and inked in the lines.

She began to compare them.

She laid one of the 1958 plans on the table. It was the one of the basement level.

Then she slid the tracing of her own plan of the basement

over the top.

They were an exact match. The black lines on her tracing fitted exactly over the lines representing the fort walls and rooms on the plan underneath. There were absolutely no differences at all.

She repeated this with the first floor. Again it was an exact match. No differences.

She pushed the plans onto the floor.

She laid the ground floor plan from 1958 out on the table top.

She slid the tracing of her own plan of the ground floor over the top.

She scanned the results, checking the black lines.

There was a difference.

15. WALL 1

Early the next morning they set off for the fort. For the first time in several days they were excited and hopeful.

It was now the seventh day since they'd first arrived.

Rox had woken Tyko during the night with the news she'd found something. She told the other two at breakfast.

The difference was in the room which shared a party wall with the back of the lift shaft on the ground floor.

On her plan of that section of the ground floor the wall was a metre thick. But on the Duc de Montbarrey's plan from 1958 the wall was only half a metre thick.

The anomaly was only on the ground floor. The walls of the rooms backing on to the lift shaft on the first floor and in the basement were the same thickness: half a metre thick. That was the case on both sets of plans, hers and 1958.

At some point the wall at that point on the ground floor had been thickened in section by half a metre. What for? Was it to hide a void of some kind? What's more the thickened wall had not been drawn on the plan. Either the wall had been thickened after the 1958 plans were drawn, or the extra thickness of that ground floor wall had deliberately not been shown on the plan. Which? Was it later or was it deliberate? Rox guessed that it was.

'Is it enough?' Camo said. 'Enough to hide anything?'

Rox said it could be.

'There's no way you'd notice it in the rooms,' she said.

They hadn't, and they'd looked in the room there on the ground floor and in the corresponding rooms above and below it, three or four times.

'It only shows up on the plans.'

The Land Rover engine whined as Camo changed down a gear to accommodate the increased slope as they left the tarmacked section of road and joined the packhorse trail. The trail rose up through the birch and conifers.

They emerged through the break in the trees where the ground levelled out and the lake began. As he had done once before Camo stopped the car at the edge of the lake. They looked across the lake to the fort.

'Back home,' Rosie said.

It felt like home too.

They'd wondered how long they would have this time. How long before Azmoun and Jem might be out on bail? They looked to Rosie for answers. She wasn't sure for a firearms offence there would be any bail available, but she didn't know. If Jem was the shooter who had wounded the policeman, then surely he would be considered a flight risk and would be refused bail.

'But even if they do get out on bail it won't be for a couple of weeks, most likely. The system won't work quickly enough for them to be out in just a couple of days.' Even if they were charged with a lesser offence than what was effectively armed robbery on them and armed assault on the police.

As for Azmoun herself, if she personally hadn't resisted, nor fired her gun, she might be out of gaol quite quickly. But Rosie didn't know.

They agreed they would give the search one more week at the most. Then they'd leave. None of them wanted to meet Azmoun again, with or without Jem. But they were all hopeful about Rox's wall anomaly. It was the first real lead they'd had since their arrival.

Camo drove in through the double doors under the archway into the courtyard beyond.

The fort was much as they'd left it when they'd been expelled. The police had left the main power switch on too.

A couple of their enamel mugs were left on the kitchen table, along with a couple of dirty plates. 'Ugh,' Rosie said and immediately took them to the sink to give them a good scrubbing.

'Before we do anything, or disturb anything,' Camo said, 'Maybe it would be a good idea to look around and see there's any evidence of what they've been up to?'

They decided that was a good idea. They split up to speed the search, and would contact each other by phone if they found anything.

The whole place was as they had left it. Except in two places. Camo reported from the workshop that a spade and shovel and a crowbar were missing. And from the smithy the big sledgehammer was missing too.

Then a short time after that Tyko texted their WhatsApp group saying they should all get down to the sound dungeon in the basement.

In the sound dungeon all four of them stood round a large pit that had been dug in the floor. It was sited alongside one wall. Stone paving flags that had been removed were leaning against the foot of the wall. There was a pile of dressed rectilinear stones next to them. And nearer the pit was a pile of broken rubble and small stones.

The hole was about a metre deep and two metres by two metres square.

It must have taken considerable effort to get this far, Rox thought, in the full day or more they'd had before the police interrupted their work. The digging did not look easy. Somehow she couldn't imagine either Azmoun or Jem being anything but reluctant workmen. But they had clearly set to work here with a will. Maybe it was because they thought they were on to something. She doubted that Bayb Azmoun had contributed much to the hole. She had sounded and looked more like the administrative brains of the operation, not the executive arm. She noticed that a few of the large dressed stones that had lined the floor under the flags above the fine stone and rubble layer were smashed. So they'd taken the sledgehammer to those, she thought, rather than dig them out. Did that signify haste, or just ignorance of good digging technique?

'Do we carry on?' Tyko said, asking around. 'Finish what they started?'

Rox stepped into the hole then knelt down to examine the floor of it. 'Not sure there's anything here,' she said.

The depth of the hole had almost passed through the white rubble layer to the bedrock beneath.

From inside the hole she pointed to the wall. 'Pass me that

spade,' she said.

Tyko fetched the spade but stepped into the hole himself. 'I'll do it,' he said. 'Where?'

Rox showed him where she wanted him to scrape away the relatively soft and multilithic white stony rubble. Tyko poked and scratched away the remaining rubble, no more than three or four inches worth in depth.

Below that it was just solid rock.

'Try there,' Rox said, pointing.

Tyko dug a little and scraped the debris to one side. Again it was solid rock below.

'There's nothing here,' Rox said. 'Solid rock.'

'So they were wrong?' Rosie said. 'Looking in the wrong place?'

'Looks like it.'

Camo wondered if they should start a trial pit somewhere else in the floor of the sound dungeon.

Rox thought not. 'Looks like they thought they knew exactly where to dig. If you weren't sure where but knew it was in this room you'd do a series of trial holes, small deep ones, all over. Just take out one paving flag, or half one. Maybe every two or three metres in all directions until you located the right area to dig the big one. You'd be looking for a place where the ground's been disturbed below the flags. What you wouldn't do is just dig one big hole in one place like this. Not unless you knew where you should be digging.'

Or thought you knew, Camo added to himself. Not for the first time Camo wondered exactly what it was that the Lion had told his daughter. Or what it was that Bayb had found out from her father's papers. Whatever it was, it now looked like a guess. But it looked like Azmoun had convinced herself it was more than a guess and had come straight to the sound dungeon.

The good news was it still looked like Danny had kept the whereabouts of his gold hidey-hole from the Lion. Or the Lion had kept what he knew from his daughter.

'Let's look at that lift wall,' Rosie said.

They left the sound dungeon, switching off the light and taking the tools with them.

They trooped into the room on the ground floor that shared a wall with the lift shaft. It was a blank featureless whitewashed plaster wall. There were no cracks nor blemishes of any kind on the face. They stared at it. Tyko began walking along it trailing his fingers behind him on the surface of the wall. At the far side he stopped and shook his head.

'Do we do with this wall what you said they should have done with that floor?' Rosie asked Rox. 'Chisel out a series of trial holes?'

'One every metre?' Camo asked. 'In a grid. Across and up and down?'

Rox was thinking. 'Not sure,' she said.

'We did try tapping it with the mallets,' Tyko said. 'We did that a couple of times. Nothing obvious then.'

Rox was still thinking. 'Let's just have a look on the other side before we do anything in here.'

They passed out through the door and into the corridor. Rox led them a few metres left to the landing area, the broad central stairwell and the lift shaft.

She tried to drag open the concertina door to the lift. It wouldn't budge. She realised why: the lift was on another floor. Azmoun must have used it rather than the stairs to descend to the basement. Perhaps they expected to be lugging boxes of gold up. She pressed the lift to summon it.

A few minutes later she attempted to draw back the lift door again. It responded to her pull and folded up against the side of the open entry to the lift.

The open lift was in front of them

After a moment's thought Rox stepped forward and examined the aluminium panels on the back of the lift car. After a few moments she turned to examine the panels on the right hand side of the lift. Then did the same to the panels on the left.

She got it.

'Adjustable spanner?' she said.

'In the car,' Camo said. 'I'll get it.'

While he was away Rox showed the other two what she'd found.

She showed them that on the left and right side of the lift the aluminium panels were fixed with rivets to whatever was the metal framework behind.

But on the back of the lift the two panels were fixed with small bolts. So small in fact that if you didn't look closely you would think they were the same kind of riveted fixings as the side panels.

Camo came back with two adjustable spanners with different jaw sizes. Rox waved him forward.

There were two large upper and lower panels covering the centre part of the back wall of the lift. They were both fixed with small hexagonal headed bolts.

Camo began undoing the bolts on the upper panel. It was held in place by eight self-tapping bolts. He put the bolts in his pocket as he unscrewed and removed them. As he undid the last one the panel began to sag open. He steadied it with his other hand. Tyko stepped forward to hold it. As the last bolt was removed, Tyko lifted the panel away and rested it on the floor on one side of the lift.

Rosie came forward with a torch.

Light from the torch and from the stairwell flooded though into the lift and shone into a large dark recess that had been hidden behind the panel. The recess was like a cupboard in the wall fronted by the aluminium panel. It was only accessible when the lift was on the ground floor.

They peered into the cupboard void now half exposed.

It was a shallow chamber half a metre deep, one and a half metres wide and two metres high. A thick wooden shelf ran across the middle. Lower down, in the dark area behind the lower panel, they could see a second shelf.

On the upper shelf there was an item. It was a large wooden box. There were two brass handles on the sides and a brass lever loop-catch at the front.

Tyko reached in, took hold of the brass handles and lifted the box out of the cupboard. It was quite heavy, but not excessively so. He placed the box on the floor outside the lift.

Camo returned to the lower panel and carried on unscrewing the eight bolts in that panel. When completed, he lifted that one away and placed it over the previous one, resting on the floor, leaning against the side of the lift.

The cupboard was now fully exposed. There was something lying on the lower shelf. It was another large wooden box. It looked exactly the same as the other box.

Camo reached into the cavity and hefted out the large box. He need two hands to shift it. He placed it on the floor next to the first box.

The box on the upper shelf and the box on the lower were the only items in the space.

All four of them now stood round the two boxes on the floor. They were all outwardly calm. But each one in their own way experienced different levels of excitement and expectation. Rox in particular was exhilarated. Her methodology had triumphed. As she was sure it would. You couldn't really hide any sizeable void in a building from an accurate drawing at a decent scale. Who did Danny think he was kidding? She was frankly pleased with herself and let it show. She beamed.

'I expected the coins would take up more space, somehow,' Tyko said. 'More boxes?'

'Maybe this is all that's left,' Rosie said. 'Maybe Danny spent the rest.'

Or took them to a Switzerland, Camo thought, and deposited them in a Swiss bank account. Or Liechtenstein. Who knew.

'Let's take them to the kitchen,' Camo said. 'We can open them on the kitchen table.'

Tyko leaned down, bent his knees a little and picked up the box. Camo took hold of the other box. Both of them needed two hands to lift and carry the boxes. The other two trooped behind them as they made their way to the kitchen.

Tyko and Camo placed their burdens at one end of the long

kitchen table.

In the bright light of the kitchen they could see that the boxes were made of heavy duty marine plywood, a deep shade of red, possibly fifteen millimetres thick and very strong.

Tyko stretched forward a hand and flicked up the lever catch on the box nearest him and unhooked the brass loop.

He lifted and pushed back the lid.

There was no sudden golden gleam from inside the box.

The lid and the inside of the box were completely lined with purple velvet padding.

Instead of rows of gold coins, there were five old leather-bound books, one on top of the other nestling tightly against the velvet. They almost completely filled the box. It seemed the box had been purpose built to take the books.

No one spoke. Rox had stopped beaming.

Tyko reached in and lifted the top book out. He placed it on the table.

He repeated the action four more times until all the books were lying spread out on the table top in a row alongside each other and the box was empty.

Rosie reached forward and flicked up the catch on the other box and opened the book nearest to her. It too was lined with purple velvet and it too was full of five books. She brought them out one by one and laid them on the table top in a row under the first row.

She opened the first volume in the first line of five books to its title page.

Traite des arbres fruitiers the title said. There was the author's name underneath the title. *Henri-Louis Duhamel du Monceau.*

Rosie opened the first volume in the second line of books to its title page. It repeated exactly the wording of the first book.

Soon they had opened all ten books to check the titles and volume numbers.

They had two large velvet lined wooden boxes and two sets in five volumes of the same book.

It looked like they'd found a big old book about fruit trees.

In five volumes.
Twice.

16. HOME

They were disappointed to say the least.

'Not Danny then,' Camo said. 'The Duc must have hidden these?'

'Looks like the old duck liked fruit books,' Tyko said.

'Perhaps he went swimming *au nature* as well,' Rosie said.

'We can take them back with us. I'll give them to Jane Shadwell,' Camo said with a sigh. 'They're hers I guess. Maybe they've got some rare book value if she flogs them. Might as well keep them in the boxes. Easier to carry.'

'Meanwhile we've got other things to do,' Tyko said. 'Other things to find.'

Rox had said nothing. She was feeling crushed and very small.

First, Camo said, he would go and refix the two aluminium panels back into place in the lift. They all felt it was important to put things back as they found them. It was a subconscious case, perhaps, of covering their tracks.

Perhaps the most disappointed one among them was Rox. Dispiritedly she started packing the five fruit books back into their boxes. She thought she'd cracked it when she'd spotted the discrepancy between the two plans. But now her energy level had slumped. She had no more ideas. She was completely spent and worn out.

'We're going to have to work on the message,' she said. 'A lot more.' She knew that would be down to the others. She knew she wasn't good at cryptics, acrostics and conundrums. Her own strengths were more linear. They lay in calculation, in what you could see and feel and measure and build. And what you could work out.

She felt she had done as much as she could. She expected to be a bystander from now on. Now it was down to the others.

Right up to the moment when Tyko had opened the box and there was only books inside, she had felt she was leading the hunt. One big book was just about ok. Disappointing, yes. But on its own it was manageable. But four more books in the box? It was a waste of a well-built box. And then the same again in another box? It was almost silly. With her knowledge of construction and surveying she'd felt she would be the one to crack this problem. It was only a matter of making good accurate plans and the truth would leap out. Well, it had done. But it was a different kind of truth. And it wasn't one that was particularly exciting.

She closed and fastened the boxes. Then she went outside with a bottle of beer. She sat on the steel decking of the barrier bridge on her own.

The other three met up again in the first floor corner room, their sitting room. They all had the message open on their phones.

Madeline got the gold with her in the hold
Madeline got the gold waiting in the cold
Madeline got the stacks never to pay tax
Madeline over under still more asunder
Madeline under over will mark a trover

'Are we going to concentrate on the ground floor?' Rosie said. 'Because I know I've said this before. But I think it's the way forward.'

It wasn't just a good idea, she thought. It was also because she wanted to lift their spirits. They were all downcast. Old books were not what they had come all this way for. She wanted to give them a target, perhaps with a little hope attached to it.

She had their attention.

'If you've got a three storey building. Which we have here. And if you're on the ground floor where are you? You're 'over under' aren't you, at the same time? You're over the basement and under the first floor.'

They agreed that was a good idea.

'And it works the other way too. If you're 'under over' then you're still on the ground floor.' Rosie finished.

'That's good,' Tyko said. 'I like it. But how do we search exactly?'

How exactly did they look through the rooms? Did they chisel out Rox's kind of trial holes everywhere? Apart from anything else, how far they think they had to right to damage the structure anyway?

'I don't know about holes,' Camo said. 'But it seems to me that Danny surely must have hidden the coins in a place where he could easily get at them? Surely?'

Which meant, Rosie finished for him, in a place which was both easily concealable but also easily revealable and readily accessible.

'A bit like the back of the lift,' Tyko said. 'That was perfect really. Twenty boxes of coins would just have fitted in there nicely too.'

'Looks like Danny never found that niche,' Camo said. 'I reckon the books have been there since the duck's time.'

And in a way, just like Danny, he had died suddenly in the lake and had been unable to retrieve his books, and they had lain there hidden ever since.

'And just like Danny's coins,' Tyko said, 'No one else apart from the duck knew where the books were.'

Like Danny, as far as we know, Rosie thought. But Azmoun and the nasty Jem know something. Or think they do.

There was one possibility, they all knew, but which none of them wanted to express out loud. Someone could have been here before and found the coins. Someone unknown. Was it possible that the Lion had taken them after the crash? Did the Lion know where the coins were hidden? It was possible.

Yet they were consoled by the logic. As long as the logic wasn't logic disguised as wishful thinking. The logic said only three people knew about the coins: Danny, the Lion and Dredge Lyly. Everyone else who might have known about them was dead. Danny was dead, and so probably was the Lion. Dredge Lyly wasn't talking. It was possible that one of Grog and Dave and Pram had mentioned the coins to someone else on the US tour before the crash. But they also suspected that even if the other band members knew about the gold, it was most likely Danny had never told them where he hid it.

That left the gold disc.

Of course they couldn't know whether someone else had learnt of the message cut backwards on the disc. Someone could have heard the message. They might conceivably have deciphered it.

If they had, then it was most likely that they had come looking for the gold. A long time ago.

Instinct – or was it wishful thinking? – said they were the first to have heard the message on the disc. And were the first to come looking.

But wishful thinking or not, what was certain was they hadn't found where the gold was hidden. Nor had they found where it had been hidden if it wasn't there any more and someone had come and taken it. They were stuck.

The more they talked about it, the less it seemed to help.

Suddenly they heard running footsteps in the corridor outside the room. The door burst open and Rox ran into the room.

'There's two things we haven't tried,' she said breathlessly, panting. She had run all the way from the barrier bridge as the realisation hit her. 'We haven't looked in the roof space. And I haven't done an elevation.'

They understood that meant more measuring and scale drawing by Rox.

'We're going to need the ladder,' Camo said. 'To get into the roof space.' He knew they'd seen a modern extendable aluminium one in the workshop hanging on hooks sideways on the wall. New enough, probably, to date from Danny's time.

'There'll be no lights. So you'll need all Rosie's torches.' Rox looked across at Rosie.

'What about an access point?' Rosie said. 'Anyone noticed any?'

Tyko said he'd seen a ceiling hatch, he thought, on the first floor of one of the stairwell landings, but couldn't remember which one.

'How will an elevation help us?' Camo asked. He was concerned a little that Rox was exhausting herself.

'The plans I did told us if there was anything odd about

the walls,' Rox replied. 'And there was. The wrong thickness or suchlike, just as we found. Elevations will tell us the same thing about the floors.'

Rosie pointed out that the clues seemed to suggest they should concentrate on the ground floor. She explained her idea to Rox.

'I like that.' Rox said. 'It does make sense.' But it would be good surely to eliminate the roof space anyway? Rox insisted. Then if they did find nothing there they would definitely know they should be looking only on the ground floor.

Privately Rox was convinced her scale drawings were the only way they would find anything. She wasn't humouring Rosie exactly. She was just convinced she was right.

Rox wanted to make a start on her new scale drawings straight away. The other three went on an exploratory search of the first floor ceilings in all the rooms and corridors, looking for trapdoors in the ceiling. They found three hatches, one above the first floor landing of the main staircase, and two more, each above the two subsidiary stairwells closer to the side walls of the fort.

Rox went down to the Land Rover and brought back her laser rangefinder. But first she wanted to check the elevations on the 1958 plans. She needed to see where the cross section was made in those drawings.

She dug the plans out of the bottom drawer of the sideboard where they'd put them back. She found the elevations sheet and laid it out on one of the garden tables.

It was as she thought. There were two elevations. One made as a cross-section looking from the sides; and the other is if looking from the front or back. Both the cross-sections had been made at the midpoint of the fort, directly under the ridge line of the roof one way, and on the main central stairwell the other way, which was also at the midpoint of the building when looking at the fort from the front and back. She would do the same.

It felt good to be back in action again she thought. It felt like she was attacking the fort, attacking it with numbers, forcing it to reveal its secrets. She felt this time it wouldn't be able to hide.

With rangefinder, tripod and phone she wandered through the three floors of the building, yet again, taking dimensions. Except it was heights this time.

She started the work outside.

It required a piece of trigonometry to work out the highest point of the building, the ridgeline. She could read the height of the outer wall easily enough up to the eaves with her laser instrument. She knew the width of the roof from the side wall measurement, and her rangefinder gave her the angle of elevation of the roof. She worked out the size of the resultant triangle, and hence the roof height, from those numbers.

Inside the building she could measure the heights directly with the rangefinder, one room above the other. She went up the ladder into the roof space to measure the interior roof height. She could see the torchlight of the others as they investigated the roof interior further along the building. As with the plans she had done before, the differences between the interior and exterior dimensions gave her the floor thicknesses.

She had completed all the necessary measurements by the end of the day. Their seventh day at the fort.

She started work immediately at her improvised drawing board in the kitchen.

The others reported in, saying they'd found the three ceiling hatches. They put the ladder up through the hole in the central one and had entered the loft space above. That part of the interior volume under the roof was occupied by the winding gear for the goods lift. They'd had a preliminary look by torchlight. The base of the roof was a series of beams crossing the entire building, front to back. Sturdy rafters, trusses and purlins completed the roof structure. There were boarded walkways along the full length of the roof, and at a number of places travelling in the other direction at ninety degrees across the roof space. They thought this was presumably to allow access to the underside of the roof to make repairs when necessary, and obviated the need to step precariously from beam to beam.

They would continue to investigate the roof space the next day. But as yet had seen nothing out of the ordinary.

Rox carried on drawing. She took a break while they ate dinner. She completed both elevations by midnight. She would do the tracing in the morning. She was too exhausted to do any more.

By lunchtime the next day, their eighth, Rox had completed the tracings where she traced the lines of her elevation scale drawings, inked them in, and compared them with the 1958 elevations.

After all that hard work she was utterly disappointed.

Her highest hopes had been focused on the floor between the basement and the ground floor. That was the thickest at over a metre thick and so likeliest to hide a void. But that floor disappointed her as much as the upper floor.

There was nothing. There were no differences whatsoever between her new cross-sections and the cross sections done in 1958.

Her tracings and the 1958 elevations matched perfectly at all points.

Nothing on her elevations or the 1958 elevations indicated any hidden voids in the floors or in the roofspace. There might still be hidden voids, of course, but they had no obvious way of finding them.

It was a crushing disappointment.

There may still be gold hidden in the floor, she knew. But she also knew there was no shortcut to finding them through her surveying skills.

The only way forward now was to crack Danny's code.

She went to her sleeping bag on the bed and slept the rest of the day.

Later in the evening she woke and joined the others in the kitchen.

Camo and Tyko had found nothing in the roof space.

With the failure to find anything in the roof space, and

with Rox's elevations showing no hidden voids and no discrepancies at all between her cross sections and the 1958 ones, their spirits sank lower and lower. And after two more days, much of it spent tapping the ground floor with mallets, they decided they'd had enough.

There was a balance in those two last days between those who gave up and began finally to treat the sojourn in Madeline as a holiday, and those who still hoped, so still kept on the lookout.

The split in taking one action or the other for some unfathomable reason was cut cleanly and abruptly between the males and the females. Camo and Tyko started playing football in the courtyard every day for hours at a time. They had effectively given up. Rosie and Rox had not given up, but they had no direction. They were the ones that tapped the ground floor. And after that they kept wandering the rooms hoping something, some anomaly, would strike, jump out at them and say look here this is it.

They could be seen sitting on the exposed beams of the barrier bridge with their phones in their hands examining and repeating Danny's quintet of clues from the gold disc. The trouble was, the more they pored over it, the more they repeated it, the more they broke it down into its constituent parts, the less sense it made and the less help it became.

One thing Rox had insisted on when they returned from their forced exile in Ax was that the barrier bridge must be retracted.

She wanted no more surprises. No more late night visits from strange vehicles. No more aggressive black suits with guns.

They oiled the winding mechanisms with Camo's oilcan and let the oil seep into the workings and the cogs and gears. They left it for half a day. Then they unlocked the pin and tried to wind one of the wheels. It resisted at first, but under the constant turning moment from the combined efforts of Camo and Tyko, the wheel began to turn and retract the steel deck into its housing. They kept turning the wheel until the steel deck had completely disappeared, fully retracted. They then removed both winding wheels and stored them in the fort's workshop.

Only then could Rox relax.

Other times they all went out of the fort in their walking boots to wander round the lake and to explore beyond.

Before they left, sooner or later they were all thinking the same thing.

There was nothing there.

Perhaps Madeline had no gold, Camo thought. Or maybe it was hidden somewhere outside the fort. In which case it could be anywhere and they had no idea where. Or perhaps it was never there at all, and was all some mad practical joke by Danny Weathervane. Perhaps he hoped the taxman might come looking, lured by rumour, for the non-existent gold and Danny would have the last laugh.

He didn't talk about it with the others but Camo was worried about Bayb Azmoun too. It didn't appear that Azmoun thought it was all some practical joke on Danny's part. And if and when she was out of gaol and back on the streets, wouldn't she come looking for them to find out what they knew? She had spotted both the plans and the spade and shovel on her first visit. Didn't that tell her something? Wasn't that a giveaway that they weren't just enjoying an exotic holiday, but were in fact looking for something in the fort, just like she was herself?

And if she came looking for them, what then? He thought he better talk to the others about his fears. It was frightening to say the least. He knew that Rox especially had had a bad scare at the hands of the repulsive Jem. None of them would want to see him again. They were all out of their depth. And none of them knew how to get back into shallow water again.

But for the time being he said nothing.

The last action they took was for both Tyko and Rosie to take detailed shots of the fort with their fancy cameras. Camo asked them both to take large numbers of comprehensive shots of every room in the fort, and do the same outside.

'In one way it'll be like Rox's surveys, except it'll be a photographic survey,' Camo said. He thought it would be good to have something to do with the fort they could still scour through and analyse when they were back home.

They had spent ten days at Fort Madeline.

It was time to go home.

They didn't really admit it to each other but all of them thought there was nothing there to be found. It had been fun, but it was a wild gold chase.

Danny and Fort Madeline had defeated them.

17. SEASON

They went through the checklist in Jane Shadwell's folder to close down the fort. They turned things off. They closed stopcocks. They drained pipes and systems. They closed and locked windows. They emptied, defrosted and unplugged the fridge. Rosie took a final visit to say goodbye to farmer Lagrange. She came away with a full bottle of the viper.

They tried to fill in the hole that Azmoun and Jem had made in the sound dungeon. But all the spoil dug out of a hole will never all go back. They patted down and smoothed the resulting mound as best they could. The dressed stones and floor paving flags they left in a neat stack by the wall.

Last one out was Rox. She gripped the big power switch in the control room and brought the handle down. The lights went out and the generator stopped working. Camo locked up. Then they left.

The ten old books in their two boxes they placed under a blanket at the back of the Land Rover among their suitcases and the camping equipment.

They wound out the bridge deck again. And after some argument decided to leave it like that, also with the winding wheels in place. That was how they had found the bridge. That was how they would leave it. Anyway farmer Lagrange would need to use the bridge on his tours of inspection.

They returned to England. Back home for the rest of the summer vacation. They each had a number of things organised.

Rox was doing work experience. She was joining a charity that specialised in providing rapidly constructed but robust buildings – some of their designs were even said to be earthquake proof - after natural disasters or in war zones. Some new designs were being tested in Zimbabwe. She was looking forward to that. She had extended family in Zimbabwe and was keen to see them again.

Camo took the keys to Madeline back to Jane Shadwell. They had stopped in Ax on the way home and Camo and Rosie and talked to two estate agents about selling the fort and brought back their details for Jane.

He also gave her the two boxes of books. He didn't say why they were looking or what they were looking for. He made up a story about a loose wall panel in the lift falling off and the cavity being exposed. It was all an accident, apparently. If Jane Shadwell was pleased with the books, she didn't show it. Her face seemed to suggest they would be just more clutter in her house, especially with their big heavy boxes too. But she was pleased that Arch and his friends had had a good time there, and any time they fancied going back again, they just had to ask. Before it was sold at any rate. She was grateful for the estate agent details and would be sure to contact them herself.

'I suppose the books must have been hidden there by the Duc de Montbarrey, the owner before Danny. The one that drowned in the lake.' Jane said.

Or was swept down the mill race and over the waterfall, Camo thought.

She said she'd take them to an antiquarian bookseller she knew who was almost as antique as his books. He might like them.

Camo also told her about the hole in the floor of the basement recording room. This had been a tricky one. They didn't know whether they should tell Jane Shadwell everything, including Bayb Azmoun's interest in the fort; or whether they shouldn't mention her at all. They decided to avoid any mention of Bayb. But Camo thought he ought to mention the hole. His implication was that someone must have broken in before they arrived. But why they should dig a hole on the recording room, he couldn't say. He did say they'd filled the hole in and laid the stones neatly by the side.

Both Rosie and Tyko had work experience holiday job attachments for the summer vacation.

That left Camo with nothing organised. But he didn't mind. He had his heart set on a summer of idleness. One thing he did plan to do was tell his grandad all about the trip to Chateau

Shagfest. It might raise a smile or stir some memories.

They went their separate ways. They would have no contact for several months, except through their WhatsApp group.

One thing did happen a few weeks after they split up and left college for the summer. Camo got a call from Jane Shadwell. She said that farmer Lagrange had reported a break-in at Madeline. There was something very strange about it, she said.

'He discovered a large hole in the floor of the recording room. The one you mentioned. It seems someone got in and redug it. Must be the same person. God knows why. He's had a mason re-lay the floor stones and mortar the joints. He'll send me the bill.'

She said it sounded like it had been dug in the same place that Camo had said there was a hole.

'But you filled it in didn't you? We've had occasional vandalism in the past. And once some hikers actually had to break in to shelter from a huge snow thunderstorm. They had to hide from the lightning. They paid for new locks. But there's never been anything like this. I really don't know what to make of it.'

But Camo Lyly knew what to make of it. Bayb Azmoun was back on the case.

'Maybe one of those hikers lost something there? Or think they did and have come back?'

'Twice?'

There was nothing Camo could say. But as is the way with students, if he felt guilty it didn't last long. There was a world out there to come to terms with, to find a role in, and he was at the centre of it. Everything else, including other people and their concerns, was peripheral. So he said nothing and soon rang off.

But Camo did feel he had to warn the others that Azmoun was back. Rox was in the wilds in Zimbabwe and wasn't reachable. But the other two were still in London, so he and Rosie and Tyko talked about it over a pint in one of their regular pubs.

They all agreed they had to be on their guard. Rox had convinced them that there was nothing in the hole that Azmoun and Jem had dug. So why go back to it? They had no answer to that.

'But I fear it might mean that when she finally finds nothing in that hole she'll come looking for us again.' Camo had that out-of-his-depth feeling again.

They'd watch out for black Mercedes SUVs with shaded windows all round.

What else could they do?

18. SHARE

They kept on the lookout for a black blacked-out Mercedes SUV for a while. Then they became less watchful and essentially moved on mentally. The strange Bayb Azmoun and the hideous Jem receded into the background and became almost unreal and legendary. That was because young as they were they lived mostly in the in the moment, in the here and now.

One Saturday at the beginning of September Camo Lyly took a fancy to visiting Sir John Soane's house and museum in Lincoln's Inn Fields. He'd heard a lot about it but had never been.

Soane was a proto-architect in Victorian times who designed a fantastical interior for his house overlooking Lincoln's Inn Fields. He stocked it with trophies and weird and wonderful things from his extensive travelling and pottering round the world. The items in the collection ranged from meteorites to female circumcision knives.

Camo couldn't persuade Rosie to come with him, nor anyone else. She expressed a firm and intense distaste for viewing female circumcision knives.

'I'm not actually sure there are any there,' he said in an attempt at final persuasion. 'It's just an Instagram rumour.'

But the rumour alone was enough to put Rosie off. So he went on his own.

He spent an interesting two hours viewing the Soane collection. He didn't find any female circumcision knives, though he looked hard.

When he came out of the front door there was a stick thin woman dressed all in black leaning on the exterior railings. She seemed to be waiting for him.

'Hi there Archer,' Bayb Azmoun said.

Behind her on the road a blacked-out Mercedes SUV was parked in a meter bay. He couldn't see if the vile Jem was in the car.

A stream of people emerged from the house behind him and others went the other way to enter, as Camo approached the woman in black. Even though the last time he had seen her she had been pointing a gun at him, here in public in broad daylight he had no qualms about talking to her.

'Hi there Bayb,' he said in a deliberately imitating irony of her greeting. But it was interesting she not only knew his name, but also got it right. Has she been researching him? But how?

'We need to talk,' she said. She indicated the SUV at the kerb.

'Ok. But no way in there. If you want to talk to me we go to a café.' He knew one nearby on Holborn. 'Follow me,' he said and set off briskly, leaving her behind. He tried to walk so fast he caught his foot on the edge of a loose cockeyed paving flag and stumbled. He slowed down, but the result was him tangling his feet and almost toppling over.

He felt aggressive to her and wanted to take the piss. As far as he could judge from what little contact they had had she was an extremely nasty and dangerous woman. He felt safe doing it in public. But he knew he couldn't relax. He could never underestimate her.

Bayb Azmoun caught up with him.

'Are you feeling ok?' she said.

Camo gave it up. 'This way,' he said.

They walked side by side without talking down an alleyway onto Holborn. They entered the coffee house and took their coffees to a quiet corner table in the basement. Bayb Azmoun naturally had her coffee black.

Bayb was not one for pleasantries, small talk, or idle preliminaries.

'I guess you didn't find anything?'

Camo looked hard at her. What to say? What not to say? What to admit? Pretend ignorance or admit everything?

It was perhaps his sincere belief that Danny Leathercock (he had begun to like that one) had not left any gold coins hidden in Fort Madeline that steered him towards openness. It was all a game that Danny had started but never finished. So he felt that really he had nothing to hide. And in any case, perhaps that was the only way to get this dangerous and committed woman to leave them alone?

'I think it's a fool's errand. A wild gold chase,' he said with a sigh. 'No we didn't find anything.'

'But you looked didn't you? You looked hard.'

'I don't think the coins are real. There never were any.' Too late he realised his mistake.

'So you know about the coins?'

He sighed again. He had forgotten how sharp she was. 'Yes. I think Danny had a plan to beat the taxman, but never got to carry it out.'

'The crash stopped him, you think?'

Camo nodded and took a sip of his cappuccino.

'Well I disagree with you mister.'

Camo looked up. She knew something and was sincere, it seemed.

Despite his misgivings part of him wanted to know, to understand, to find out why and how she had been looking for the gold too.

'What set you off?' he asked.

'My dear departed pop.'

She wanted to talk, he could tell.

Holding her empty coffee cup between both hands Bayb Azmoun talked about her search for Danny's gold.

The Lion had said nothing about Danny's gold for nearly all his life, she told him. He had a strange loyalty to the dead rock star. Danny was the one who hired him. They shared a bond, Bayb almost spat. Camo wondered if Bayb was jealous of the strong bond between Lionel and Danny.

'But then he had his final stroke,' she said. 'Not just that but his mind seemed to go too. He couldn't talk normally any more, but would spout strange phrases.' These phrases had no obvious meaning. But sitting next to his bed in the nursing home for long hours and days, whole nights sometimes, Bayb gradually began to understand they all related to something that her father and Danny had done together. She divined it was a secret between them. Something big, something to cheat the taxman.

Slowly she accumulated the necessary knowledge. The Lion had bought for Danny a collection of gold coins – 'the Krugers, the Krugers' – the Lion referred to them. He never said how many, but it seemed very valuable.

It took the full and final four months leading up to the Lion's death for Bayb to piece it together from the wild snippets coming randomly out of her father's mouth.

Danny had bought a stash of gold coins. Krugerrands, apparently. Bayb didn't know how many, it was just 'the Krugers, the Krugers' but she got the impression it was thousands of them, worth hundreds of thousands of dollars at the time. And they would be worth millions now. Millions. And Danny had hidden them somewhere in his mountain love-nest in the Pyrenees. But within weeks Danny had died in an air crash. It was almost a certainty the coins would still be there.

'Why did you dig a big hole in the recording room?' Camo asked, interrupting her flow.

She tilted her head over on one side and then back the other way. It seemed a physical metaphor for her indecision over what to say.

'One thing the Lion said clearly on a number of occasions was, 'It was under the drumming. Danny said it was under the drumming.''

That made less sense to Camo even than Madeline's hold did. So it looked like Danny never told the Lion where he had hidden the coins. Just hinted vaguely.

'So your father never knew where they were?'

'No. I don't think he did. Never. But he sure thought they were real. He knew darn well they were real. That's because he bought them for Danny and organised the delivery to the chateau. Danny couldn't find his ass in a magic mirror if he had to do any business stuff. The Lion did all that. Then Danny thanked him by hiding them while the Lion was away in New York. That's my guess.'

Maybe when the rest of the band and all the groupies were

away too, he thought. He had a quite sinister vision of Danny alone in the chateau desperately hiding his gold somewhere in the dark.

Suddenly Camo got it. The hole she'd dug.

'So you thought they must be hidden in a hole in the floor under where the big drumkit stood in the basement recording studio? 'Under the drumming'?'

'Yup. That's why we dug there. Had a good look through pa's family albums.' She told how she had some old photos of the band in action in the basement, taken by her father. From those she was able to work out where the drumkit had been standing.

It made a kind of sense, Camo thought. Straightforward, really, and quite sensible. But surely too sensible? The Danny that went to the trouble of laying down the mumbo-jumbo of clues on the gold disc surely wouldn't have been that straightforward with the Lion?

'How about another coffee?' Camo went to get them.

'But they weren't there, were they?' he said as he brought the coffees back. 'You looked there twice.'

She looked hard at him. 'Your turn,' she said.

In reply Camo said nothing but handed her his phone. On the screen were the five lines that read:

Madeline got the gold with her in the hold
Madeline got the gold waiting in the cold
Madeline got the stacks never to pay tax
Madeline over under still more asunder
Madeline under over will mark a trover

'Jesus,' Bayb said. 'Where did this come from?'

'On the gold disc. The one you wanted to buy. I outbid your man Jem for it if you remember.'

He told her how they'd found the lines by accident and how you had to play the disc backwards to reveal the words.

'Why did you let me outbid you?'

'My father mentioned it. But it was almost meaningless. All he said was 'Get the back disc.' It was a strange way of putting it and I always thought he meant 'get the disc back'. So I thought it might be worth 'getting it back' but didn't know why and any-how I didn't think it was that important. Now I know better. I should have listened to him better, maybe.' She had been focused on the drumming.

But 'back' was the key word, Camo thought.

'You're welcome to it,' he said. He held it while she took a photograph of his screen.

'So you tried to crack this code? And failed?'

'Yes. We tried all right. Tried and tried. But in fact we thought we didn't need to crack it. We thought we could do bet-ter.' He told her about Rox's survey and the scale drawings she made. How that should have revealed any hidden voids in the structure.

'That's good. Real good,' she sounded impressed. 'I kinda wondered who was the brains in your outfit. But it didn't?'

'No it did do that. It was an excellent move. It did reveal a hideaway. We thought we didn't need the code. But when we opened it up it was empty.' He told her about the survey showing up a strange thickening in the wall behind the lift, leading them to finding the hidden space in the lift shaft behind the lift.

'But there was nothing there. Empty. Bare.' On a sudden instinct he decided not to tell her about the books. He wanted to steer her in another direction.

'Do you think it's possible that your father came back later and found them? I mean, we found the place – I think – where Danny hid the coins, but it was empty. I think the cold and sad reality is that someone beat us to it. We were certain that's where they were.'

It was something she had considered herself. And to tell the truth she didn't know the answer. It was a gnawing fear. She had realised a while ago her father kept a number of secrets from her. For all she knew her father had a secret Swiss bank account where he'd deposited the gold coins after Danny's death. He had definitely been to Europe a few times around then without her. 'Business,' was all he told her.

Trouble was, he hadn't told her about any secret Swiss bank

account while he was alive and as yet no information like that had turned up in his papers. But she wasn't going to admit that to this kid.

'So when we found the space behind the lift, and it was empty, we gave up. Until then I thought there was no gold. It was all a plan that Danny never got round to actually putting into action. But when we found that void behind the lift, I really thought that was the place. It made a lot of sense. But it was empty. I think we were beaten to it. By a party or parties unknown.'

It's your pa what done it. Your pa. He repeated this mantra inside his head, trying to transmit the notion to her telepathically that her father was the one. It's your pa what done it. The Lion never told you. You've been by-passed Bayb. Unincluded.

Bayb Azmoun tilted her head from side to side again as if to say she realised that it was a possibility but that she herself had not reached the same conclusion.

'So you've given up?' Her eyes were boring into his.

'Definitely. If there was anything there at all. If there was, we were beaten to it.' He didn't add but clearly implied again that the main suspect for that was her father. That was the direction he wanted to steer her in.

Azmoun looked hard at him. She stared at him for a long time. Then she reached a hand across the table.

'Ok,' she said.

Camo shook her hand.

Then without further words they left and went their separate ways.

In retrospect Camo thought it was giving Azmoun the five line clues that made her let him go and to leave them all alone and not hound them afterwards. She appeared to be satisfied.

'I reckon she was certain she could get more out of the clues than we ever could,' he said later. 'In a way I was pandering to her intellectual arrogance. She thought she would be able to do what we hadn't been able to do. We were nothing but a bunch of students anyway. And she's a woman of the world. The clues were all she needed to leave us alone.'

'Good thing Jem wasn't there with you and her,' Rosie said.

Camo agreed. He knew he would never have been so relaxed nor so confident nor so capable of steering Bayb Azmoun in the direction he wanted her to go if the hulking Jem had been sitting with them at the coffee table.

So summer came to an end. A new college year began. It was the winter term, the first term of their third and last year at university.

They felt they had had a huge adventure. They hadn't found any gold but it was an adventure they'd relive for the rest of their lives.

More importantly they'd seen off Bayb Azmoun and got her out of their lives. It had been a narrow escape they thought.

19. WHEELS

'Idiot,' Rox said, angry with herself for looking but not seeing. She stood up.

The evidence had all been there. The split level of the wheelrooms. The lower level four metres below the upper level was necessary to align the overshot wheel with its necessarily lower axle height with the water level. The water ran over the top of that wheel, but under the first one. And that second wheel too had trough buckets not paddles. She'd seen it all but she hadn't understood it. She'd looked but she hadn't seen. She'd made assumptions. And that was the worst thing an engineer could do. When an engineer made assumptions you ended up with the Banqiao Dam disaster, the wreck of the Tacoma Narrows Bridge, the collapse of the bridge over the silvery Tay, and even the banana-shaped Leaning Tower of Pisa.

Summer was over. A new college year had begun.

There was a module option on Rox's structural engineering course that looked how structural design over time had been modified and adapted to cope with different power supply mechanisms and sources.

Civil engineering is such a vast topic you had to specialise to some degree at an early stage. Rox had decided that her chosen route into the profession would be as a municipal engineer. At one level this involved structures as they related to humans and their urban living space and along with all the necessary urban infrastructure; at another it particularly involved all aspects of water: the supply of water to urban environments, and the creation of structures for the removal of water from the urban environment. In other words, dams, drains, aqueducts, cisterns, conduits, pipelines and sewers.

This third-year module she chose looked at how engineers over time had met and tackled the problems of power supply and distribution.

It started, the lecturer told them in the large lecture theatre, as most things did in human history, especially in the Old World, with the benefit of using the power of big animals.

'It often started with human power,' the lecturer said. 'Usually the forced labour of captives and slaves. Remember the story of Samson Agonistes – 'eyeless in Gaza at the mill with slaves'. But communities all soon realised the power of big animals was better.'

Oxen, mules and donkeys had been used for millennia to rotate Archimedes screws to raise water and also to turn mills and grindstones.

'Then at some point early engineers realised they could utilise the even greater power of falling water to do the same job and do it better. The riverine civilisations along the Tigris, the Euphrates and the Nile probably realised this fact first.'

And that led, is it did with many things when it comes to the history of engineering, to the Romans.

'The water wheel is one of the great human inventions,' the lecturer said. 'For the first time in human history there was a source of power that worked independently of the muscle power of animals or humans.

'We don't know who did it first,' he continued. 'Or where it happened. And we don't know who invented both types of wheel. But it was the Romans who really put the water wheel to industrial use. There is a huge site in the Rhone valley south of Lyon. It's really preindustrial industrial because it's so huge and there's no other phrase for it--'

The lecturer paused as a hand was raised in the banked auditorium. Two hundred eyes focused in on the raised hand.

'Yes?'

'Sorry. You said 'both types of wheel'. Can you tell us a bit more what you mean by that?'

The lecturer realised he had got a little ahead of himself and had missed out a good chunk of vital detail about water wheels.

'Yes of course,' he said. 'We got a little ahead of ourselves there. Essentially there are two types of water wheel. The water goes under or it goes over. The undershot and the overshot.'

Rox's heart missed a beat. She stared at the lecturer. She remembered to breathe.

'And the overshot is much more efficient,' the lecturer continued. 'An overshot wheel can generate three to four horsepower. Whereas an undershot can do maybe only one to two.'

She'd been daydreaming and glancing aimlessly sideways out of the high ceiling-to-floor windows. She'd been listening, but her focus had been drifting in and out.

To illustrate his point the lecturer flashed several images up on the screen behind him and the lectern at the foot of the lecture theatre. He explained that 'undershot' meant that the water travelled under the wheel. The wheel rotated by having the flowing water push against paddles attached to the rim of the wheel obstructing the flow. The 'overshot' wheel on the other hand had the water flow over the top of the wheel and the wheel rotated by having the water fill buckets not push paddles. The water falling over the top of the wheel filled a series of trough buckets around the circumference of the wheel. So with an undershot wheel it was the total force of the flowing water that mattered. But with an overshot wheel it was purely the force of gravity.

'Therefore with an overshot wheel it's the weight of the water that turns the wheel; whereas with an undershot it's only the force of the water pressing against the paddles that turns the wheel. Obviously you can only have one full paddle actually in the water at one time, plus several paddles partially submerged. A lot depends on the size of your wheel actually how many paddles are in contact with the water. But with an overshot wheel you can have many many buckets all full of water as they drop down and rotate from the apex. Naturally the bigger and wider the wheel the better: the bigger the wheel the more full troughs. You can generate some serious and useful power with a big overshot wheel. And the rotational forces on an overshot wheel are independent of the speed and force of the water source. You can actually work an overshot wheel when there's only a trickle of water. All you've got to do is fill the buckets. All you need is water flowing downhill and you've got a kind of industry. The Romans used them a lot. They were very popular in medieval Sicily.'

Overshot and undershot.

Over. Under.

'Idiot,' Rox said again as she stood up and rushed out of the lecture theatre. And again, using one of her mother's familiar words: 'Nincompoop.'

Rapidly she tapped a WhatsApp message to the group.

<Meet. Now. Bar. Urgent. Extremely>

If they were in lectures she told them to leave immediately. It was that important.

They met in the darkly-lit student bar in the basement of the main admin building. Their accustomed alcove was free.

'We have to go back,' Rox said as soon as they'd all brought their pint mugs over to the alcove and sat down. 'Back to Madeline. As soon as we can.'

'How come?' Tyko said. 'What's the rush? What's changed?'

'I know where the gold is,' Rox said. 'At least I know where to look.'

Camo smiled broadly and leaned back but said nothing. Tyko spluttered into his pint. Rosie giggled.

Rox repeated the refrain from the gold disc for the hundredth time.

Madeline got the gold with her in the hold
Madeline got the gold waiting in the cold
Madeline got the stacks never to pay tax
Madeline over under still more asunder
Madeline under over will mark a trover

Now it made some sort of sense. Then she told them all about water wheels.

'Under and over refer to the two water wheels. Nothing to do with under or over the ground floor. One of the wheels is overshot – the one in the lower room – and the other one in the upper room is undershot. *Under. Over.* There's a secret room or space hidden somewhere between the two wheels. There's got to be. I'm sure there is. The clues tell us.'

'In the two wheel rooms?' Camo asked 'Some kind of

'hold'?'

'Possibly hidden there. In the floor or the walls. I don't know. We need to go back and really look.' Rox didn't add that the hidden space could feasibly be outside the fort, just as long as it was still somehow between the two wheels or in their vicinity.

'I just didn't see it when we were there,' Rox said.

'None of us did,' Tyko said.

But Rox felt it was somehow her responsibility. She was the one among them with knowledge of what was feasible in construction terms. She was the only one who could have possibly outthought Danny Weathervane. He hadn't as far as they knew any knowledge of construction at all. She was the one with the knowledge of what was likely and unlikely. She was the one in charge of feasibility. And she'd missed it. She now thought she knew why the 'hold' had not revealed itself during her meticulous measurement survey. It must lie somewhere where she couldn't measure the difference between the inside and the outside walls. That meant it must be in the floor. In a floor where there was no basement below in which an elevation would reveal the floor thickness. The only floor in the fort that had no rooms beneath was the basement floor itself. And the two wheel rooms. She was now convinced the secret room must lie under the floor of the wheel rooms. Most likely she thought, it would lie near or behind the connecting steps that dropped down from the upper level to the lower. That was now the obvious place.

Her instinct leapt and she imagined one of the stone steps might be movable, to reveal a 'hold' beyond. She also thought the 'asunder' in the five line refrain somehow indicated the hold was somewhere between the two wheels. But she kept that to herself for the time being. It was too ephemeral, too flighty, too much of a leap. It was amazing, she thought, for an engineer how much she was relying on instinct.

'Wherever it is,' Rosie said. 'At least now we have somewhere to look. Somewhere to focus on. We didn't really know what we were doing before. It was too big. At least now we have a target area.'

Rosie had her laptop with her and she opened it up to view the huge numbers of photos that she and Tyko had taken before they left the fort.

They all clustered round her and the laptop as she scrolled through the small indicative icons until she found the series of shots they'd taken of the end of the fort where the mill race ran, and where the waterwheels were housed in their recesses. Now they realised the waterwheels were actually both under and over, one of each, they could see it clearly in the photos. Now they could see that the lower wheel's axle level was set much lower in the wall than the first wheel. They could see that it meant the axle height of the undershot wheel would stand above the water level and the axle of the overshot wheel below it. The lower wheel, the one they now realised was the overshot wheel, was fixed right on the edge of the cliff. Water pouring out of its buckets ran straight into the waterfall.

They all agreed they had to go back and finish the job.

But when?

And what should they tell Jane Shadwell? Should they tell Jane Shadwell at all?

After some debate they decided they would go as soon as the university winter term finished. That would be mid-December.

'We may be being watched,' Tyko said. He didn't need to spell out who might be watching them. 'If she spots us heading off pell-mell for the Pyrenees tomorrow or next week she'll smell a big fat dirty rat and come racing after us. But if we go in next holiday time it'll look more routine and I think she'll be less on her guard and we might be better able to give her the slip.'

They all agreed with that. Although Camo for his part thought that Bayb Azmoun had been satisfied with the outcome of their conversation. With their handshake they had a kind of a deal. It was unspoken, but it was there. He didn't think she was still watching them. He hoped so anyway. He didn't talk about it with the others.

For the same reason some argued that they should say nothing to Jane Shadwell. They should just turn up at farmer Lagrange's and ask for the keys.

But Camo particularly was against the idea. He was he confessed feeling a little guilty about his dealings with Jane Shadwell. Particularly about his story about the hole in the floor. He felt they should ask her permission and get the keys. He said he could make it sound the most natural thing in the world that they should want to go back, especially in winter time to see what it was like in a different season. Only if she was reluctant to give them permission should they consider going without her say-so.

'I don't think we should forget,' he said. 'The if we do actually find anything, then Jane Shadwell is technically the owner of it.'

'Can't we keep quiet about it?' Tyko said. 'She needn't know.'

'That probably depends on the quantity of what we find,' Rosie said. They weren't sure what she meant, so she carried on. 'I mean if we find ten thousand gold coins, it's going to leak out sooner or later that we've got them. It's much harder than you think, I think, to keep that sort of thing quiet. Quantity will out. In fact it will shout.'

Camo was glad they were bringing this issue out into the open. They'd delayed talking about it for too long.

'I think,' he said tentatively. 'That if we find all of it we give it to Jane Shadwell. I hope she'll then split it with us. There should be plenty to go round. The moral obligation will be on her then, not us.'

After some debate they agreed that Camo should approach Jane Shadwell.

20. RETURN

They were ready to go in mid-December, two days after the winter term ended.

'Don't know about you,' Rosie said. 'But I want to be back on or before Christmas Eve.'

The others agreed they did too.

'I don't think it'll take long this time,' Camo said. 'If Rox is right.'

There was no camping this time. Instead they stayed in two-star family run hotels. But in lieu of tents and camping equipment they had brought all the heavy and light tools they could muster. This inventory included spades, shovels and pickaxes, block hammers and chisels, crowbars, all chucked into Camo's plumber's bass, altogether with Rox's specialist surveying tools. The only part of their camping equipment they'd brought again was their sleeping bags.

They approached the Pyrenees towards the end of the second day after crossing the Channel. Each driving day they'd pushed the road harder, faster and further than the first time. They were in a hurry now.

On the road down through France many times they'd looked back and scanned the vehicles behind, checking for a black dark-windowed Mercedes SUV. Maybe they had given Bayb Azmoun the slip. Maybe it didn't occur to her that if they were going to return to Madeline they'd do it this close to Christmas. For the same reason they ventured off the autoroute for spells on to the parallel main roads for several exits before returning to the motorway. Apart from a few scares with similar vehicles they saw no sign of Bayb Azmoun. Though Camo thought all this obsessive caution was silly he was outvoted.

It was nearing dusk as they came to the narrow turn-off into the trees and up the mountain. When Camo had stopped the Land Rover in Ax-Les-Thermes and asked them if they wanted to find a hotel then in Ax and approach the fort in the morning; or press on to Madeline now before it was dark, they'd all agreed to push on and make it before dark.

'Open it up. Get the lights on. Get the heat going. Get cosy.' Tyko said.

So that's what they did.

There was snow now on the high ground and on the peaks round the lake. But the packhorse track was clear still. Rox was pleased to see that her guess that the engineers had taken the packhorse trial up through sheltered areas was correct. They emerged from the woods in the still soft colourless light of dusk. Camo stopped the car and they looked across the broad lake to the fort beyond, gleaming bright and yellowish in the evening winter sun. The lake was still ice free. The dark green trees swayed in the chill mountain breeze.

In the back seat Rox shivered. 'Get moving. It's going to get cold.'

It was full dark outside by the time Rox had engaged the switches to start the generator and power the lights and heating. They brought their provisions and belongings into the kitchen.

Before settling down in the kitchen to eat they made a rapid tour of inspection. Everything seemed as they left it. Which was a surprise, because they knew Bayb Azmoun had broken in some-time in the late summer. They wouldn't have expected her, nor Jem if he was still at large and with her, to be tidy. Maybe farmer Lagrange had cleared up any mess they'd left.

The great stone complex warmed up slowly around them as they ate their first meal of the stay and decided on a plan of attack.

Clearly their only focus was going to be on the end wall area of the courtyard and fort. They would check closely the wall outside which the mill race ran, plus the recesses housing the wa-terwheels; and of course the two chambers behind the wall, the upper and the lower wheel rooms. They would probably focus on the connecting steps between the two levels.

It was still Rox's main guess that the obvious place to search was the area in the split-level chambers around the linking set of stone steps.

That was where she led them next morning.

They came armed with a sledgehammer, a spade, a shovel, a hammer and chisel, a crowbar, a rubber hammer and a wooden mallet.

Tyko had the crowbar.

'Tyko, see if there's any cracks or slots or any orifices at all,' Rox said. 'That'll fit the end of your crowbar.' It was Rox's thought that one or more of the broad stone steps might be movable, sufficient to allow access to a cavity behind. The supposed cavity would stretch back under the floor of the upper chamber.

On either side of the broad connecting stairway between the two chambers there was a vertical stone wall four metres high, which was the difference in floor level between the two chambers. While Tyko inspected the stone steps for orifices, sometimes literally with his nose to the stone, Rox and Rosie took rubber hammer and wooden mallet and began tapping the face of the stone retaining walls either side of the steps, listening for any telltale echoes and differences in sound. Camo meanwhile ran his fingers along all the joints in the stonework, seeking anomalies. He started first on the joints between the stone flags of the floor in the upper chamber near the top of the steps.

They tapped and touched, scratched and scraped, probed and prised, inspected and inserted, dusted and dragged, examined and exhausted the stones and flags, and themselves, for two hours. They found nothing. At one point Camo fetched a bucket from the workshop and tried Rox's water trick on the floors of both chambers. Everywhere he tried, the water ran to the lowest local point and pooled there. It didn't disappear or run away down invisible cracks.

'Can we physically actually shift these steps?' Tyko asked at the end of the two hours. 'I mean like dismantle them? Unbuild and deconstruct them? Whatever you call something when you take it apart after you've built it. The reverse of how you built it.'

'You mean, whether they're supposed to move or not?'

'Yes. Just to see what's actually behind them.'

Rox wasn't sure. She was still convinced that Danny's hiding place would be easy to access, once found. She had no real reason to think that, other than her conviction that Danny would want to get at the coins readily, with relative ease. He couldn't do that if the boxes were just permanently and irrevocably walled up somewhere. There had to be an easy way in. There had to be.

This was the nearest point the four of them came to a falling out.

Up to now the other three had followed Rox's lead. She knew more about construction than any of them and knew what was feasible and what wasn't in terms of a hidey-hole. Everything they did, they let her decide if it should be done and how it should done.

Now for the first time Rox was almost overruled.

Rox went over to where Tyko was kneeling on the second step. There were sixteen steps in all. Each step was two metres wide with a tread 250 millimetres high and a going 300 millimetres deep.

'You want to move one of these steps?'

'Yes. Force it. Break it if we have too. Tyko stood up then sat down on the fourth step.

'I'm not sure we can. They're heavy. I mean really heavy.'

'We break it then.' Tyko's weariness was making him more abrupt than usual. He also knew he was getting very tired of the search. Would it never end?

Whacking it with a sledgehammer to break it into more manageable pieces would be easier said than done too, Rox thought.

'Let me think. Let's take a break.'

The four made their way out into the winter sunshine in the courtyard. Rosie handed round some mugs and a thermos of coffee as well as some granola, nut and yoghurt energy bars. They sat in a line on the flagged courtyard floor leaning back against the wheelhouse chamber wall.

'I agree with Tyko,' Camo said. 'I think the time for delicacy and pussyfooting around is over.'

'So you want to shift one or more stone steps – or more

likely break them up into smaller pieces to shift them – and see what's behind them?'

Rox really disagreed with this forceful approach. She felt certain that if the steps were the designed entrance mechanism to the hidden 'hold' then they would move easily once the right movement was initiated, probably through some kind of counterbalancing arrangement. But above all, they would be designed to move back to reveal the space and then forwards again to conceal it. That was their job. The trick was to find the right point to initiate the movement. The fact that after two hours searching they hadn't found anything remotely like that suggested to Rox that the steps were not the right place.

'Well, if you insist on doing that, there's an easier way to reveal what may or may not be behind or under the stones,' she said.

'What's that?' Tyko was already toying with the sledgehammer, taking its weight.

'Go in through the side.'

She explained that the side structure of the flight of steps was made of much smaller stones than the steps. Much easier to manage and much easier to extract. There would be no need for breaking anything. Any stone removed could be quite easily remortared back into place.

'Chisel one of those side stones out. It won't be easy. It'll take time. But yes we've got the tools. If the space is hollow under the steps – though my guess is that it'll be solid – but if it's hollow, taking one stone out will let you shine a torch into the void to see if anything's there. If there is you can take more stones out to get at it.'

Tyko grinned. 'I thought you'd come up with a solution if you set your mind to it.'

Rox grimaced. She thought it was a waste of time. But they hadn't found anything else in two or more hours of looking.

'It pains me to admit it,' Rosie said. 'But chiselling stones out of a wall by whacking pointy steel things into cracks and joints with ungainly and blistery hammers for hours on end looks like a job for the boys.'

Since both Camo and Tyko were the ones most keen on seeing what might be lying under the steps, they agreed that they should be the ones to tackle the job.

'I better identify the best stone to remove then,' Rox said, standing up.

The other three followed her back into the lower chamber.

Rox identified the face of a square stone set four stones back from the back edge of the eighth step.

'This should be a comfortable working height,' she said. 'And once removed should let us see the whole of any space under the steps. Hammer and chisel as far as you can go into the mortar joints all round the face of the stone. Fortunately we have chisels of various thicknesses, widths and lengths. Try the crowbar every now and then and lever it about to see if you can prise the stone loose. If and when you get it loose, jump, prise, waggle and tease it back by any means you can until you can get a grip on it and pull it out. All yours lads.'

The two women went to the kitchen while the men started hacking at the mortar joints with hammer and chisel. They brought back two of their supply of two litre bottles of mineral water and some bread and cheese. It would be hungry, thirsty work.

It turned out Rox was wrong. She was wrong on two counts. Firstly there was a space behind the stone and under the steps. And secondly there was something hiding in the void.

Camo and Tyko took it in turns, either for half an hour at a time, or until one had had enough, whichever came first, to chisel at the joints round the stone. At first Rosie and Rox watched their progress – which was agonisingly slow. But after the first hour they became tired of the incessant hammering and the dust and ventured outside.

'You think this is a waste of time, don't you?' Rosie said. They were in the courtyard, finishing the coffee in the thermos, sitting against the outside wall of the fort.

'I do. A waste of time and energy. And of search resources.

We should be looking elsewhere.'

'But where?' Rosie understood, she thought, the men's need to do something physical, right or wrong. But she also thought following Rox's ideas was the best way forward. She was split.

'I don't know,' Rox answered flatly. But she thought it would be better if all four of them were looking instead of two of them doing nothing and the other two wasting their energies on a phantom. But she didn't say it. She knew that Rosie knew it too.

'Well let's us at least carry on looking,' Rosie said. 'Why not have a look on the other side?' She pointed towards the other side of the wall. 'Outside.'

'Good idea.'

They walked across to the double gates of the courtyard, which they'd opened and fastened back and then followed the exterior path round the courtyard's perimeter wall back towards the mill race.

They climbed up the steel steps to the point where the double walkway began. One arm carried on over the sluice gate to the knoll, while the other went in the other direction along the wall of the fort. They decided to follow the walkway fixed to the wall above the mill race.

There was only a grating beneath their feet. And the noise from the mill race was tremendous. Holding on to the steel railings, rusty but well made and still sturdy, they made their way along the walkway, examining the wall as they went.

This side wall of the fort was roughly on the east side of the complex. The front of the fort looked generally south towards the Ariege river. The packhorse trail approached from the north, and the lake lay on the north side of the fort. The mill race and the walkway above it were on the east walls of the fort and the courtyard.

The winter sun was declining now and they lay in deep and chilly shadow as they progressed along the wall. Despite the monstrous gushing and gurgling sounds coming from the race, as they went past the undershot wheel recess and approached the lower, overshot, mill wheel set in its recess, they thought they could hear hammering coming from inside.

Then the hammering seemed to stop, or maybe they hadn't really heard it in the first place and it was all wishful thinking.

They passed the first wheel in its recess. They examined the stone housing round the wheel. They could see nothing obvious. The stonework looked old and untouched.

Rosie carried on towards the second wheel recess to have a look in there, but for some reason Rox stopped and turned to look back along the walkway. Maybe it was a trick of light and relative lack of brightness, or a shimmering reflection from the scudding clouds above, but for a brief second from the edge of her right eye she thought she saw something in the water. It was a flash of dirty dark red in the shape of a disc. Then it was gone. She tried to find the spot, for no more reason that it was something unknown and she didn't recognise it and would like to know what it was, but there was only the glittery reflections off the surface of the water and the darkness of the cut rock and stone course beneath.

At that moment as she sought to repeat her position and angle of sight and find again what she thought she had seen, a shout came from the corner of the fort where Camo was shouting and waving his arm.

They couldn't hear his words, but he seemed excited.

The two women retreated back along the gangway to the corner. Camo had gone back ahead of them as soon as he saw them begin to follow him.

Maybe they'd found something after all?

They had.

There was now a hole in the parapet of the flight of steps. A large cuboid stone lay on the floor. A dark space appeared in the parapet wall where the stone had been.

As Rosie and Rox entered the chamber and rushed down the steps to the lower room, Tyko and Camo were standing at the side of the steps and were trying to position a torch to shine into and through a hole beyond.

So the steps and the stones did hide a void after all.

'There is something in there. Definitely,' Camo was saying. 'But pretty small. Can't get a decent view.'

Camo handed the torch to Tyko. He tried to angle the torch and his head to throw maximum light into the void at the same time as allowing him to see as much of it as possible.

'I think so. But what is it? We're going to have to take out another stone so we can see.' Tyko was already reaching for the hammer and chisel which lay on the floor at his feet next to the extracted stone.

Standing behind the two men, Rosie assessed the situation. The hole looked large enough, just, she thought.

'If you'll allow me, I think my head is small enough to poke it right into the hole, at the same time as getting an arm through there with the torch.'

Immediately Tyko handed her the torch. 'Have a go,' he said.

The more she thought about it the more she realised there was a better way.

'First I've got a better idea,' she said.

She reached into a pocket in her shoulder bag and pulled out her phone. Tapping on the screen she opened up the phone's camera app. She reached through the hole with her camera in her hand and snapped a shot downwards into the space. The flash illuminated the entire space. She withdrew her hand.

'Shit. Didn't think of that,' Camo said.

Rosie reached through the hole into the space beyond again and this time took a series of photos in all directions in the void.

Sitting and clustering on the steps the four of them peered at Rosie's photos. The void appeared to fill all the available space under the steps. There was nothing solid there at all. There was a cavity under the entirety of the stone steps. But the void did not reach back under the floor of the upper chamber. In some of Rosie's photos the underside of the steps looked like the interior of a mini-ziggurat or the inside of a stepped pyramid.

The space under the stairs was certainly big enough to hold

them but there were no boxes of gold coins in the space.

However there was something there.

Lying on the stone floor a few feet away from the back face of the first and lowest step there appeared to be a bag. It looked to be a kind of backpack or rucksack. It was black and appeared to be made of leather. It looked a little like an old-fashioned school satchel. Was it an army pack, they wondered? It was right side up in the sense that the front flap and its two leather closure straps and buckles were facing upwards. The flap was closed and buckled shut. And judging by its flatness there might be nothing, or very little, in the rucksack at all.

But empty or not, they all now knew they wouldn't rest until they had retrieved it.

Rox borrowed Rosie's phone and peered intently at one image of the small rucksack.

'I think if it is empty or there isn't much in it, we could drag it out through the hole you've made. So we won't need to remove any more stones. And by the way, I was wrong about this!'

They laughed and Tyko patted her gently on the shoulder. It wasn't patronising. He knew, as they all did, that without Rox they'd have got nowhere. In a way they still hadn't and she was their only hope.

The question though, they all knew, was how did they get hold of the pack to lift it up to their hole?

'I think we can make a grapple of some kind,' Camo said. He knew there were steel pins and a spool of wire in the workshop. Rox had used some of the pins during her surveys. There was also plenty of string there. Rope too. 'If we can improvise a grapple, with a bit of luck we can toss it into the hole and it'll snag on one of the straps or buckles.'

Camo and Tyko went out to the workshop next door. Forty minutes later they came back sporting a homemade grappling hook. They'd taken three pins and bent the ends into hooks. They'd then wound wire tightly round the straight part of the pins in two places to hold the hooks in place, thus binding the three pin hooks together into a facsimile of a triple-tanged grappling hook. They'd then found some thick string and tied it firmly round the upper unbent end of the triply bunched pins.

Tyko said he'd have first go.

He asked for Rosie's phone and studied one of her images of the pack lying on the floor in the step void. He was trying to comprehend, visualise, and memorise the orientation of how the pack was lying.

Satisfied he faced the hole in the wall. He reached in and tossed the homemade grapple down into the void in such a way, he hoped, it would be landing square to the orientation of the pack. Slowly he reeled the line in. There was no resistance and soon the grapple reached the level of the hole in the wall. He pulled it out and tossed it again.

It took him fourteen attempts to persuade the grapple to snag firmly on one of the straps. Sometimes it seemed to grip then slide away. Sometimes it seemed to make a solid and firm connection, only to come unstuck and slide away as he applied lifting pressure. Most often he snagged nothing at all.

On the fourteenth try he felt the grapple take the full weight to the pack as he reeled in the line. He both felt and heard the leather bag begin to slide across the floor of the void. The he felt its full weight as he began to pull it up the wall beneath the hole. Judging the moment, Tyko reached in an arm through the hole and waited, pulling the line steadily and carefully with his other hand. He felt the leather touch his outstretched fingers. He grabbed the bag. He pulled. With very little resistance it came intact through the hole, almost with a slither as though it were alive. Shaken slightly by the slitheriness he dropped it on the ground by his feet.

They stared at it in the bright beam of the overhead strip lights, silent.

Rosie was the one who reached down to lift it and place it on a step at convenient height and proceed to unbuckle the straps.

'I guess it is an army pack,' she said. 'But I've no idea, really.' It looked old. And well used. But also it was in surprisingly good condition. The void in which it had lain for who knew how many years would have been more-or-less airtight. Damage by damp, bacteria, bug or parasite would have been minimal. To an untrained eye it looked in as good a condition as the day it was left in the space beneath the steps.

But why had it been left there? Perhaps its contents might reveal that.

Rosie reached out and began to undo the two buckles. She flipped back the flap and opened the pack. On the underside of the flap a six-figure number had been burnt or branded into the leather. A soldier's service number? They had no idea. Rosie peered inside the pack. She reached in and brought out a single object.

It looked like a broadsheet newspaper, folded to fit into the pack.

Gently Rosie unfolded the object to its full extent on a step.

It was a newspaper. A French newspaper. Or at least a newspaper in French.

Its title, centred in the top middle of the front page appeared to be:

\<L'AURORE\>

In the top right hand corner of the front page a date was printed. It said:

\<13 JANVIER 1898\>

At the top the main headline – indeed the only headline on the page – said:

\<J'Accuse…!\>

in large black type. And under that was printed:

\<LETTRE AU PRESIDENT DE LA REPUBLIQUE\>

And below that:

\<Par EMILE ZOLA\>

'We're going to have to do a bit of research,' Rox said.

'Google it!' Tyko said and they all laughed at the now standard line.

Something about it was ringing a bell for Rosie.

'I think,' she said. 'I think what we have here is the most

famous newspaper headline ever written.'

'Can you read it?' Camo asked.

'Not sure I can no,' she replied. 'Not the body at any rate. Or very slowly. But I don't need to because the headline is straightforward. And I know what it's about. Amazing. It's the Dreyfus Case.'

'Let's go to the kitchen or the day-room,' Rox said. 'I'm knackered. I need food and a drink. In either order. And Rosie can tell us all about the Dreyfus Case.'

21. LIGHT

Rosie carried the newspaper while Camo carried the army pack. They were now convinced that's what it was, an army pack dating from the time of the Dreyfus Case, or at least from January 1898, the exact time of Emile Zola's deadly open letter of accusation against the French government, all under editor Georges Clemenceau's legendary headline.

They made straight for the kitchen. It was the end of the day anyway and going dark and none of them fancied going back for further search and investigations that day. Tyko heated up some chilli and rice while Rosie opened a bottle of red wine. Camo and Rox took a beer each out of the fridge.

Yet again a day had been wasted and they were no nearer to achieving their goal. Yet again they hadn't found what they were looking for. But they'd found something interesting nonetheless. And they were less downhearted than they expected to be with yet more failure. This second side-discovery seemed in its way more remarkable and exciting than the discovery of the old books. It was a kind of time capsule dating from the last few years of the 19th century. It was a direct relic from one of the most notorious miscarriages of justice in French, European and world history.

Rosie rapidly filled them in on the background. She told them how Dreyfus was an army officer. He was Jewish. He was accused and convicted – in fact framed by the army and abetted by the government – of selling secrets to the Germans. Rosie said if she remembered rightly it was secrets about the revolutionary 75 mm field gun, but she couldn't swear to it.

'But it doesn't matter really what the secrets were. Dreyfus didn't do it. Someone else did. But the army and the government believed it must be him, he couldn't really be completely and patriotically French because he was Jewish, so they fabricated evidence and basically framed him for it. Unbelievable.'

Dreyfus languished in the desperate prison on Devil's Island in the colony of French Guiana in South America for five years before the case was reopened.

'The writer Emile Zola was instrumental in getting the case reopened,' Rosie said. 'He wrote this open letter to the French president basically accusing him and the government and the army of framing Dreyfus and covering up their tracks. The army at the time was nakedly anti-semitic. This newspaper L'AURORE was edited by Georges Clemenceau who later became president himself. He wrote this amazing J'Accuse headline.'

'Was L'AURORE a daily newspaper?' Camo said. 'Or a weekly?'

But Rosie didn't know.

'Google it!' Tyko shouted from the stove.

'Don't know if it makes any difference really,' Camo went on. 'I guess this time capsule – if that's what it is – was hidden away under the steps some time after the 13th of January 1898. But we don't know how long after.'

'Possibly hidden by the soldier whose number is burnt into the pack?' Rosie suggested.

'Yes. I'd go with that,' Rox said.

'What else can we say?' Camo asked. 'Can we say the hider – this soldier say – was a sympathiser with those defending Dreyfus? But perhaps being in the army himself couldn't show his sympathy?'

'They were called Dreyfusards,' Rosie said. 'And yes, I like that. He was sympathetic, but couldn't admit it. But hid the newspaper and his pack when he got the chance. So the future would know that even in the army at the time there was someone who was against what the army had done to Dreyfus.'

They all agreed that this scenario was plausible.

'Maybe he was working on repairing the steps, or something like that, and took the opportunity to hide the paper there.' Rosie wondered who it was. Maybe when they got home they might be able to search through French army records for this soldier's number and find his identity. That couldn't be secret surely? It would be good to find out his name, at least. Yet whoever he was he was probably killed in the First World War along with four million other French soldiers.

They talked late into the night, about this and other things. Tomorrow they would begin the search for the gold again. No one admitted it, but there was beginning to be a consensus among them that if they didn't find anything in two more days they would give up. Despite any defeat it was an adventure they'd remember for the rest of their lives. It had also brought them closer as a group.

They'd done their best and maybe there was no gold there anyway.

In a way for Rox finding something but not what they were looking for was worse than finding nothing. The Dreyfus Case in its own way was fascinating. And finding a direct relic that linked them to people alive then, who were living through it, was astonishing. But it wasn't what they'd come for. It couldn't disguise the fact she had failed again.

She was so certain this time she'd cracked it. She had been convinced that the hideaway must be somewhere near, around or between the two water wheels. Danny's ridiculous clues said so. She felt deeply the responsibility of the failure of their first trip to the fort. She felt her superior structural knowledge to whatever Danny possessed would reveal his hiding place to her. All she had to do was create a sufficiently detailed plan and the hideaway's whereabouts would reveal themselves. They had to. She was a structural engineer. And what was Danny? A pre-scientific musician? A rampant sex-starved goat? His hiding place should have been obvious to anyone with the slightest knowledge of construction. But it wasn't. She took it personally. And now Danny had beaten her not once but twice.

She knew in a way why she'd failed. She was out of her depth. She was too inchoate. She was too young, too inexperienced. She didn't know enough. And of course, too arrogant as well. Science can do that, she knew. When you're surrounded by unscientific and pre-scientific people, even friends, you could assume an arrogance based on your superior knowledge of science.

She knew now she needed a little more humility. She needed to listen more to the others' ideas. She needed to listen more to them and let them lead.

Rox couldn't sleep. Her sense of failure and the realisation of the depth of her arrogance wormed their way into her head, preventing her from relaxing. There was something else too rising and falling at the edges of her mind. An image of something dull red and round set in a white circle under flowing water played around the limits of her conscious sensibility. If it was something and not just her imagination, it shouldn't have been there at all, she thought. It should have moved.

Eventually she stopped trying to sleep. Carefully so as not to disturb the still form of Tyko next to her in his sleeping bag, she eased out of her own sleeping bag and put on some warm clothes and wrapped a down-filled jacket round her and carried her laptop into the bathroom next door. It was chilly rather than cold. Though the timer for the central heating had not yet switched on the boiler, the thick walls of the fort retained some warmth from the night before. She sat on one of the WCs and switched on her laptop.

She looked out of the high window. It was still dark outside. Then as her mind worked constantly like a gyroscope, always returning to, and centring on, the immediate problem, she began to wonder about light. She thought about different light conditions. She began to wonder whether in totally different light conditions the object she'd seen in the stream, if that's what it was, would reveal more detail. She and Rosie had been in full shadow on the gangway in the late afternoon when the fleeting image had struck her.

In winter the east wall of the fort lost the sun early in the afternoon. But what if she went out to the same place in totally different light conditions? What if she went out when the east wall was in full sunshine? What if she went out there soon after dawn? What might she see then?

She looked at her watch. Dawn was in an hour and a half. When the light came she would go out and see what she could see. It was a diversion, she knew. But she had to do something. She just couldn't sit and do nothing. There was also a feeling of mild dread about facing the others again in the new morning after her latest failure.

Patiently now, she waited for the light. Gradually the dark through the window gave way to grey and after that colour and depth made their presence known. It was time to go, Rox thought.

She walked alone through the stone corridors. The fort was silent around her. We've never thought about the soldiers stationed here, she thought. The garrison. Did they think it was a good or bad billet? Now in the silence where she walked, once there would have been scores of soldiers boots, even in the dawn, running along the stone in some kind of daily drill. There would always have been a watch. There would always have been someone in the fort who never slept. One thing this place would never have been in those days was silent.

Then when the soldiers had gone a lone eccentric French aristocrat had made his home here. Did he walk the corridors in the dawn too? she wondered.

And then there was Danny. She wondered if he preferred it on his own, when the entourage had gone, once the non-stop parties were over and the guests and groupies and hangers-on had gone. Maybe he liked it both ways. Maybe he deliberately alternated between being on his own in the fort and having a party staying.

She could imagine him walking the long corridors on his own. Planning perhaps his great gold scam to beat the taxman.

Rox emerged from the fort in a full snowstorm. It took her breath away. She shivered and was glad she had wrapped up warmly. She pushed her fingers deeper into the ski gloves, straightened the cuffs over her jacket sleeves and pulled her woolly hat over her ears and shrank her neck and chin deeper into the down jacket. The snowflakes swirled in the slow wind. They settled on the ground for several tens of seconds before dissipating. It wasn't cold enough yet for the snow to stick. Close, but no freeze yet.

She stood still for a moment by the corner of the fort, by the sluice gate, between the stone wall and the lake.

The wind was being baffled by the wall and flurries of snow were eddying up and around in all directions. There was a voice in the wind, sometimes human, sometimes inhuman. Sometimes it was a distant voice calling desperately for help. Sometimes it was just the sound of a tinny aerial engine keening hopelessly for oil.

Assistance or lubrication, she thought with a sudden insight. Was that the definition of the underlying essence of the universe? In the same way is the dawn by nature a scary time? she added to herself. Or was it the source of hope? The beginning of the same old daily grind or the start of a new day? An old start or a new beginning? Both, she guessed. But this time the scary outweighed the hopeful.

She felt both extremes. She felt utterly professionally compromised. She had failed again. Why had she come out here in the cold hopeless hopeful dawn? She sincerely wished to go back inside. To go back into the warmth and hide in the comfortable stillness. No one blamed her, she knew that. But she also knew she had only herself to blame.

She forced herself to go on.

The water still chattered and clattered down the mill race. But for some reason it was less choppy in the dawn, and smoother. The surface broke up the light less, allowing clearer seeing into the depths.

She tried to concentrate. She was gnawing at the problem, constantly fidgeting with mental solutions to what it was she had seen. Or what she might have seen, she corrected herself, it was so quick, so fleeting.

Had someone dropped something into the water at some point? Was that what it was she thought she'd seen? Then why hadn't the water swept it away long ago? Perhaps it was snagged on something?

At this moment there were only two realistic images circling inside her head that made sense of what she'd fleetingly seen. One was the brown wooden O of a lavatory seat. She hoped that wasn't it. The other was the broad leather circle round a horse's neck they used as a base for traction in the old days. A horse-collar it was called. It could conceivably be that. But why hadn't it been washed down the race and over the waterfall decades ago?

That was what had piqued her interest. It wasn't the object itself, whatever it was. That was most likely something broken or useless, something heedlessly cast aside. But why was it still there? What was snagged in her mind, like the object itself, was what an object stuck on the bottom of the mill race might mean? If something was snagged or stuck on the floor of the mill race, then why? And if there was, did that mean there was an inconsistency in the flow? Was there an obstruction of some kind in the mill race at that point? Why? And what could it be? What did it mean?

Then suddenly the snow stopped. The clouds lifted and disappeared over the ridgeline. The east wall was in full bright dawn sunlight as Rox climbed up the steel steps, rounded the corner of the fort and made her way along the elevated steel walkway bolted to the outer wall of the fort.

The rising sun had emerged momentarily but completely into one of the serrated cols of an adjacent eastwards ridge. The full rising sun was caught in the V between the peaks. Bright light flooded along the line of the mill race. The water was clear. It was clearer than at any other time she'd looked into it.

She carried on along the steel grating. She held the railing on the left with her hand. She passed the undershot wheel in its deep recess. She stopped short of the recess for the overshot water wheel, as near as she could estimate to where she had stood when she had first glimpsed the round dull red circular object in the water.

She looked down into the mill race.

She saw it.

Then the sun disappeared behind a cloudbank and the light changed. The water became more opaque, as before, and what she saw became invisible again.

But she had seen it for long enough to know exactly what it was.

Set in the bottom of the mill race between the two water wheels and nearer and just short of the overshot wheel was the dark rusty red disc of a heavy-duty manhole cover and frame. And in the stone environment around it was the dull greyish off-white circle of its mortar bed.

She'd found it.

Under. Over. Past the under; before the over.

She'd found Danny's hiding place. She'd found the entrance to Danny's hold.

She had found the place where Madeline was waiting in the cold.

22. HOLD

Overcome by emotion she sagged against the steel railing, almost in a state of collapse. After so many failures and false leads the sweet pain of final success overwhelmed her and she cried and cried with great chest-heaving sobs.

Her sobs ebbed away and she collected herself and straightened. She wiped her eyes with the back of a ski glove. Once more she looked down into the water. The manhole was no longer visible, but she knew exactly where it was.

She also knew what they had to do next.

'I wondered where you'd gone,' Tyko said. D'you go for a wander?'

He was sitting up in his sleeping bag. She came and sat on the edge of the bed next to him. Gently she reached for one of his hands with both of hers.

'I found it,' she said, simply. Then she told him all about it.

Tyko was amazed, excited, he couldn't wait. He leapt out of the sleeping bag in his purple tee-shirt and black briefs and went charging barefoot down the stone corridor to rouse Rosie and Camo in their quarters. He banged on the door shouting get up! get up!

'I would guess the other sluice gate has not been raised in decades?' Camo looked at Rox.

They were in the kitchen, some eating, some drinking tea and coffee.

'Nor the mill race one lowered,' Rox agreed. 'But we've got your oilcan.'

Once they were gathered in the kitchen Rox told them about the manhole in the mill race. Her conviction and enthusiasm were infectious. Now they all believed they had found at last the entrance to Danny's hidey-hole. But how could they access it? Rosie asked. It was under water.

'We close one sluice gate and open the other,' this was Tyko stepping in before Rox could give the same answer.

'Exactly,' Rox agreed. 'We've got the winding wheels to both sluices.' They knew the winding-wheels were hanging on the wall in the workshop. 'We fit those in place.' They could have a go at winding the sluices straightaway, she said. 'But my suspicion is they haven't been moved for so long we'll need to let the oil penetrate into the gears, the cogs, the thread and all the workings. We might have to wait several hours for that to work. Even a whole day.'

'Then we try again,' Tyko said. But then added: 'Can't we just bash the winding wheels round with a sledgehammer if they're stiff?'

Rox said she'd rather not. But she knew they might have to do that as a last resort if the oil didn't work. If necessary, she thought, the best thing to do then would not be to try to knock round the circular winding-wheels, but to see if there was a big pipe wrench in the workshop and fit that to the square winding nuts. Then bash that round with the sledgehammer. And if there was no sufficiently large pipe-wrench here, then they'd go down to Ax and buy one.

What they were going to attempt to do was this. There were two sluice gates. Currently one was open and the other was closed. They were going to reverse that configuration. First they would open the second, further away sluice gate on the other side of the grassy mound where the original stream bed lay. Having done so, water may or may not immediately flow through it along the old river bed to the falls. But if that went successfully then they would close the other sluice gate at the head of the mill race. That would effectively and definitively cause water to flow through the further sluice gate. It would be the only way out of the lake. With its gate closed and water denied access to it, the mill race would then run dry.

Then they would descend into the bed of the mill race and inspect Rox's manhole. They would see what they would need to do to open it.

Then they would see where the manhole led.

It was cold and they were dressed warmly when they emerged from the fort and made their way along the outside of the courtyard wall to the mill race on the east wall of the fort. The snow started again. Camo and Tyko were carrying the big wrought iron control wheels for winding the sluice gate mechanisms.

Camo mounted the steps to the top of the mill race sluice gate. He fitted the wide square hole in the centre of the control wheel over the square nut on the sluice spindle. It was a good tight fit. Reasoning that clockwise rotation would be to lift the gate, and anticlockwise would be to lower it, he exerted a relatively small amount of power in an attempt to turn the wheel anticlockwise.

'Stop!' Rox shouted up to him. 'We have to do this in the right order. We need to raise the other gate first.'

Camo stopped trying to turn the wheel raised a hand in acknowledgement of his error.

They moved on across over the sluice gate bridge onto the grassy knoll on the other side and over to the second sluice gate. Tyko mounted the steps up to the top of the gate. He fitted his control wheel securely onto the square nut on top of the gate's winding mechanism. He noticed a cotter pin dangling on a small chain near the nut and inserted it through a hole which now showed above the wheel. The control wheel was now locked into position. He looked down at the closed gate. There was a foot or more of lake water pressing against the bottom of the sluice gate.

'Give it a go,' Rox said from below. 'Try clockwise.'

Tyko strained to turn the wheel. It responded with a creak and a tiny amount of movement. They saw the bottom of the gate move a crack out of its concrete bed. A thin horizontal spurt of water leaped and squirted through the tiny gap. But then the wheel froze stiff and Tyko could turn it no further. Tyko returned the wheel to its start position and the seeping crack in the bed at the base of the gate closed again.

'We need oil,' he said.

'At least we know that clockwise is up,' Rosie said.

They returned to the kitchen out of the snow while Camo went to fetch his oilcan from the Land Rover parked in the courtyard. He went back with it and soaked the screw threads, the cogs, and every part of the mechanisms he could drip and squirt oil into on both sluice gates.

Then they waited.

It was lunchtime three hours later when they came back to the second sluice gate, the closed one on the other side of the grassy knoll.

This time both Camo and Tyko ascended the iron steps to the top of the gate. They both gripped the control wheel and attempted to turn it clockwise. The mechanism tried to resist, but not for long. The oil had done its work. The wheel started to move. They rotated the wheel firmly, slowly and steadily. And slowly and steadily the large cast iron gate rose inexorably out of its bed, sliding smoothly in grooves in the side stone breastworks that supported the whole gate.

Water hissed, then roared, then settled into a kind of bouncing chattering and drumming hum as it forced itself through the increasing gap under the gate and ran down the old stream bed for the first time in who knew how many decades.

It probably hasn't been raised ever since they took the water wheels out of commission, Rox thought. She said the same to Rosie as they watched the gate slowly rise and the gap beneath it steadily increase.

'Perhaps the gate was last raised at almost the same time as the soldier left his newspaper under the stairs.' Rosie said. Or when Danny hid his gold, she thought. If Rox is right and this is the place. They had been wrong so many times she wasn't as hopeful as the others were that this time they were on the right track.

It was a nice thought. It was possible, Rox thought. The fort had converted to steam and electric power sometime in the 1890s, which made the wheels redundant. Perhaps it was the very works involved in doing the conversion that gave the soldier the opportunity to hide his pack where he did. Who knew?

The control wheel came to the limit of its thread, and could go no further. Camo and Tyko stopped winding. The sluice gate was held in the air well above the level of the water. The old stream bed was filled to capacity with rushing water. The water bent flat the foliage that had grown in the stream bed over the decades since the gate had last been opened.

No one said anything as they walked back over the grassy knoll to the mill race sluice. Camo and Tyko ascended the iron steps to the control wheel. They began to put pressure on the wheel to rotate it anticlockwise.

With this gate too the oil had done its work. As the two men turned the wheel the thick solid cast iron gate began to descend towards the rushing water. Soon it bit into the surface. On it went. Down and down through the water. They felt it slide home into its concrete bed. The water flow was stopped in it tracks. Now the noise of falling water increased and was louder in the other water course as that sluice supplied the way to the lake's only outlet.

They stood on the iron walkway over the sluice and watched the mill race run dry.

In the distance beyond the recess holding the undershot wheel, and before the recess with the overshot wheel, Rox thought she could see the rusty red manhole cover.

As the mill race ran dry it also ran silent. It was strange no longer hearing the rushing and yes, drumming, sound of the flow, Camo thought. It was a kind of drumming sound. He remembered how Bayb Azmoun had quoted her father, quoting Danny Weathervane: 'Danny said it was under the drumming.' Well here was the drumming, just as they said, but now it was silent.

'That's good,' Tyko said. He was pointing to a set of steps cut into the stone. The steps were situated midway between the two wheels and were cut into the rock of the grassy knoll down the vertical side of the mill race on the other side from where they were standing on the bridge over the sluice gate. They had not been visible before.

'I wondered how easy it was going to be to get down into the bed of the race,' Rox said. 'Seems the builders, Vauban or someone later, thought of everything.'

Now the entire mill race was completely drained of water. The bed of the race was neatly constructed of smooth stones. There was no moss, nor weeds; the water ran too quickly for those to grow. The race was bare stone. The far side, the grassy knoll side, was cut directly into the rock. The fort side, below the steel walkway, was constructed in heavy blocks of stone.

'If there is a chamber under that manhole,' Rosie said, not wanting to count her chickens. 'Would it have been built by Danny Weathervane?' It seemed unlikely.

Rox thought that was extremely unlikely. She thought there'd be some sort of inspection pit down there under the manhole for access and to enable maintenance work on the original water wheels. Probably it was dug and built, hacked out of the rock, in the early days as part of the fort's construction, before the retractable wheels were installed; before the steel walkway as well.

'Part of the original construction I think. Danny may have found it, though. He might have put on the manhole cover or had it rebedded.' When she had first seen them at dawn that day she thought then that both manhole cover and its mortar bed looked relatively recent.

Maybe Danny did find it by accident. It was conceivable that in abnormally hot and dry summers the lake level sank too low to feed the mill race. The manhole shaft would then be exposed naturally as the race ran dry. But she guessed the builders would have allowed for an abnormally low lake level and dug the race deep enough to cope with all weather eventualities. Yet maybe the morphology and slope configurations of the lake had changed over the years, over the centuries? And Danny just got lucky one year and found it. But however it had happened, she was sure it was Danny who had replaced the original cover and instead put in the modern heavy-duty manhole cover and frame.

Then the more she thought round the problem the more she arrived at a better answer, one that didn't depend on changes in lake morphology and which seemed so sensible and logical it must be right. Perhaps when the book-dealing duck drowned when he was sucked down the mill race the authorities, or someone with interim responsibility for the place, reversed the existing set up for safety reasons closed the mill race sluice gate and had the water flowing out of the old stream bed instead. So when Danny bought it and arrived here for the first time that's how he found it and the mill race was dry. Under those circumstances it was probable that the manhole shaft and whatever cover was on it in those days would be plainly visible. So it was Danny who then investigated the pit and had the manhole cover repaired and the mill race reopened. Come to think of it he probably had both sluice gates serviced and modernised at the same time so he could depend on them and make use of them whenever he needed to enter the pit.

'Well, let's go and have a look at it,' Camo said. 'Let's check it out and see what tools we need.'

Rox realised how nervous she was now. There might well be an inspection chamber under the manhole, but would there be anything in it?

Camo led the way over the sluice gate bridge to the grassy knoll on the other side. They followed him along the bank on the far side of the race until he reached the set of steps, cut into the rock, which descended to the bed of the mill race.

They followed him down the steps.

'They're a bit slippery,' he called back over his shoulder as he went, and he grasped the rock to steady his footing as he went down. The others did likewise.

The stones in the bed of the race were also slippery. They walked carefully and a little gingerly downslope along the bed.

They grouped in a circle around the rusty red manhole cover.

It definitely looked modern to Rox. Mid-twentieth century perhaps, she guessed. So definitely Danny's doing. 'Looks like it's six hundred millimetre diameter,' she said. 'Two feet.'

There were two deep slots opposite each other cut into the

top of the manhole cover.

'They're the lifting slots for manhole keys,' Rox said. 'We might find a set in the workshop.' If not, she thought that a couple of crowbars could do the same lifting job. She'd seen that done before. Precarious, but workable.

'OK,' Tyko said. 'We'll go and look for those. What else do we need?'

'Everything we've got,' Rox said. They didn't know what further obstructions they might find down in the pit. They still might have to dig or hammer and chisel once in the chamber. It was better to be prepared. 'Apart from the set of two manhole keys. Definitely a spade. Hammer and chisel, And two crowbars just in case. And torches. All the torches we've got!'

They returned to the workshop. Camo and Tyko carried on over to the Land Rover, Tyko to bring back all their torches and Camo to lug the plumber's bass that was filled with an array of tools, including chisels, pipe wrenches, hammers and crowbars. The others searched the workshop for a set of stout manhole keys. Camo and Tyko returned and joined in the search. No one had noticed any in their previous trips to the workshop. There was a pile of wood and cut timber in one corner. For some reason Rosie wandered over to the pile as the others were peering under workbenches and sifting through collection of other tools. Peering over the edge of the neat stack she saw something round on the ground between the wall and the timber. Reaching down she pulled out two matching metal tools tied together with string. They were shaped a little like the Egyptian *ankh* hieroglyph, the symbol for life, but without the cross piece. Each tool was about a foot long with a circular hand ring at the top and small tee-shape at the bottom end of the long straight shaft.

'What's this?' she asked, aiming her question at Rox and lifting them up to show her.

'They're the keys!' Rox said, recognising them straightaway. She was intrigued when Rosie said where she had found them. Had they been deliberately hidden she wondered? She couldn't say. But there were plenty of other manholes and drain covers throughout the fort. There was a large one for instance in the centre of the courtyard. So seeing manhole keys at an earlier point in their searches would not have automatically struck her with a eureka moment.

Tyko had returned with the torches, and now armed with those and the plumber's bass, plus a spade from the workshop they returned to the manhole in the bed of the mill race.

Rox undid the string and handed the keys to Camo and Tyko, 'Try one each,' she said. 'It'll be quite heavy.' The cover had to be heavy to sit firmly enough in its frame to be watertight. Not only that, it probably hadn't been lifted since Danny was there. She hoped.

She showed them how to insert the tee-shaped end of the keys in the ready slots in the manhole cover. 'Then you twist them through ninety degrees. Then they're housed tightly in the slots and won't come out and they'll take the weight as you lift the lid.'

They did as she told them. Then eyeing each other, Camo and Tyko prepared themselves to lift.

'Three. Two. One. Lift!' Tyko said. The two men strained. The lid resisted. Then suddenly it gave way. The two men carried it a little to one side and set it down. They left the keys still in their slots.

A dark hole had opened up in the stone bed of the race. Kneeling down and peering in Rox could see a set of galvanised steel step rungs fixed into one stone side of the pit, descending into darkness. She shone a torch beam into the hole. The cone of light showed that the manhole shaft dropping through the stone bed of the mill race was a metre thick and below that she could see a stone floor about another two metres below the bottom of the manhole shaft.

'Looks clear,' she said. 'Who wants to go first?'

'I'd like to,' Camo said.

They recognised his right. He was the one among them who had family involved in this place.

Camo took another torch from the bag. He sat on the edge

of the manhole and dropped his feet in, reaching for the topmost steel step rung. He found it, let it take his weight, and continued on down, stepping down the rungs and holding on to the upper ones as he went.

He reached the floor. From above they saw his torch beam change direction and sweep somewhere back below them, out of sight.

'Wow,' they heard him say. 'Oh wow. Oh my. Wow. Wow.' Then the light moved on. Then came a cry, almost a shout, 'What the-- Jesus!' Then calmer: 'Better get down here. Shit.'

Rox went down next. Then Rosie. But before Tyko descended Camo went back to the access shaft, called up and asked Tyko to pass down the bag with the remaining torches and the bass with all the tools. He did so, handing them to Camo one by one. Then he too joined them in the pit. Tyko brought the spade down himself.

They stood in a line just under the access shaft. The four of them now wielded torches. They flashed their torches round the chamber. It was bone dry inside.

It was bigger than they expected. The descent rungs were set in the middle of the end wall. The manhole access shaft was at the end wall as well. The chamber was four metres wide and stretched back from the access manhole as much as ten metres long. Its width appeared to match the four metre width of the mill race above. But they only worked out the dimensions later. For the moment they were all beaming their torches onto a series of objects that were piled up in the centre of the chamber.

It was a stack of small stout wooden boxes.

But it was what was beyond the boxes that made them catch their breath.

Seated on the ground, leaning against the far wall with its legs stretched out in front of it, was a skeleton.

23. COLD

First they checked the skeleton.

'Gave me a hell of a fright,' Camo said.

They could see now in the light of their torches as they approached that it was a mummified body rather than a skeleton. The adipose tissue had dissolved and dried away and the sallow skin had shrunk and tightened over the bones.

They went past the stack of boxes and stood round the mummified skeleton. It was still dressed in the substantial remains of the clothes the owner wore in life. In the light of their combined torches they were able to see that the clothes though faded had once been black. Under the black jacket the body had a white tee-shirt with a black unidentifiable image of a woman's head on it. On the skeleton's feet a pair of shin high boots were still intact and in good shape. They were a shiny cherry-red colour. The head was leaning back against the wall. It was surrounded by a mass of blonde hair. The eyes had gone, the nose had shrunk back to a sharp tetrahedron and the mouth was hanging open in a ghastly grin.

Rosie bent down closer to the right front side of the body and shone her torch on the top of the right breast pocket which was centred on a brass press stud. She focused her light on the seams edging the flap.

'They're stitched with green cotton,' she said. 'And those boots on the feet are Doc Martens.' It was just as Chris Sentinel said.

'And see here,' Camo said. He shone his torch to the right of the skeleton's head.

The letters FFF were scratched on the wall.

Tyko shone his torch at the body's left hand resting on the stone slab floor. They could clearly see the hand had six fingers.

'This is Felix Fairfax,' Camo said. 'She went missing in 1971. Just before the band's last US tour, the fatal tour. The story was that she walked out on the band. Now we know different.' He didn't add that it looked like Chris Sentinel was right. Danny

Weathervane did know something very definite about the disappearance of Felix Fairfax.

Tyko had stooped down to peer at something shiny that lay on the stone floor under the fingers of the mummy's right hand.

It looked like a gold coin.

Camo flashed his torch again at the triple F initials. The letters had a kind of faint gold sheen to them.

'She scratched her initials with the edge of the coin,' he said.

'I think she tried to use it to dig her way out too,' Rox said. She showed them what she'd seen. The mortar joints round one stone above the mummy's head had slight score marks and indentations in them.

It was too awful for words, Rosie thought. How could you even begin to imagine what it must be like to be in a situation where you're all alone in a stone tomb in the total dark and all you can do is try to dig yourself out with a gold coin?

Also on the ground by the body's right hand was a cigarette lighter. To Tyko who thought he knew about these things, it looked like a Zippo, but it must be the IMCO lighter that Camo and Rosie said Sentinel had mentioned.

So she had light, of a kind, for a while, Rosie thought. Then when the fuel or whatever ran out, what then? Just the dark.

Rosie expressed what they were all thinking.

'Is this Danny's doing? Did Danny kill her here?'

'Or more likely sealed her in here to die. Yes. I think he did,' Camo said. 'Who else knew about this place apart from Danny?'

'I don't think you can seal yourself in here by accident,' Rox said.

Rosie was wondering how things could come to this. Danny and Felix were supposed to be in a relationship. A troubled one, certainly by all accounts. But they must still have cared for each other. Perhaps cared greatly. And yet here was Felix Fairfax dead and Danny was the only serious suspect.

Did she walk out, she wondered? Then regretted it and came back to surprise him? Maybe when all the groupies and party types had gone? When she knew it would be just Danny at the chateau?

But it wasn't just Danny, was it? She reasoned it through to herself. It was never just Danny. It was always Danny and his money. It was the only thing he ever wanted to be alone with.

Maybe it went like this: perhaps she came back and found him here, counting his money?

'I have a feeling she was going to tell the authorities,' Rosie said.

'Rat on Danny to the taxman?' Camo wanted to see the good side of Danny, but was finding it difficult. He kept wanting to try.

'It's a pretty good motive for silencing someone,' Tyko said. 'I'd imagine,' he added. Especially from what we know about Danny he didn't add, but they all thought it, even Camo.

Rosie could see it now. The discovery. The flaming argument. The threat. The final act. The harsh heaving scraping sound as Danny dragged the manhole cover back into place. The living death.

She was fascinated by the detail. What happened? How did it really go? She imagined Felix stopping and paying off the taxi from Ax lower down in the trees because she wanted to walk up along the packhorse trail through the trees and past the lake and step over the drawbridge and approach the weird looming fort on foot. The only place where Danny felt at home. And all the while anticipating, looking ahead, imagining the event, routing and rebating the coming reunion in her mind, with expected tears and laughter, especially laughter, as always. And then soon, as always, the promises, the regrets, the denials, the vows to change his ways, and finally the shared vision to put the past behind and create a new and better future together. And all the while as she walked, anticipating, hopefully envisaging, looking forward with an inward smile, she had no idea she was walking to her death.

Shocked and silent they returned to the pile of boxes.

There were twenty boxes. Each box had a pair of rope handles. Each box was about a foot long, nine inches wide and nine inches deep. The stack of boxes was three layers deep. Nine boxes were laid in a tight square on the ground. A second square of nine boxes, rotated through ninety degrees, was piled neatly on those. There was a third course of two boxes on top.

They approached the stack. They were silent now. There didn't seem to be anything worth saying. Camo's series of 'wows' had said it all.

Approaching the stack of boxes, Rox was the only one who had eyes for anything but the boxes. Civil engineer to the last, she was examining the room they were in. She noticed a small grating in the centre of the floor near the boxes. Made sense she thought, if water ever leaked in from the mill race above you'd want it to be able to drain away. She knew the drain couldn't cut back towards the mill race because it was already below the water level here. She guessed the drain therefore most likely went directly down and then to and through the front wall of the fort. She noticed the floor had a slight fall in all directions towards the drain.

As they approached the pile of boxes Tyko was thinking: twelve million quid in gold. Jesus Christ.

Camo was thinking about Jane Shadwell. He was feeling decidedly guilty. By rights the coins in the boxes was all hers. What should they do about that? He and they had not decided anything about that yet. In fact they hadn't even really talked about it in reality, just as a possibility. Perhaps that was because none of them really thought the gold was real. They'd probably all thought deep down that it was all a fantasy, just like he had insisted to Bayb Azmoun. And even if it wasn't they couldn't really believe they would be the first to find it after all this time. Now they would have to face the Shadwell problem.

Because it was real. And it was here now. And they were the first to find it.

'Shall we open one?' Rosie said. She realised she was whispering. It was because of the mummy. It seemed to own the chamber. It seemed to fill it completely and leave no space, nothing spare at all. It had far greater rights to the space than they did. They were newcomers arriving too late. The gold was Felix

Fairfax's now. They stood round the pile of boxes, now always conscious of the other entity in the room.

Camo shone his torch on one of the top two boxes.

'Might as well,' he said.

He looked closer to see what tool they'd need to prise open the box. Chisel or crowbar?

It was neither. There was no tool necessary. He examined the top of the nearest box. There was a neat brass catch on top and it looked like if you pressed down the catch that released the lid of the box and allowed it to slide backwards in grooves to expose the inside.

Camo pointed the torch down more closely on the box top. He pressed down the brass catch. Then he slid back the top of the box.

A gleaming surge of gold light greeted them. Several streams of coins standing edge on in neat rows were exposed to the light.

They were exposed to the light for the first time in nearly fifty years.

One of the rows had a coin missing. That must be the one that Felix Fairfax had used to scratch her initials, Camo thought. And begun her futile attempt to dig her way out of her tomb, armed only with a gold coin. He stopped himself. It didn't bear thinking about.

Tyko was staring down at the banks of coins.

'Twelve million quid,' he said aloud this time. 'Jesus Christ.'

'As much as that?' a voice with an American accent said from the end wall of the chamber, below the access shaft. 'I never knew. We'll take over from here kids.'

They recognised the voice.

Bayb Azmoun was standing at the end wall of the chamber. The light from the access shaft above lit up her black hair like a dark warning beacon. As before when they'd seen her she was dressed in a black suit. But now she wore a black overcoat over it. She was holding a pistol in her right hand which she continued to wave about alarmingly as she talked like a lecturer with a laser pointer. In her left hand was a torch which she now snapped on.

'Ok Lurch,' she called up the shaft. 'You can get down here now.'

Soon a bulky athletic looking person also in the trade mark black suit and overcoat with velvet collar began to step down the steel rungs and soon joined her at the end of the chamber.

Camo felt a degree of surprise that Bayb's bulky muscle-bound assistant Lurch was a woman. She was the biggest, heftiest and most muscle-hulked woman he'd ever seen. She too had a pistol. She didn't wave it about.

'What happened to the vile Jem?' Rosie asked. It was an utterly incongruous thing to say, but it felt superbly ironic to them all given the situation they were in. They all hoped Lurch was an improvement.

'Still in gaol I imagine,' Azmoun said, as if she couldn't care less. 'Dumb asshole shot at the police. He can rot.'

Even in that dire and stressful situation, Rox felt a tiny amount of relief that they weren't going to have the benefit of Jem's company.

'I took you at your word,' Azmoun said, pointing the beam of her torch directly at Camo. 'You said you'd given up.' Her voice breathed fire and retribution.

He shrugged.

'Good thing I'm an untrusting disbelieving bitch,' she said. 'But you did lose me a coupla times on the road. But, hell, I kinda knew where you were headed. Now,' Azmoun said, waving the gun around like a bonfire night sparkler. 'Make your way over there and stay by the far end wall.' She pointed with the gun towards the end wall upstream ten metres from her. 'And stay there. Don't move. I don't have the time nor the energy to cope with any melodrama or histrionics. Be still. Behave. Be said. No more warnings. Move.'

The four moved to the far end wall and stood there in a line quite meekly.

Then Bayb Azmoun noticed the mummified body for the first time at the base of the wall beyond the boxes. She started and seemed to jump.

'Who's your skinny acquaintance?' she asked. Her attempt at levity failed. Her voice had a tremor she couldn't hide.

'We think it's Felix Fairfax,' Camo said. 'She was in the band. You must remember her?'

Azmoun sucked in her breath through her teeth and made a kind of exaggerated whistling surprise noise.

'I do. Oh I do. Danny had the hots for her. Well now. That is interesting. She went missing. Danny said she stormed out. Joined a commune or something. I guess this is Danny's doing. Pity it's too late to put him in the can for murder. Oh well.'

'Do you think Danny was capable of murder?' Rosie said. She couldn't stop it. She needed to know.

'Oh yes. Oh yes indeed.'

Bayb Azmoun came and stood by the stack of boxes and covered them with her pistol. She glanced down at the open box of coins. Her face was impassive. She revealed no emotion.

At the same time Lurch pocketed her gun, took off her overcoat, and after a worried fearful glance in the direction of the mummy, began lugging the boxes to the bottom of the shaft, two at a time, and then one by one carried them upwards and out into the chill afternoon air above. A flurry of snowflakes drifted down through the manhole.

The boxes were heavy. They could see that from the effort it required for Lurch to move twenty boxes.

Eventually all the boxes bar one had been removed from the chamber. The remaining one was the one that had lain on top of the stack, the open one, the one whose lid Camo had slid back to reveal the seemingly glowing rows of coins inside. Lurch had put it down to one side when she first started removing the boxes. It had taken her perhaps forty-five minutes to remove them all.

Lurch came back a final time. She stooped to slide close and then pick up the last box from the floor. It was still open. The coins inside gleamed in her torch light in the remarkable untarnished unoxidised way that only gold has.

'Leave it Lurch,' Bayb Azmoun commanded. 'Let them enjoy it. That's what they came for.' Lurch gave a small grin. Then she covered them with her gun as Bayb Azmoun retreated from the centre of the chamber. Lurch put her overcoat back on as Azmoun moved backwards towards the exit shaft.

Bayb Azmoun stood still below the shaft. She flashed her torch at the body on the floor.

'So long darlin,' she said. 'He didn't deserve you.'

Then she looked back at them one last time.

'The coins are mine,' she said. 'Danny-goat owed me big time.' Then she turned and made her way up the rungs and out. Before disappearing out of the manhole she ducked her head back one time and looked directly at Camo.

'You shouldn't have lied to me,' she said. 'No one lies to me.'

Lurch rapidly followed her up and out. As she stepped on the lowest rung to step up and out of the manhole Lurch glanced to her left and noticed the spade leaning against the wall. She retreated and picked it up and started to remount the rungs. But then Azmoun's voice came down the shaft from above.

'Leave them that too.' And a faint harsh laugh could be heard. Lurch threw the spade onto the floor, turned to gash a sickly smile at them one last time and disappeared.

Well, thought Rosie, better the sickly smiling but silent Lurch than the sickly smiling but verbalising Jem.

Both Bayb and Lurch ignored the plumber's bass that was lying on the floor near the manhole shaft. Like everyone else, they probably had no idea what it was and dismissed it from their minds. It could be they thought it was a bag – unnecessary for Lurch – they'd brought to help them lift the boxes of gold out of the chamber?

At the far end wall of the chamber, before any of them could think what to do next they heard a scraping sound of metal on stone, and then a grunt.

The chamber went pitch black.

Lurch had replaced the manhole cover.

One of them flicked on a torch.

'Are we stuck here?' Tyko asked. He was beginning to realise he was slightly claustrophobic; something he'd had no idea about till now.

'Is this chamber airtight?' Rosie asked. 'How soon will we run out of air?' She kept her voice calm, which was a surprise to her. Is that how Felix Fairfax died? she wondered.

'No and no,' Rox said, glad now she'd noticed the drain in the floor. Switching on her torch she made her way to the grating over the drain. She kneeled down and placed a hand over it. She could feel a slight draught on the back of her hand. Air was coming in through the drain. Thankfully the building predated the notion of the S-bend or the P-trap. The drain ran directly to the outside air without a water bend sealing the pipeline.

'We're ok for air,' she said, pointing with the torch beam down at the drain in the floor. 'There's plenty coming through there. And as for being stuck…'

She moved across to the exit and stood under the closed manhole cover, flashing her torch upwards.

'Do one of you boys reckon you could shift this manhole cover – if you had a solid enough place to stand?' They would only have to shift or tilt it up a fraction. Just enough to get the end of a crowbar in the gap. Then they could use the crowbar to lever the manhole cover aside. 'We'd only need to shift it a bit. To get a start, kind of, then we can use one of the crowbars to shift it. How heavy was it?'

Both Camo and Tyko thought each on their own would be able shift it enough. They knew they'd be standing not on the ground but on one or more of the rungs in the wall. But they reckoned they could do it.

'Ok. Not stuck then either,' Rox said. Although she wondered if Bayb Azmoun agreed with that. Rox was convinced she had intended them to die in the pit, either through lack of air, thirst or eventual starvation. She didn't think Bayb Azmoun cared how they died. But what she didn't want was for them to get out again. Azmoun was sure they were stuck there and would die there.

'Anyone got a mobile signal?' Rosie asked, practical as ever.

'We could just phone the police?'

Such a good idea Camo thought. But amazingly it turned out that none of them apart from Rosie had bothered to bring their phones.

'I thought we wouldn't need them,' Tyko said. 'And thought it might get damaged if we had work to do.' He'd left his phone in the kitchen.

When the rest said they hadn't brought their phones either, Rosie rapidly checked her shoulder bag for hers. She never went anywhere without her shoulder bag.

'Oh shit,' she said. 'Shit.' The phone's battery was dead. 'Sorry.'

'Well, no worries,' Rox said. She had a plan.

Rox said not having phones didn't matter so much at the moment as she preferred them to get out of the chamber under their own devices, if the others agreed with that?

'I don't fancy answering any questions about what we've been up to,' she said.

Rox had a plan, she said, and what did the others think?

'We wait an hour before trying to get out. And I think we can get out when we want.' She pointed her beam to the under-side of the manhole cover. 'I think we'll be able to shift that quite easily.'

She explained that she was convinced that Azmoun meant for them to die. It might be a good idea if they didn't disabuse her of that conviction.

'I don't want her anywhere in my life ever again,' she said. Nor Jem nor Lurch, she thought but didn't add. 'It might be a good idea if she thinks we're dead.'

The others agreed with her thinking so far.

'So I'd like to wait an hour before attempting to leave. I timed Lurch shifting the boxes out of here. It took her forty-five minutes to get them all out. So say they've got their SUV at the corner of the courtyard wall in the park by the mill race, then I reckon it'll take Lurch another hour to carry all twenty boxes from the stream bed above to the back of their SUV. Then they'll leave. That's when we leave too.'

They thought it was a good plan. At least none of them could think of a better plan.

'So let's take it easy till then,' Camo said, sliding his back down the far wall until he was sitting on the floor. He wrapped his arms tightly round him in his jacket. It was cold.

It was cold here, Rosie agreed. In here with Madeline in the cold. But they were warmly dressed.

Strangely, Camo thought, none of them seemed to be as distressed, fearful or as worried by the presence of the mummified skeleton as he might have expected. Alone with it in the dark wasn't so bad. The remains of Felix Fairfax had already become familiar to them. She had almost become a friend. Here was someone who had suffered the same fate as them. She was a fellow victim. Like her they had been sealed in a tomb in the dark. But unlike her they had light. Unlike her they were not alone. They had each other's company. And there was one final and inestimable difference: they had hope. Unlike them she had been unable to get out.

But at Tyko's request they kept one torch burning while they waited.

Time moved on. Rox imagined Lurch lugging the boxes either two by two, or more probably one by one, back up the mill race to the steps, then up the steps out of the race and then over the rough ground of the grassy knoll, then back up and over the sluice gate bridge to the corner of the outer courtyard wall and the gravelled area where the Mercedes was most likely parked. She assumed Bayb Azmoun would not be doing any lifting and lugging.

It was quiet in the pit. Sometimes they chatted and sometimes they were all silent.

After fifty minutes of waiting, Tyko's patience ran out, driven by his incipient claustrophobia.

'Let's give it a go,' he said, getting up and aiming his torch up at the base of the metre-deep shaft.

No one disagreed. They all stood up. They clustered round

the shaft. Tyko said he'd try it first. He began to step up the shaft on the wall rungs until he was perched on a good firm footing on several of the wall rungs, with his back braced against the side of the manhole shaft and his head bent to one side and his hands and shoulders just under the manhole cover ready to heave.

Just then a booming gurgling gushing sloshing drumming sound came from over their heads.

'What the hell?' Tyko said.

'Stop! Stop!' Rox yelled. 'Don't do anything. Tyko keep still.'

'Why the hell not,' Tyko said shortly. His patience and his tolerance of the confined space were wearing thin.

'They've reopened the sluice gate,' Rox almost shouted. 'The mill race is back. There's six feet of water rushing over our heads right now.'

After the initial gasps there was a shocked silence in the underwater chamber.

24. DRUM

It was definitely a drumming sound, Camo thought. Danny was right. It was even more of a drumming sound in the mill race when you were under the water than it was when you were above it.

They all thought that even Rox would have no answers to their predicament this time. But they stood in a circle under the manhole shaft and looked at her. At least she could explain clearly what was happening.

'There's six feet or two metres of water over our heads right now,' she said. She sounded calm and matter-of-fact, but was she really? 'The mill race is back. We'll never be able to push the lid up against that weight of water. And-' she looked directly at Tyko in her torch light '-even if you did manage to push it up a tiny bit the water would immediately force its way in and fill this place in a millisecond. We'd all drown. But…' she said, thinking.

'But what?' Camo asked.

'But if I can lift this lid even a tiny bit against the weight of water,' Tyko interrupted her, still up the shaft at his perch under the lid. 'Won't the rapid flow against the raised edge help lift it further? Perhaps even the rest of the way? Won't the flowing water itself act like an upwards lever?'

Conceivably it might. She could see what Tyko meant.

'But if it does open even a tiny fraction it'll instantly flood this chamber,' Rox continued. 'We'd never get out in time. The drain over there is just for leaks. It wouldn't cope with the full flow of the race. The chamber would be fully flooded in seconds, way before we could even make the first attempt to get out.' She was repeating herself, but she needed Tyko to understand.

He said, 'Ok,' and clambered down from the shaft.

'You said 'But'?' Camo asked her.

'Yes. But. Our situation depends on what else they've done or haven't done.' She explained she didn't think it likely that Bayb and Lurch would have bothered to cross over the mound and lower and close the second sluice gate. 'Which means that both sluice gates could be open now.'

'And that means what?' Camo said again. He wanted to keep Rox talking. She always seemed to have the best ideas about what was going on.

'It means at some point the lake level will fall. With two sluices open there'll be more water leaving the lake than there is coming in from the stream under the drawbridge. It may fall enough for the mill race to run dry. Or at least low enough to severely diminish the flow.'

'How does that help?' Tyko was breathing heavily, still looking up the manhole shaft to the underside of the cover. He climbed back up and touched the underside of the manhole cover with the flat of his hand. He could actually feel the water drumming over the top of it. But no water came through. The watertight seal was good.

'It helps because the flow might diminish enough eventually for us, you, to be able to push up the manhole cover even against the weight of water still running over it. And also running slow enough for us all to get out of here once you've done that before this place fills with water.' She grimaced as if to say it would be so tight in timing that one or more of them were unlikely to be able to get out in time. But what else could they do?

'If that's the case, how long do you think we have before the level drops to a feasible level,' Rosie said, the practical one.

'I just don't know,' Rox said. 'I really don't know.'

'A guess?' Camo asked.

'Two days. Three days,' she spread her hands. 'I'm so sorry. I just don't know.'

'Can we survive for three days?' Rosie asked. 'Until then?'

'We have to,' Camo said.

'How will we know if and when the level drops? And how will we know if it's low enough to be able to push up the cover?' Tyko asked.

'By sound,' Rox said. 'We listen to the water.' But she knew it would still be a guess. A horrible guess. Right or wrong they would only get one shot at it.

It was cold in the chamber, but they were warmly dressed, well enough. Apart from the things she'd mentioned, Rox was worried about food and water.

'We don't have any food or water,' Tyko said. 'For three days?' He descended from the shaft and stood in the circle with the rest. 'Three days?' he repeated.

For the first time Rox showed a flash of anger and impatience. 'I've no fucking idea how long it'll take. It could be a week.'

It wasn't so much the flash of anger that worried Tyko, it was the swearing. Rox never swore. He raised a hand in apology. But she didn't see it.

'Sorry,' he said.

'We do have a bit of water,' Rosie said delving in to her ubiquitous shoulder bag. She produced a half-litre bottle of mineral water. It was full and unopened.

Rox smiled a sad smile. 'That's something.'

She suggested they keep silent for a moment and listened to the water.

But suddenly she spoke again.

'I'm so sorry. Probably we could have all got out of here in time if I hadn't made us wait the hour. I was convinced that Bayb would have shot us if we emerged and just dumped us back down here again. I'm sure she thinks she needs to kill us. But maybe one of us might have got away.'

All three reached out and touched her in reassurance.

'It was the right call,' Rosie said. 'Come what may.'

Rox smiled sadly. Again she suggested they all sat down in the dark and were silent and listened to the water. They needed to know if any changes in sound meant the level was lowering.

They did as she suggested.

She also suggested they switch off all the torches to conserve the batteries and only use them as necessary.

'Can we have just one light on?' Tyko was sweating in the cold now. He was trying to control his fear, but his voice gave it away.

'I think that's a good idea,' Camo said. 'We had four torches altogether in the bag. I think we've got one each.'

They were all already beginning to see that Tyko was struggling. A couple of the flashlights were big hefty things that threw a lot of light.

Four torches, Rox thought. Would that be enough? Would they last? She was already wondering about something else.

Tyko put back the powerful torch he had been using and swapped it for the small one Rosie was holding. He switched it on and minimised its beam to save energy. It was now the only illumination.

They were silent then, and listened.

It was a drumming, Camo thought again, the sound of water running overhead. A drumming solo that went on and on and never stopped.

And now he realised they were all suddenly a lot closer in fellow-feeling to Felix Fairfax than he had thought was possible less than an hour ago. Suddenly the hope that was the main difference between her and them had diminished to near zero. Rox's plan to wait for the water level to drop had given them a degree of hope. But it wasn't the same kind of hope, one based on the certainty of getting out, that he'd had before.

They listened to the water for half an hour. They couldn't tell if there was any difference in the sound it made.

After half an hour Rox spoke again.

'I've been thinking,' she said. 'I think, for various reasons, not least the fact we've no idea whether the other sluice gate is open or not, nor whether the level is actually dropping or not, that if we're going to wait three days then we should try to do something else while we're waiting for the level to drop. It's better than just waiting and doing nothing. But it does have risks of its own.'

'What's that Rox?' Camo asked.

Rox switched on her torch and pointed the beam at the long side wall of the chamber, the fort side wall. The spot was four metres down from where the body of Felix Fairfax lay against the same wall.

'I think we should try to break through that wall.'

Everybody's interest immediately quickened. Not least Tyko who was now shivering a little. He knew he needed something to do that would give him a focus that might take his mind off the space and the tiny size of it and the inexorable finality of the absence of an exit.

'The lower wheel room is directly on the other side of it, isn't it?' Rosie said.

'Yes,' Rox said. 'And I think the floor levels are the same here and in there. But we have to be realistic here,' she said. 'From my survey on the first trip I know that wall is over a metre thick, a metre and a half in fact, or whatever units they had in good old king Louis's day, but call it sixty inches, five feet, if you add in the joints to the thickness of the stones.

'And you two-' she flicked the beam to fall on both Camo and Tyko '-are going to have to do all the work. You'll hit the chisel harder and truer than either Rosie or me. You can keep it up for longer too. But you'll get thirsty. Very thirsty. You'll need all of Rosie's water bottle and more. So you have to be careful. You have to pace yourselves. We have to take it steady. We have no food. And more important we have next to no water. My guess is it'll take us three days to chisel the stones out and get through that wall. We can do it. We've got the tools. I hope.' She flicked the beam to where the spade and Camo's bass lay under the manhole shaft.

'But we have to save the batteries. We can only use one torch at a time. And that must be to illuminate the work, nothing else. So it's going to be close. We can survive three days without food, that's easy enough. We can even do a week without food. But there's no way we'll last a week without water. Three days may be the maximum time we've got. In three days either we break through that wall, or the water level has lowered enough for us to be able to lift the manhole cover. If we haven't done either in three days, then I'm afraid we're fucked.'

It was the longest speech any of them had ever heard from

Rox. It was also only the second time that any of them had heard her swear. It kind of sobered and focused them all.

'So we don't need to listen to the water any more?' Rosie said.

'No. Forget it. We've only got three days. At the end of that if the water level has dropped enough by then, we can try to lift the lid. If it hasn't dropped we won't be able to shift it. Or we'll have broken through the wall. It has to be one or the other. We won't have any energy to do anything after that.'

Rosie was looking hard at Rox in the torchlight. It was a look that said, why are you saying the men will do this better than us?

But Rox wasn't being uncharacteristically old-fashioned, nor suddenly reverting to Victorian values, nor being polite nor sexist. She was being practical and realistic. She really did think the two men would break more ground and shift more of the stones more quickly than the women would. Time was not a luxury now. She had no idea whether Camo and Tyko could do it all on their own. They would have to see.

Rox hoped the speed and energy of the two men would be enough to break through the sixty inches of the wall without assistance from her and Rosie. She hoped. But in reality she thought that she and Rosie would be needed at some point to keep chiselling through the wall. But let the men do as much as they could as fast as they could first.

'What's stopping us attacking the wall right now?' Tyko said. He needed something to do. He couldn't just sit and wait.

'Let's do it,' Camo said.

Rox stood up and walked over to the plumber's bass. The spade Lurch had discarded lay on the floor beside it. Rox now realised the significance of Azmoun's order to leave it behind and Lurch's sickly smile in response. Azmoun and Lurch knew at that stage they were going to trap them in the inspection pit and were laughing and smiling at an image of the trapped four desperately trying to use the spade – the only tool they thought was left – in a futile attempt to dig through the solid stone wall. It was another facet of Bayb Azmoun's overarching and tantalising cruelty.

Well, Rox thought, a spade might be better than poor Felix's gold coin in attempting to dig through a solid stone wall. But not much.

She opened the heavy jute bass and spread it out on the floor and examined the contents with the light of her torch. She pulled out two block hammers and several chisels of different gauge and length. She took a crowbar out too. Then:

'Oh yes. Nice. You've got a bolster. Two bolsters! Camo your dad's a genius.'

Despite the dire situation they smiled.

'What's a bolster?' Rosie asked.

'It,' Rox said, bringing the tools across to the target wall and piling them on the floor. 'Is a specialist type of chisel. It is designed specifically for this kind of job. For chiselling out mortar joints between blocks of stone.' It was also designed, she knew, for cleaning lime and cement mortar off the faces of used stones and bricks, but she didn't think she needed to say that.

She showed one of the bolsters to Camo and Tyko. It was a chiselly looking tool. It had a hexagonal shaft at the hitting end at the top, just like a standard chisel. But then it became a wide blade at the cutting end, much thinner and wider than a chisel.

'A chisel is actually for cutting stone. Although you can use it for this. But a bolster is actually designed for chiselling out joints,' she said. 'Couldn't be better.' A thought seemed to strike her.

'Hold on a minute,' she said as Tyko picked up a block hammer and held a hand out for the bolster. 'I just want to check something. Camo or Rosie, can you shine a light on this joint?'

She walked across and then stood at the face of the wall. Camo followed her with a light. She took the other block hammer. She pointed to a joint in a stone course at an easy striking point from a comfortable standing position. It was the fifth course up from the floor.

'Just there,' she said.

Rosie and Camo both shone their lights on the vertical

white joint.

Rox rested the bolster edge against the mortar and tapped its top end firmly with the hammer. The wide point of the bolster dug a few millimetres into the mortar and a long thin chunk of white mortar flew out.

'Excellent,' Rox said, handing the bolster and hammer over to Tyko. She picked up the sliver of mortar from the floor and examined it in the torchlight. She rolled and crumbled it between her fingers. 'Yes. That's one good thing. It's lime mortar. I thought it would be.'

'Why is that good?' Camo asked.

'It's a lot softer than cement mortar. And it loses its strength and cohesion over time. Remember this place is old. When this place was built in bad old king Louis's day lime mortar was all they had. Cement hadn't been invented. And this is one of the original walls.'

'Let's go,' Tyko said. His eyes were lit.

Rox advised them on technique. They were to take shifts. Take it as easy as they could. They only had a half litre bottle of water. They were going to get thirsty. One person at a time would work at the stones. Another person would shine a torch to illuminate the work. The other two would sit in the dark. They should use the bolsters and remove as much mortar from the joints surrounding the target stone as they could. At various intervals they should insert the end of a crowbar into the joint and see if they could prise and lever the stone loose from its mortar joints.

'The key is getting the stone lose,' Rox said. 'Just like you did with that stone – actually straight through there–' she pointed through the wall '-on the steps yesterday. Once a stone is loose you'll be able to waggle and lever it out.'

Tyko set to work. He stood in front of the wall as Rox had done. Camo shone a light for him to work by.

Rox didn't add that looking at the stone wall her guess was that each stone was a cube 250 millimetres high by 250 millimetres wide by 250 millimetres deep. And the wall therefore would be six stones thick.

She thought they would have to remove a square of four stones. That would create a square hole 500 millimetres by 500 millimetres across. That was plenty wide enough for all of them to crawl through to the other side. And if the wall was six stones thick, as she thought, that meant they would have to remove twenty-four stones to create a hole in the wall. They would essentially be making a tunnel through the wall half a metre square. It was a hell of a hard job.

She knew there was a real danger the wall could collapse as they removed stones from it, no matter how well-built it was. There was a lot of masonry above. But her guess was that just making a hole two stones wide would be all right. But they daren't go any wider. She was convinced that creating a hole two stones wide would be safe. But was she desperately trying to convince herself and ignoring the engineering here? She wasn't sure. In any case, this wasn't a time for Tyko's accusation of enginerring. They couldn't learn from their mistakes. It had to be engineering this time. And she had to be right.

But she knew they might have to remove more stones as they went further into the wall just to create sufficient working space to keep removing a square of four stones. They could never go wider than two stones in width across, but they could go more than two stones high. They could go to three.

She also crossed her fingers that there wouldn't be any bond in the stonework. In other words none of the courses would be offset with each other. She had a feeling that kind of coursework finesse came much later, and that when this wall was built it was standard practice just to butt the stones on top of each other and flush against each other, all without any overlap so the joints were all lined up horizontally and vertically. Certainly that was the case with this wall she could see in the chamber. And as far as she could remember it was also the case with the wall in the wheel room beyond.

But they would stagger over that bridge when they came to it. If they had to cut stones in half with the chisels just to get past the staggered bond then so be it. At least they had the tools for it. Whether they would have the energy to do it was a different story.

In each case, removing the first stone in the set of four in the square would be the hardest job. Removing that incredibly difficult first stone would have to be done six times.

They began work a little to the left of centre of the wall. Felix Fairfax lay about four metres further along the wall, upstream.

We'll get you out, Camo thought to himself, after all these years. I promise.

25. WALL 2

It was the bolsters that did it. And the crowbar of course, for waggling. Those were the things that gave her confidence that the job could be done. Time and again in the dark Rox imagined Camo's dad Vinny – was he really christened Vinyl? – examining his tool collection in his toolshed at the bottom of their garden. Why would you collect bolsters? Why collect any tool for that matter and not use them?

It was the bolsters – a tool designed for the job they needed to do - and the fact that the mortar was lime mortar not cement – that allowed them to make such good progress.

And again, Rox was willing to bet that if Camo had actually looked in the plumber's bass when he went into the toolshed he would have rejected the bolsters and chucked them out. But he hadn't. He'd essentially just grabbed it and run before Laura asked him what he was doing.

And equally if Bayb Azmoun had known what a plumber's bass was and what it was likely to contain, she would have checked it out and ordered Lurch to remove it from the chamber too. If they had left them then in this intended tomb with just a spade their cruel smiles and laughter would have been justified. But now? Now it was different. Now at least they had a chance.

It seemed that luck was on their side at last. They hadn't had much of that recently.

For a while Rox watched the men closely as they worked; one holding a torch, the other tapping the bolster. The boys attacked the wall in shifts, twenty minutes or half an hour at a time.

One thing she wouldn't admit to any of them was that part of her suggestion that they should try to tunnel through the wall was not because she thought it could be done, of course it could be done, but only time would tell if they had enough water to make that a reality. Water was the key, because that alone would determine how long the men could keep working. No, the essential part of her suggestion was just to create a diversion. She understood that Tyko needed something to keep him busy, something he could focus on, something that would take his mind away from dwelling on the tight space he was now confined in.

At some point she hoped, and it was no more than a hope, that the diversion could actually become a reality.

Now as she watched the beginnings of the work progressing, what she wanted to know was how exactly was the wall constructed? One answer to that would be good news; the other answer less good.

One thing she wondered about more than anything else now was the construction of the wall, but she didn't let herself hope anything until they had removed the first stone. That was because there was a chance the wall would just be packed with rubble behind this neatly cut face. Essentially between this neat face of cut stone and the neat cut stone face on the other side of the wall in the lower wheel room, there would just be a metre of rubble infill. She knew that was normal enough with thick stone walls. It improved the speed a thick defensive wall could be built for a start. If that was the case they would make rapid progress once they had removed the covering stones. All they had to do was keep shovelling the rubble out with the spade and very soon they'd reach the back of the stones on the far face.

But on sober and serious reflection she thought that mode of wall construction was unlikely to be the case here. The rubble infill method was more normal in the days before cannonballs. This wall was constructed well into the age of the cannonball. It was a high quality, even prestige, military construction and was expected to be abnormally and exceptionally strong.

So it was probable that this wall was going to be neat, cut, dressed stone courses and layers all the way through. There would be six layers of cut stone to break through. There would be no shortcuts of shovelling out rubble. This was going to be a hard chisel all the way through.

It took over two hours to remove the first stone. Part of the amount of time it took was because they were learning techniques. What worked and what wasn't so good. They used the bolsters as far as they could, eating away the lime mortar all round the target stone. Then they switched to the longest chisel and the crowbar. Eventually they had removed enough mortar to ram the crowbar into a joint and lever it side to side or up and down. This was sufficient to break the stone's bond with the remaining mortar joints. Then they set to waggling and levering the stone backwards with the wedge end of the crowbar. Millimetre by millimetre the stone was persuaded to move backwards. When it had moved backwards far enough they could grab it with their gloved hands and physically pull it and remove it from the wall. They stacked it on the floor further to one side, between the hole and skeleton.

Everyone in the dark space cheered.

Immediately Rox moved forward and examined the empty space with her torch. It was as she feared. There was no rubble infill here. The wall was solid stonework all the way through. Ahead there was only another course of stone set in its dirty white joints of lime mortar. But at least she could see that the next course in was set square with the first course. The stones were not offset into a masonry bond. They were flush, butted and square with each other.

One gone, twenty-three to go, she thought. Minimum.

The boys returned to the task. They began to widen the hole by removing three other stones contiguous and adjacent to the first one to make the half-metre square.

She didn't need to give the boys any more tips on working methodologies. They quickly worked things out for themselves and created their own solutions. As they went further into the wall they worked out best methods to progress. One effective method was not to try to remove all the mortar in a joint, but to hammer a chisel deep into the joint either at the sides of the stone or at top or bottom. They'd pull the chisel out. Then they would take the crowbar and ram the wedge end as far as it would go into the chiselled hole, then begin to lever it to and fro or up and down until the stone cracked loose from its surrounding mortar beds. Then they could begin the laborious but satisfying process of waggling and levering the stone backwards towards them. The spade helped immensely with this technique. Once the surrounding mortar had been successfully cracked the spade could be inserted into the crack on the opposite side of the stone to the crowbar. Then both the crowbar and the spade could be used as levers to grip the stone tightly between them and its passage backwards accelerated.

Only when the stone was completely removed would they set about bolstering or chiselling away the remaining mortar.

They had a debate at one point during the first night about how long they should work.

It had been around two in the afternoon that they had first lifted the manhole cover and entered the chamber. It was roughly four o'clock when they had started work on the stone wall after Bayb Azmoun had ambushed them, removed the gold and reopened the sluice gate.

The first stone had been removed at 6 pm.

At 8 pm, with two more stones removed and stacked on the floor, Rox asked them to stop and take a break.

'Just let's get this last one out,' Tyko said. Ignoring any response she made, he began to hammer a chisel into the mortar joint under the last remaining stone of the first four. The steel tip dug rapidly and massively into the degraded lime mortar. He pulled the chisel out and rammed the edge end of the crowbar into the hole. He tapped the curved end of the crowbar with the block hammer to drive it further into the chisel hole. The crowbar was stuck firm and when tapped vibrated like a piano string. He then brought the hammer down in strong side hits to loosen it. The crowbar didn't loosen under the attack, but the stone did. It cracked away from its two remaining mortar joints. Tyko immediately applied leverage pressure to the crowbar. The stone moved sideways, loose and free. Camo reached in and pulled the stone out. He placed it with the other three on the floor.

There was now a square hole in the wall. One course of four 250 millimetres deep stones had been removed from the wall, leaving a hole half a metre by half a metre in size.

'Four and a half hours to clear four stones,' Tyko said in triumph. He was sweating and panting a little.

Rox was impressed. She did a mental calculation. At that rate, allowing for increasing tiredness and difficulty of access, so say five to six hours to remove each layer of four stones instead of four and a half, then it would take them twenty-five to thirty more hours to break through the wall.

That was much less time than she thought it would. Even with rest breaks, sleep and increasing tiredness and decreasing energy levels, it might only take them two days to break though the wall, not three.

For the first time she felt a tiny breath of hope in her lungs. Really and truly for the first time she thought it could be done.

But it all depended on how long the two men could keep going.

One modification she did propose, which they immediately accepted, was that she and Rosie should take it in turns to hold the torch, while Camo or Tyko worked and the other rested and did nothing until it was his turn again with the chisel, bolster, hammer and crowbar.

But now they had stopped and were taking a break, as she requested, what she wanted to know was how did they propose to proceed?

'Sleep or non-stop?' she asked them.

They talked round this for a while. In reality none of them had any idea which would be medically safer, more energy efficient, or more likely to succeed. While they were thinking about it, Rosie suggested the two men drink half the bottle of water between them there and then. It was an unspoken agreement between Rosie and Rox that they would try as hard as they possibly could for as long as they possibly could to take no water at all.

Rosie took a pen from her shoulder bag and marked the halfway point on the plastic water bottle. Then she made two more marks splitting the bottle into quarters.

'That's it,' she said and handed the bottle to Tyko.

'Do you think we'll lose energy inevitably as we get dehydrated?' Camo looked at Rox.

'I'm sure of it. I'm no doctor, but it seems logical to me.'

'Then clearly,' Tyko said. 'We carry on now as long as we can while we can. We don't stop and we don't sleep.'

It made sense. While they still had reserves of energy and hydration they would be able to do more work, hack more joints away, and remove more stones from the wall more quickly than they would be able to do later when they were feeling the effects of severe dehydration.

But it was a vicious circle, they knew. Working non-stop now would hasten the onset of dehydration. They knew there was no real answer to the conundrum.

'I'll feel happier carrying on working until I'm really tired, then take a break, rather than try to conserve energy,' Tyko said.

'Then let's do it that way,' Camo said.

Both men drank from the water bottle down to the levels that Rosie had marked. The bottle was now half empty. Then they returned to the wall.

It was amazing how quickly you got used to it, Rosie thought. At first she thought the unceasing noise of hammering and chiselling would drive her mad. The sound overwhelmed the space. It flooded the walls and echoed round the chamber already filled with the noise. It seemed one sound of steel hitting steel hadn't died away before the next one added to it. There was Camo's steady thunk, thunk, thunk alternating with Tyko's more frenzied thunka-thunka-thunka. Each similar sound, characteristic of their pace of working, was interrupted frequently by mishits. In a way she welcomed these indeterminate ching sounds as they mishit the top of the chisel or caught hard stone instead of softer mortar with the tip of the chisel. She welcomed those mishits because it broke up the deadly monotonous cacophony of the incessant thunks.

At least the hammering drowned out the sound of the water drumming overhead. And when you could no longer hear the water you could even begin to believe it wasn't there, that there wasn't water two metres deep flowing over your head, sealing you into this stone tomb. Then amazingly after a few hours Rosie thought, you hardly heard the hammering sounds at all.

It took five more hours to remove the next layer of four stones. The square hole was now half a metre by half a metre, face on, and two stones, half a metre, deep.

They were a third of the way through the wall.

But it was at a huge cost.

It was one o'clock in the morning and they were exhausted. The men were also beginning to enter the first stages of severe dehydration.

Everyone tried to sleep. Camo and Tyko did sleep, Camo well, but Tyko only fitfully. Rox and Rosie didn't sleep so much, but they rested.

Daylight hours had no meaning of course in the darkness of the pit. But they still had their natural diurnal rhythms which dictated natural patterns of sleep and wakefulness. Their bodies knew it was night time and late. They were ready for sleep whether they knew it or not.

Work started again at seven o'clock next morning.

They rested more than they worked during the course of that second day.

Rox didn't say it but looking at Camo and Tyko's lined faces and listening to their heavy and rasping breathing as they returned to the task, she knew that if they didn't break through the wall that day they never would.

Rox knew that this layer, the third layer of stones was going to be the hardest so far. And each layer after that would become progressively harder.

That was because it was tight to access. The men had to reach in half a metre into the hole they'd made before they could start hammering at the next layer of exposed joints. Then when a stone was loosened it had to be pulled over half a metre backwards to remove it from the hole.

It was tight, difficult and exhausting work. It was also extremely mentally demanding. Already both men had cuts and grazes on their arms and hands. Tyko had a nasty graze on his forehead where he had misjudged his entry into the hole and had banged his head on the stone edge above the hole. He was also increasingly miss-hitting the end of the chisel. And he often missed the right place when he attempted to ram the crowbar into the chisel hole they'd made. His coordination was diminishing. His mental judgement was declining faster than Camo's. That was probably because of Tyko's incipient and utterly enervating claustrophobia. But no one wanted to say anything about that. It was too dreadful. How he'd lasted so long, Rox was amazed. When Camo worked at the stones he did it with a constant tempo, but with Tyko it was a frenzy.

At ten o'clock in the morning Camo and Tyko consumed half the remaining water.

They had removed another course, the third layer of stones, and were halfway though the wall.

Camo and Tyko returned to the job. It was backbreaking, shoulder wrenching, arm crunching, knuckle scraping work. It went on and on and on with minimal progress and insignificant results. But they kept at it. They had to.

One good thing was that they were becoming more efficient with practice. They each had found out for themselves what techniques worked best. So the equation of their declining energy and strength was balanced to some degree by their increasing efficiency. For a while.

One variation they had come up with that worked far better than a strict time regime was to allocate the work into tasks rather than times. They realised that system was a way of optimising their progress, because Camo was left-handed and Tyko was right-handed. It was natural for Camo to twist and get into position to attack the left side vertical joint; and Tyko the right. Therefore that's the way they did from then on. It was Camo's job to remove the left joint, however long it took, with as many breaks as he needed. Then it was Tyko's turn to attack the joint on the right of the block. Equally with the top and bottom joints. One of them would take the top joint and the other would take the bottom. They found that having specific physical personal targets was a more efficient way of working.

And in this way they progressed faster and more smoothly.

But their energies were inexorably dropping. They were severely dehydrated. Tyko much more so than Camo. Tyko's frenzied assault had taken its toll. He had white rime covered lips. He hardly spoke. His breathing was laboured. His tongue felt like a monstrous leathery boot. His movements were slow and inaccurate.

Seeing him hardly capable of having any effect on the joints now as he desperately tried to chip away at the mortar, Camo came to a decision.

'We have to enlarge the working space,' he said to Rox. 'We can't go on like this.'

She knew what he meant, but had hoped it wouldn't be necessary, that they could reach the other side without wasting time and effort in enlarging their work space as they progressed. She nodded.

They stopped trying to reach in to the excavated space and chip away uncomfortably at the joints in the fourth layer. They retreated and removed two more stones from the bottom of the square. They had to create more space to be able to work more efficiently at the fourth, fifth and sixth faces. As yet they had not removed a single stone from the fourth face.

It didn't take long in fact to remove two stones from the base of the square in the first face and then two more from the second face, and then finally two more from the third. Rox was thankful for that.

When they finished removing the extra stones what had been a square hole in the wall half a metre by half a metre in size was now a rectangle, still half a metre wide, but now threequarters of a metre high.

Now for the first time they could attack the fourth face with a greater degree of comfort and a lot more force.

One at a time Camo or Tyko would enter the rectangle on their knees. They would face the third course of stone on their knees. Then they would contort themselves and twist their bodies to either the left or the right to create hammering room. And now the extra quarter of a metre they had created by removing the stones gave them just enough space to swing a hammer and hit the chisel properly, and hard.

As with the first stone face, prising out the first stone in the fourth face was the longest and hardest job. It took three hours just to remove that first stone. The other three then took just over an hour each to remove.

After six hours they had removed all four stones in the fourth face.

They were two-thirds the way through the wall.

As before they had a square hole in the wall half a metre by half a metre far into the wall. Then they set about removing the two extra stones from the bottom of the square. The hole was now a rectangle.

They both rested.

They rested for a long time. They rested for hours.

Rosie and Rox whispered together in the dark as Tyko and Camo slept fitfully. Should they let them sleep as long as they wanted? Or should they wake them? What held them back was the reality that they themselves were not doing any of the hard labour. They were just torch-bearers. Did they have the right to rouse them and ask them to get back to work?

As the hours went by Rox was becoming increasingly worried. Was the task too much? Would they die in here with the tunnel through the wall over two-thirds done?

She roused both men and forced them to take the remaining drops of water. They slept again.

Then with a sudden spurt of desperate energy Camo woke from his stupor. He roused himself and went back into what was now a tunnel a metre deep into the wall. He took hammer, chisel and crowbar. With desperate energy he attached the first stone in the fifth layer. After two hours he had removed it. He quickly levered the stone alongside it out. Then he removed two more stones at the base of the square. Then he took the extra two stones out to convert the square that was impossible to work in to the rectangle they could work in.

He finished, retreated from the hole and threw himself on the ground.

Now the fifth square was a rectangle too. Now they had dug a rectangle half a metre wide by threequarters of a metre high by a metre and a quarter deep.

Just six stones in the sixth and final rectangle lay ahead.

And they only needed remove four stones in the final face not all six. All they had to do was create a hole large enough for them to crawl through and drop out into the room on the other side.

But Tyko was spent. He had looked at Camo as he began his attack on the fifth layer, then closed his eyes. He didn't move. He lay on his back, stretched out. He was panting rapidly in shallow heaves. Rox went over to him. She tried to sooth him. She tried to stroke his forehead. She tried to calm him down. She succeeded. His breathing became steadier and smoother. He seemed to fall into sleep.

After his monstrous exertion Camo rested for twenty minutes. The he crawled back into the hole. He too was near the end. But he had tried to pace himself all through the task and had worked much steadier and at a far less frenzied rate than Tyko. They could hear his heavy breathing as the slow but solid and persistent hammering began again.

Rosie shone the light for Camo as he worked. It was their fourth and final torch. The batteries in the other three had died.

The light shone brightly for an hour. Then it too abruptly died.

They were in total darkness.

It took Camo two and a half hours in the dark to loosen the first stone in the final face. He had to carry out much of the work by touch and feel. He had a rough idea of where his hitting targets were. He would reach forward to confirm. He could feel the difference between lime mortar and stone by touch alone. Occasionally when he was unsure he dig a fingernail into the substrate and if he scraped soft material then it was lime mortar, and if he just tore his nails then it was stone. Then when he had identified the mortar joint by touch he kept his hand in place then he placed the end of the chisel or bolster alongside his fingers. His fingers stayed in place and gripped the bottom of the tool. Then he began to tap the end of the chisel. Inevitably his hitting force was diminished. He could not see where he was striking.

He chiselled on and on. Eventually he guessed it was worth a try. He removed the chisel and pushed his forefinger into the hole to gauge it. Then he inserted the crowbar into the deep hole he'd chiselled on one side of the stone, feeling his way all the time. He tapped the crowbar into the hole as far as it would go. For many hours now both men had hammered the crowbar into the chisel hole: they didn't have the strength to ram it home by hand. Camo took a breath and levered the crowbar to the left and right. He felt, and even thought he heard, the mortar joint crack all the way round the stone.

As he hammered and chipped away there was a strange thing. He never mentioned it to Tyko, nor told the others about it, but there was definitely something odd. As he laboured, exhausted, he occasionally but increasingly often glanced aside towards the body of Felix Fairfax. And it felt to Camo as if she was willing him on, helping his ebbing energy. Just when he had no more energy left to even lift the hammer he'd glance at her and somehow suddenly the energy would come. He didn't know what to make of it and never talked about it.

He retreated from the tunnel. He needed to rest again before trying to remove the stone. As he sank into an exhausted stupor he glanced again at the withered desiccated body a few metres away and mentally renewed his promise to Felix Fairfax that he would get her out.

When Camo was resting for what he hoped would be the final push, Tyko finally awoke. He picked up both the crowbar and the spade and in a daze he forced himself to walk on his knees into the tunnel, feeling his way with his hands. He ignored Camo's call to stop, he would do it.

Rox went over to lean against the wall next to the hole to

encourage Tyko as much as she could.

Rox could hear Tyko begin to force the spade and the crowbar into the cracks round the stone. She heard him hold his breath as he tried to lever the tools tight to grip the stone. He tied to pull the stone backwards towards him, just as they had done with all the others.

'Stop it Tyko. What are you doing?' Rox shouted as she realised what he was trying to do in the dark. She tried to put a sharp edge in her voice to rouse him, to make him think and see more clearly.

'Focus. Tyko. Focus. You don't have to pull it out. Just push it.' Rox understood that his weariness and need for water had confused his mind. He was working on autopilot.

Amazingly Tyko laughed. Or tried to. He licked his rime-covered lips with a dry as dust tongue. He dropped his head onto his outstretched arms and Rox could feel his back moving up and down as he laughed. Then he gathered himself and retreated back out of the tunnel.

Camo now crawled over on his hands and knees, feeling his way towards the tunnel. He went in feet first. He lay on his side in the one and a quarter metre deep tunnel they had made. Camo drew both feet back and then stamped back as hard as he could on the face of the stone with the soles and heels of his Red Wing boots.

The stone moved a fraction. Camo stamped again and again. The stone began to move further and carried on moving. Suddenly under the impetus of Camo's stamps it slid out completely and dropped away down the far side of the hole. A new cold fresh draught of air swept past Camo's face and into the chamber behind him. And a new dull dark light appeared at the end of their tunnel.

They were through the wall.

26. OUT 2

It took a much shorter time now for both Camo and Tyko to remove the last three stones in the final square. They knew they'd make it. They were going to get out of the pit. And that renewed their strength.

It was Tyko who kicked the fourth and last stone loose and then pushed it with his feet out of the sixth and last face and heard it thump to the floor in the wheel room as it dropped down the far side of the wall.

He carried on and crawled out of the tunnel feet first into the lower wheel room. He staggered on straw legs over to the large bottles of water that Rosie had left on the steps – when was it? Two days ago? Three? He opened one, he barely had the strength to break the seal, then threw away the top and gulped and gulped and gulped.

While he drank the others crawled out through the hole. Once she was through the hole Rox rushed over to the light switches and threw them all on. The upper and lower wheel rooms were flooded with light as the striplights overhead flickered on. A good deal of light now swept into the pit and they could see the inside for the first time in six hours.

Camo was the last to leave the chamber that had so nearly become their tomb, their mausoleum. Next last out was Rosie. Before she crawled through the escape tunnel she looked hard one last time round the dimensions of the pit. The light coming through the hole caught on the metal spokes of the drain set in the middle of the floor. Strange she thought, we've been stuck in here for two full days and yet none of us needed to pee. Dehydration she assumed. Then she left.

After Rosie had crawled through, Camo came after her pushing the box of coins in front of him. He left the tools including his father's beloved plumber's bass behind. He just didn't have the energy to think about them.

They sat on the steps next to Tyko and passed the other water bottle around between them. It wasn't enough but it would do for a start.

'Why do you think she left us one box of coins?' Rosie asked them, thinking aloud in a way. 'She knew, or thought she did, we'd die in there. She intended us to.'

Some kind of weird and final tantalising cruelty, Camo thought. There was almost an element of Greek myth to it, Tantalus perhaps, of hubris and overreaching, plus the notion of just deserts. Here we are stuck in our tomb for eternity with the very thing we've been searching for. We have what we looked for, we got exactly what we wanted, but we'd give it all up in an instant to be free of the pit. It was an exercise in cruel and vicious irony.

'Basically she did it because she could,' he said.

'It was a show of power, as well, I think,' Rosie said. 'And weird nonchalance. Kind of ultra bravado and showmanship to a very small audience. I don't think she really needs the money. Her father must have left her a tidy package, and she was probably hugely successful herself in whatever line she was in. She was going to leave us as the richest corpses ever.'

'Then why was she looking so hard and so relentlessly for the coins?' Rox asked.

'I think Danny hurt her badly,' Rosie suggested. 'I think he really must have hurt her emotionally, so hard she never got over it. I think her dogged and ultimately successful search for the gold was all part of some kind of revenge on Danny, way after normal people would have learned to live with the hurt.'

'Whatever the reason, I owe you all an apology,' Camo said. 'I really thought I'd got rid of her by trying to insinuate her dad had found the coins first and maybe dumped them in a vault in Switzerland she didn't know anything about. But in fact all that happened was that she got everything we knew and we got nothing in return. Nothing but a drumming sound. I thought she was arrogant enough to believe she could crack the code whereas we had failed to crack it. But of course she could do both, couldn't she? She could make her efforts to crack the code at the same time as carrying on watching us. She must have guessed we'd go back at any moment if we cracked the code. She knew we wouldn't be able to resist no matter what I'd said to her about giving up. And if she didn't crack it either all she had to do was keep watching us. And that's what happened. Us rushing off down here was a real giveaway that we thought we were on to something new. It meant we had cracked the code and knew where the gold was. So she just followed us.'

'She let us do all the hard work then stepped in at the crucial moment,' Rosie said.

'Professional, really.' Tyko said, still breathing in short gasps.

'But we didn't know where the gold was, did we?' Rox said. 'We just thought we did.' She looked glum.

'You found it Rox,' Camo said. 'Never ever forget that. Ever.'

'No one else did it,' Tyko said hugging her. 'You did it. But you didn't find the newspaper though!'

'J'Accuse!' she cried

They laughed. They were recovering already.

'I'm afraid to say this,' Camo said later when they were all sat round the kitchen table drinking water and eating bread and cheese and the box of coins was on the table top, open to view. 'After all we've been though. But I think the coins belong to Jane Shadwell. I think they're hers. I think we should give them to her.'

They had talked round this before, in a hypothetical way. Now it was real. Here and now. They all had each realised at some point they were going to have to face that reality.

'Maybe she'll split them with us?' Tyko said. 'Six hundred thousand pounds is still a lot of money. If she took two hundred thousand's worth, we'd still have a hundred thousand each.'

'Maybe she will. I don't know. But that has to be her decision, not ours.'

Easy enough, Tyko thought, for the one with the most money already to be the moral arbiter of the group. But he kept silent. Despite his urge to benefit financially from the ordeal they'd been through, he still knew deep down that Camo was right.

'But does your moral rectitude and oh-so fair and proper

outlook depend on the size of the proceeds though?' Tyko said. 'I mean what would you have said if we were sitting here with all twenty boxes of coins on the table?' Tyko knew it was an accusation but he smiled to defuse it a little.

Camo laughed. 'Yes. Fair point. But actually if we did have all twenty boxes, all twelve million pounds, then I'd say we should keep six of them and give Jane Shadwell fourteen.'

'So she'd have eight million four hundred thousand pounds?' Rosie said, doing the calculation. 'And we'd have three million six hundred thousand? Is that right?'

'Yes,' Camo agreed. 'I think if she had over eight million pounds suddenly out of the blue she wouldn't begrudge us having the rest of the twelve million to share between us. Psychology I guess.'

'So we'd all have nine hundred thousand pounds apiece?' Tyko said.

'No. Not quite. I would have shared it differently. I'd say you three would have a million each and I'd have six hundred thousand.'

From their faces it looked to Camo is if they were about to seriously disagree with that.

'Come on. You know that's fair.'

'Maybe,' Rox said. 'But it's all moot. We haven't got twenty boxes. We've got just one.'

In the end they had no choice really, they knew it. They authorised Camo to offer the box of coins to Jane Shadwell. Maybe she'd be generous.

'We've got another problem,' Rosie said. She'd been sorting through the permutations with her legal, linear and analytical mind. 'Which makes the Shadwell problem insignificant in comparison. The problem is, what do we do about Felix Fairfax?'

Should they leave her there? She asked them. Should they pretend they had never been in the chamber? Should they just go home with their box of coins, maybe split it with Jane Shadwell, like they just agreed, and just pretend they hadn't solved a fifty-year old mystery about the disappearance of one of the most famous people in the world?

Should they leave Felix Fairfax to rot? Just like Danny did.

They talked through the options. Camo thought they had to report the discovery of the body.

There was another problem for Camo. He had made a silent promise to Felix Fairfax's bones that he would get her out. Could he go back on that promise now once he was safely out?

'I tend to agree,' Rosie said. 'But you know that will lead the police to ask us a whole lot of questions we won't necessarily be able to answer.'

'Or have to give them answers we're not really happy to give,' Tyko said.

'What were you doing here? For one,' Rosie continued. 'Two, what were you looking for? Three, did you find what you were looking for? Four, where is it now? Five, how did you come to get sealed in the pit? Six, who sealed you in?'

'And then, say we manage to satisfactorily squeeze through answering those questions,' Tyko said. 'Then there's the problem that all the publicity surrounding the discovery of Fairfax's bones will alert Bayb Azmoun to the fact she failed to kill us. Clearly we survived.'

'And so, ultimate problem I guess,' Camo said 'Will she try again?'

'We can never be sure that she won't,' Rosie said.

'We'll never be able to rest easy,' Rox finished.

'So what do we do?' Rox said.

They didn't know.

'I do have one idea,' Rox said.

They were well accustomed now to the value of Rox's ideas. She had their attention.

'I think we can re-arrange the stones so it looks like we broke in to the chamber, not out. We'd have to think it through really carefully, and bring out all the mortar debris and so on as well as the stones. But I think we can do it effectively. And if we do that, it—

'—means we don't have to say anything about being shut in

there,' Tyko finished for her.

'We never found the manhole shaft. But we suspected there was a hidden chamber there – by echo perhaps when we tapped the wall – so we dug through,' Rox said.

'And we found nothing there except the bones of Felix Fairfax,' Camo said. 'No gold. We can admit we were looking for the gold. Chris Sentinel pointed us on our way to that. But we never found any.'

'And we don't have to mention Bayb Azmoun at all,' Tyko said. 'And when the police don't come calling on her, despite all the publicity about the skeleton, and our obvious survival, it means that we haven't said anything at all to the police about her.'

'And therefore she may leave us alone once and for all,' Rosie said.

'It's precarious,' Camo said. 'But it's doable.'

'The police will be suspicious,' Rosie said to Camo. 'They'll search the place.'

They're welcome to do that, Camo thought. Fat lot of good it would do them. But he thought he would hide the box of coins just in case. He would put them in the cavity behind the lift shaft.

Now that was agreed, Rox realised they had forgotten about the water level in the lake.

'Do you two lads think you have the strength to lower the other sluice gate? If it's open?' She really wanted to find out.

'Sure,' Camo said. 'I'd like to see how thorough they were too. Whether they just left both sluices open and scarpered.'

They took their coats, left the kitchen and walked out of the archway, around the outside of the courtyard wall till they came to the corner by the mill race.

There were fresh tyre marks in the gravel. It seemed the Mercedes had been parked there. Also lying on the ground were the two manhole keys. Lurch had obviously dumped them there.

From the corner they looked across and could see that both sluice gates were open. Bayb had not ordered Lurch to close the further gate when she reopened the mill race gate.

'So you were right Rox,' Rosie said pointing to water in the mill race. 'The level has dropped and would have dropped more.'

'But look at it,' Rox said pointing to the fort wall beyond the water. 'The level's only about a foot lower than it usually is with only one gate open.'

She thought that's a foot down in over two days. The level would probably have carried on dropping, and perhaps they would have been able to lift the manhole lid at some point. Maybe they could have shifted the lid when there was less than a foot of water over it. But at the current rate it would have taken between ten and fourteen days to get to that point.

'We made the right decision,' she said. 'It would have taken a week at least, maybe a fortnight for the level to drop low enough for us to move the lid.'

Tyko and Camo crossed over the sluice gate bridge to the grassy knoll and mounted the step to the old stream sluice gate. They wound the wheel anticlockwise and lowered the gate into its concrete housing. The old stream bed quickly ran dry.

They brought both winding wheels and the manhole keys with them back inside the fort

'So we made the right decision to go through the wall.' Tyko said as they walked back towards the kitchen.

'Definitely,' Rox agreed. 'We would have died in there.'

That would have been probably later today, Rosie thought. We just got out in time.

A day later they were ready. First they took out two more stones from the exit hole in the lower wheel room. Now the tunnel was two stones wide and three stones deep all the way through. Then they moved all the stones except the last six from the interior of the chamber and stacked them neatly against the wall in the lower wheel room. The remaining six they left inside the chamber. It would look like those six had been pushed in rather than dug out.

They swept up all the mortar debris and brought it out

and made a pile of it next to the stacked stones. They took a bucket and mop inside the chamber and washed the floor clean. They removed the bass and the tools and the spade. Then Rox made them walk through the pile of mortar debris and step back through the hole and make footprints into the chamber, including all round the skeleton.

The next morning, once Rox was satisfied Rosie was deputed to ring the police *capitaine* in Ax to report their discovery.

Camo hid the coins behind the lift.

It went as they had predicted.

The police arrived with cars and vans and flashing lights.

They were asked to show what happened, how they had made the discovery, to re-enact it in a way.

Camo and Rosie led the police to the lower wheel room and so into the chamber. They were instructed to wait outside as a forensic team, gloved and masked and white suited, entered the chamber.

Several hours later the bones were gently removed and taken away.

Then the questioning began in earnest.

It seemed surprising in a way to Rosie that the police seemed to accept quite readily that the four of them should have come to Fort Madeline on a treasure hunt. She thought it was a brilliant brainwave by Camo to show Danny's silly gibberish five-line clues, and relate how they had found them on a gold disc. She added that the words 'under' and over' in the quintain convinced them that the gold must be hidden somewhere very close to the two mill wheels. And so eventually they had homed in on the outer wall of the lower wheel room and broken through the wall there into the chamber beyond. And had then entered the chamber.

And so had found the body that they believed was that of the famous 1960s rock star guitarist Felix Fairfax.

But unfortunately they hadn't found any gold.

Rosie was sure the police *capitaine* believed their story. But just to be sure he ordered the whole fort to be searched. And their car. He seemed finally convinced when nothing was found.

He allowed them to leave. Investigations would continue, he said, and it may be that he would want to talk to them again. He would of course be liaising with the British police. He took their addresses. But for now they could go.

One thing the police *capitaine* told Rosie was that when they entered the chamber to move the remains, they found a message scratched on the wall behind her. It was effectively concealed by her body, her hair and her jacket. The message said:

DAN
SHVT
MEIN

Just like that with the words under each other, and a V instead of a U because it was easier to scratch. And no space between the last two words.

'That was really clever,' Rosie said. 'She knew Danny would be coming back into the chamber from time to time to count his money if nothing else. She knew if she left the message in plain sight – like she did with her FFF initials – then Danny would obviously erase it. So she hid it behind her. And closed up the last two words for the same reason, to make it easier to conceal. She thought it all through.'

'I think also,' Rox said. 'That she chose a place to sit against the wall for the final time that was well away from the stack of boxes. That meant Danny would never have to move her. So he would never see the message. I did think when we chose a place to break through the wall that Felix should have scratched the joints there in the same place with her poor coin. It was the obvious place. But she didn't. She went further upstream. I think that was because she wanted to be further from the boxes so that Danny would never have cause to move her. Clever.'

Such a pity, Rosie thought, that her bones and her hidden message didn't get their final revenge. Such a pity really that Danny died in the aircrash only a few short weeks after she did, after he had sealed her in. Having out-thought Danny, even in the exceptional circumstances of being sealed into a living death, it would have been marvellous if now with the discovery of her last message, the police were to arrive at the famous living legend, national treasure, rock star's country mansion to answer some searching questions about the discovery of his long-lost bandmate. And to explain the meaning of a certain message on the wall.

On the first day of the drive home Rosie raised the question that had always been there all along lurking under the surface like an impacted splinter.

'Why did he do it?' she asked them. She was in the passenger seat and threw the question over her right shoulder. 'Danny. Why did he leave the clues?'

'You mean not just on the gold disc, but also dropping the hint to the Lion about it being 'under the drumming'?' Camo said. Because it really was under the drumming in a way, he thought.

'Yes. He risked people finding the clues, working it out, and going to the fort when he wasn't there and pinching all his gold.'

'Not only that he risked them finding Felix Fairfax's body too,' Camo said. 'And being in the frame for it.'

'But maybe he just assumed that whoever might find the coins wasn't going to be someone who would go running to the police to report a murder?' Rosie said. 'Too many questions.'

'Maybe it was his fear of flying?' Tyko suggested.

'A premonition, you mean?' Rox said.

'Exactly. Maybe he felt if he did die in an air crash, then nobody would find the gold. Maybe he felt if he wasn't around to enjoy the benefits--'

'The benefits of beating the taxman.'

'Yes. That too. If he wasn't around then maybe someone else, someone close to him perhaps, like his sister, or the Lion, might be able to work it out and they would benefit. Perhaps he preferred to have someone he knew, someone close to him, benefit rather than someone he didn't know. Like some future owner of Chateau Shagfest, maybe.'

'But who knows really. He seems to have been a simple character on the surface, but much more complicated underneath,' Rosie said.

'So maybe he did want to leave the possibility of someone finding the gold,' Tyko said, 'But no more than that. A possibility.'

'After all,' Camo said. 'Bayb never solved the clues. All she did was wait for us to make a move. Then follow us. That's a definite cheat. And it took us a long time to do it. And we had the benefit of having a specialist!' He smiled across at Rox. 'They were not easy.'

'They weren't designed to be easy,' Tyko said.

But Rosie knew they were only guessing. They never would truly understand why Danny had done what he did.

It was on the second day of the drive home that Camo received a text from Jane Shadwell.

<We need to talk urgently. Please call me>

He was in the passenger seat map-reading. Rosie was driving. He showed it over his shoulder to Tyko and Rox in the back seat. He pulled a face.

'Looks like she's pre-empted us.'

He knew he had to do it. It was the right thing to do. But he wasn't looking forward to it.

27. BOX

A few days earlier back at Fort Madeline before they set off for home Rosie had wondered aloud to Camo next morning after their breakout whether they should tidy up before leaving?

He didn't think so.

'The hole in the wall we made probably has to be repaired professionally, once the police have finished. I guess farmer Lagrange will organise that.' But no question Camo knew he'd have to tell Jane Shadwell about it.

There was one thing he wanted to do before they left. He asked the others if they wanted to join him in a last visit to the pit? Tyko replied an emphatic no. But the two women went along with him. It was one thing to be in a small place when you were trapped there. It was quite another to visit the same place when you could leave any time you wanted to.

They crossed the courtyard to the far end wall and entered the upper wheel room. They had recharged a couple of the torches, but they put all the overhead lights on in both rooms as well to throw as much light as possible through the hole in the wall. They descended the steps to the lower wheel room. Tyko had replaced the stone they'd removed back into the stair parapet. They referred to that hidey-hole now as 'the Dreyfus cavity'. The stone sat loosely in the hole. That too would need mortaring back, Camo thought. It was something else to admit to Jane Shadwell. The list of damage was getting alarmingly long.

He was the first to crawl back through the tunnel they'd dug so desperately over the course of a night and two days. The others followed him through.

Rox and Rosie came through and stood either side of Camo. They stood silently in the space. They listened to the water drumming overhead.

By their torchlight and the light leaking through the hole from the wheel room beyond they could see it was highlighting Felix Fairfax's last message. The body had been removed and now they could see quite clearly the letters she had scratched desperately on the wall and then hidden with her body in an attempt to seek justice beyond the grave.

DAN
SHVT
MEIN

Rosie was thinking about Felix alone in the dark. She had her lighter for a while. But how long did that last? She had a momentary image of Felix when the fuel had run out carrying on striking the flint to give her enough instant and fleeting spark to scratch her initials and the last message. Then at the end leaning against the wall to die, making sure she hid the words.

Rox was thinking it was fortunate they had been so busy digging their way out when they themselves had been trapped in here. Too busy in a way to consider their situation. But Felix Fairfax had had all the time in the world. Poor Felix, sitting alone in the dark, and her hopeless scratching at the mortar with the edge of a gold coin was too heartbreaking to contemplate.

Still no one said anything.

Then they left.

The drive home was uneventful. They crossed the Channel on the night of the second day and were back in London in the early hours of the following morning.

One thing they talked about on the way home was Bayb Azmoun.

'Does she get away with it?' Rosie asked aloud.

'The gold?' Tyko said. 'Not sure we can do anything about that. She's got it. We haven't.'

'No. Attempted murder.'

They all thought she shouldn't get away with it. But couldn't see what they could do about it.

'Anonymous tip-off? To the police.' Tyko said.

'We'd still have to be witnesses in any court case,' Rosie said.

'Anonymous tip-off? To the tax authorities.' Tyko persisted. 'About the ill-gotten gold.'

Better, thought Rosie. But was that enough?

'If she's any sense,' Camo said. 'Which I'm sure she has, she'll do exactly what I insinuated the Lion had done. Deposit it all in a Swiss bank account.'

'It's probably already there now,' Rox said. 'Her Swiss bank won't be telling anyone about it, least of all the US inland revenue.'

It seemed there was nothing they could do.

Rosie was wondering whether what they were actually doing as they talked about what they should do about Bayb Azmoun was tickling the tail of a dragon.

They knew from news outlets on the internet that the sensational news of the discovery of Felix Fairfax's body was out. Bayb Azmoun would already know they had escaped the tomb she had made for them. She would be spending a fretful week as she waited for the knock of the detectives on her front door. When nothing came, she would be able to relax. But would she fully relax knowing there were four people out there who knew that she had stolen millions in gold and had attempted to murder them as well?

Would she let it lie?

They couldn't say.

They drove on.

Camo replied to Jane Shadwell's text saying they were on their way home and he'd call or text her as soon as he was home. He didn't explain why they'd cut short their scheduled stay in the fort. But she probably knew about it all from the news anyway.

The day after they arrived back in London he sent an early and somewhat abrupt text to Jane saying he'd like to see her straightaway and would be down in Tunbridge Wells by early lunchtime.

'Do you want, would you like, any of us to come with you to see Jane?' Rox thought they should all share in what was likely to be a humiliating experience.

But Camo was determined it should be him and him alone to face Jane Shadwell. She hadn't met any of the others anyway.

And it would look odd and possibly intimidating if they suddenly all turned up mobhanded at her house.

He thought he might get it over with as soon as possible.

So it turned out.

He arrived at the house. For the moment he left the box of coins in the Land Rover.

As soon as Jane Shadwell opened the door Camo spoke.

'Look Jane, I have a confession to make,' he said. 'Well actually it's a series of confessions, I'm afraid.'

Jane had thrown a big beaming smile at Camo as soon as she opened the door. She still smiled even after he'd said his opening words.

Camo nearly fell over at this strange reception. This huge smile wasn't what he'd been expecting.

She continued to smile gently at him, standing there on her front door mat looking timid and apprehensive. He really did remind her of dear dear Jim in those fabulous far-off days when they were all at the sharp end and everything was possible.

'You've been looking for Danny's gold, haven't you?' she said, reaching out and touching his arm. She was still smiling. 'And dear Felix! How dreadful. What an amazing discovery! I'm so glad you found her.'

It looked like at the moment Jane didn't know that her brother was the main, in fact only, suspect in the death of Felix Fairfax, Camo realised.

'I guess that was Danny's doing? He broke her heart. More than once. And did other things. I'm glad he's not around to face the music.'

So maybe she did realise.

'But come in,' she said. 'And tell me all about it. I've got something to tell you too.'

Camo would tell her all about it. There were two stories to tell. There was the supposed background to the sensational news story; and the real story. He would tell her both.

'Sure. Sure,' he said. 'I will. We have. But just a minute.' He stepped back to the Land Rover in the drive and carried back the wooden box of four hundred and ninety-nine Krugerrands.

Earlier that day before packing the box in the Land Rover, Tyko had asked if he could see the coins one last time. The others agreed with that sentiment too.

So Camo opened it up on the kitchen table of their flat.

Tyko reached out and took out the end coin in a row. He held it up between finger and thumb. It was about an inch and a third in diameter. The gold had an astonishing elemental cleanliness. It looked immune to the fate of the universe and nonapplicable to any law of thermodynamics you could name. It looked inoculated, inoxidable, incapable of experiencing disease or illness. It was heavy and serene in his hand. It was neat. It was deeply and inherently the opposite of unkempt. It was kempt.

On one side, Tyko thought it was called the obverse, there was an image of a statesman. He guessed that this was an image of the Kruger the coin was named after. He must have been president of South Africa, he assumed, at some point. It said SOUTH AFRICA in English and SUID AFRIKA in Afrikaans in a circle round the statesman's head. He turned it over in his hand. On the back – the reverse – there was an image of a high-stepping buck or deer. Tyko guessed this might be a springbok, which he had a feeling was one of the national symbols of South Africa. Their rugby union team was called the Springboks, he knew that. The date – 1970 – was split into two numbers either side of the springbok. There was some wording in a circle towards the edge below the springbok. It said in English FINE GOLD followed by 1 oz – which he guessed was the gold weight. The Afrikaans version FEIN GOLD was repeated after the weight.

'Nice,' he said and placed it gently back in the box.

The neat parallel standing edge-on rows along the top of the box were not of the same length. One of the rows was a single coin shorter than the others. That was where Felix Fairfax had taken out her coin.

She raised an eyebrow at the box as he carried it into the

house, but said nothing. She led him to the dining room.

'Put it on the table,' she said. 'But you can keep it. Take it back. Share it. I don't want it.'

He couldn't believe what he'd heard. Did she really know what was in it? And apart from that, she was still smiling. He looked round the room very surprised. She seemed to have relatively modest means. She lived in a nice four-bedroom house in a leafy cul-de-sac in a good neighbourhood of a well-to-do town. But it was shabby, he could see. The paint on the window frames had disappeared in places and was peeling elsewhere. There were stains on the ceiling. Maybe the bath overflow had blocked and water had run through the ceiling? Perhaps she hadn't the spare funds to redecorate? There were stains on the carpets too. It looked like Jane Shadwell lived in a sort of bubble of ex-wealth, a kind of genteel poverty. Once she had money but didn't any more.

Danny probably hadn't left her much, Camo thought. There would have been so many claims on his estate by the assorted army of illegitimate offspring there mightn't have been much left over for his sister. And of course there were no royalties coming in for any songs Danny may have written. That was for the simple reason he hadn't written any. It was probably just the old band's playing, performance and screen license payments that kept her going.

She would be glad of the extra money, surely?

What was going on here?

28. DUC

A month later in mid-January of the following year, Camo Lyly was sitting in the main auction room of Christie's in New York.

He and Jane Shadwell sat on two wooden seats at the back of the packed auditorium. They had no need of bidders' paddles.

They were there to watch and listen.

A month earlier on the day before Christmas Eve Camo had stood in Jane Shadwell's dining room. He had a feeling his jaw had dropped open.

'No really,' she said. 'I know what it is. I don't want it. I don't think I'll need it.'

But before she could explain the mystery she asked Camo to fill her in on all that had happened to him and his friends on their two trips to Fort Madeline.

'The real story this time,' she said.

They sat down opposite each other at the dining table. The box of gold coins sat unopened on the table between them.

'Yes, you're right,' he confessed. 'We were looking for Danny's gold.'

'I did wonder. I looked for it myself,' she said wistfully. 'Many times. It was the only reason I kept going down to that awful stony prison. But what put you on to it?'

He brought out his phone, reached across the table and showed her Danny's lines.

Madeline got the gold with her in the hold
Madeline got the gold waiting in the cold
Madeline got the stacks never to pay tax
Madeline over under still more asunder
Madeline under over will mark a trover

'It's really gibberish, isn't it,' she said. 'Mumbo-jumbo. No wonder he couldn't write any songs.'

'We thought that too, almost to the end. But the key words are over and under.'

First he told her what she had seen on the news was only partly true. They had found Felix Fairfax, that was true. And Danny was the most likely suspect for her death. But they hadn't found her remains in the way that was being reported. He explained how they had generated the story and the background details for public consumption, particularly so they could feel safer from the person who had tried to kill them.

Jane looked shocked and clutched her hands to her chest.

'I'll explain,' Camo said.

Then he related the whole of the real story. The music memorabilia auction. The gold disc bought for Dredge. The knock backwards that revealed the word gold. Tyko's adapting of the record player to play the disc backwards. The hair-raising effect of hearing Danny's voice recite his clues for the first time. The visit to Chris Sentinel. The discovery that Madeline was a chateau in France. The first visit. Rox's surveys and plans. The arrival of a third party, Bayb Azmoun—

'I do remember her,' Jane murmured.

--the daughter of Dr Edge's old band manager, with guns. The eviction and arrest of Bayb. The hole in the recording room floor. Their discovery of the boxes of books behind the lift shaft. Their failure to find the gold.

'There's more about Bayb Azmoun later,' Camo said holding up a hand.

He went on to tell Jane Shadwell all about the second visit. Rox's realisation that the over and under in Danny's gibberish referred to the two water wheels. Their search behind the steps connecting the upper and lower wheel rooms. The discovery of the J'Accuse newspaper.

'That's interesting,' Jane said.

He went on to talk of their continued failure to crack the code. Rox's depression and her dawn walk. (At one time Camo was so worried about Rox that he actually feared in retrospect that Rox might have thrown herself into the freezing lake on that dawn stroll if she hadn't seen the manhole cover). The discovery of the entrance to the inspection pit. Their entry into the pit. The discovery of the remains of Felix Fairfax. The discovery of twenty boxes of gold coins--.

Here Jane raised an eyebrow and looked at the single box that Camo had brought.

--The arrival of Bayb Azmoun. 'My fault,' Camo said. 'She was watching us still and followed us again.'

Bayb's stealing of all but one of the boxes—

'Odd,' Jane said.

--Their imprisonment in the pit. Vinny's plumber's bass full of the vital necessary tools—

'He was ridiculous with those tools,' Jane said. 'A huge collection. And he had absolutely no intention of ever using them. I think he knew he didn't have the skills. But maybe he just didn't want to spoil them by using them.'

--Rox's determination that they had to either wait long enough for the water to drop to try to lift the manhole lid or break out through the wall of their tomb while they still had the strength to do it. The desperate arid two-day dig to tunnel out of the pit.

'That's horrible,' Jane said. 'But so brave to do that. I would just have curled up and died, I'm sure. I think many people would. That awful woman. Your Rox sounds a formidable and resourceful lady.'

She's not my lady, Camo thought. Rosie's pretty good too. Tyko did well too.

'So that's it,' Camo said. 'Bayb Azmoun stole all the other nineteen boxes.'

'Why on earth did she leave just one behind? She obviously meant for you to die in that terrible place.'

'She did it because she could,' Camo said. 'But we really don't know. No idea. But I think Danny really hurt her emotionally in some way when she was young.'

'Oh yes,' she said. 'He did that. He did that a lot.'

'So it was part of her revenge in some way, maybe. If you can take revenge on the dead.'

'He's probably still very much alive in her mind,' Jane Shadwell said.

'So, to finish, we thought you would want to have the one box of coins that Bayb left us with. I'm sorry about the other nineteen. They're rightfully yours too.'

Camo explained there were four hundred and ninety-nine gold Krugerrand coins in the box. He estimated they were worth six hundred thousand pounds in total at the current price of gold.

Jane Shadwell looked thoughtful for a moment, then kind of dismissed the box with her hand.

'Why on earth don't you want it,' he asked, perplexed. 'It's yours.'

'Well I would normally. Of course I would. But I think I'm not going to need it.' Jane Shadwell was still smiling. 'I don't think you are either.'

She could see he was totally bewildered by her attitude. He probably thought she was mightily ungrateful too, after the hard work they'd put in and the ordeal they'd all been through to obtain it. It was time she explained herself.

'Those books,' she said. 'Those French fruit books.'

Camo tilted his head a little to one side. He hadn't thought about the 'fruits' of their first trip to the fort at all for quite a while.

'I took them to an antiquarian bookseller I know,' she said. Actually she couldn't get them out of her house quick enough. 'His response was astonishing. He nearly fell off his office chair when I plonked them on his desk and showed him what was in the box. I had to take two trips to the car to carry them. He was in a frightful state after seeing just one copy. When I brought in a second copy, I thought he might need an oxygen mask. He was gasping for air. I think he actually did faint.

'That book, the Treatise on Fruit Trees, turns out to be the most expensive book in French ever sold. He told me the last time one five-volume set of it came to market was in 2006. It sold for nearly five million dollars.'

Camo stared at her. He couldn't believe what he was hearing. He hadn't even bothered to leaf through the illustrations.

Who gave a shit for fruit trees? Leathery stinky old books were such a disappointment when you were looking for gold.

'My antiquarian book chap put me in touch with Christie's. They're quite excited. Not a single copy has turned up for sale in all this time since 2006. And now to have two full intact copies in perfect condition up for sale. Well, they can't believe it.

'Their best guess is that both copies will go for at least eight million dollars each. It could be as much as ten million.'

Camo was still staring at her. His eyes felt the size of full moons.

'What I'm proposing,' she said. 'Is that I take one copy. And you and your friends take the other.'

The full moons of Camo's eyes became even bigger.

'In fact I've already drawn up a legal document transferring title and ownership of one copy from me to you.'

She said she hadn't said anything about this before 'Because it took quite a long while to go through the provenance process. And to establish that I had full legal rights to the ownership of them.'

It seemed that the Duc de Montbarrey was what Jane Shadwell described as a 'confirmed bachelor'. Camo had no idea what she meant by that, so she was forced to explain, with a certain amount of distaste exhibited by a tightly pursed mouth, that it meant that the Duc was 'a homosexual'.

And that meant in his day 'He never married and never had children. There was no family and no heirs it appears.'

It had seemed a little strange to them at the time of their first visit, Camo now said, that 'The duck got rid of the fort so quickly. Who then did Danny buy it off after the duck had drowned?'

Jane Shadwell said she thought the Duc had bought the fort in 1956; but had drowned two years later, in 1958.

Camo couldn't resist a side thought as Jane Shadwell spoke that she clearly thought of the previous owner of the fort before Danny as 'the Duc', whereas he always thought of him as 'the duck'. It sounded exactly the same, but there was a differing amount of respect involved in each spelling.

'His creditors, mainly his bank, took ownership of it when he died. It turned out that though he was a very well-known and respected antiquarian book dealer, he'd made some bad financial deals and was perilously close to bankruptcy. I imagine he was about to bring the two copies of the Treatise on Fruit Trees to market himself to put his business back on its feet. Or at least one copy. But then he drowned. People knew he owned one or two copies of the book. But they never turned up. Till now.'

'So did Danny buy Fort Madeline off the bank?'

'Yes exactly. Danny bought it in 1966. It had gone to rack and ruin in the eight years between. So even though Danny got it for a song – the bank more-or-less gave it away - he spent everything he had, nearly, making it habitable again.'

'But he loved the place, didn't he?'

'Oh yes. In many ways despite his success my brother was a troubled soul. He was very happy there. I was glad about that.'

Danny had died at the height of his fame. Camo wondered if he might have become a very sad case if he hadn't died then. A major player in the rock pantheon who became an ex-player. Constantly trying all sorts of bad and ill-advised moves in an effort to recreate his glory days. Even a laughing stock. And now, because he had died when he did he was still considered a giant. But who knew? Maybe he was being unfair.

Camo adopted a more formal tone of voice.

'Jane if you are sure about this. If you are sure you don't want both copies of the books. Then thank you. Thank you with all my heart. I say that for all of us.'

For some reason he thought of Rox, torn by feelings of inadequacy and professional failure perhaps about to throw herself off the steel walkway into the freezing water. Then the light changed and she saw what she saw.

'Never forget Arch, you found the books. Not me.'

'So what happens now?' he said.

29. BIDS

And so here they were. Camo Lyly and Jane Shadwell sitting side by side in a huge auction room in New York City.

Though he was excited at the prospects of seeing how much the fruit books would go for, Jane Shadwell was much more excited than he was. She seemed to love every minute of the process. She kept gazing round the room. For some reason she kept wondering to Camo which of the people she spotted might be francophone and therefore likely bidders. She claimed she could tell they were francophone by the shape of their mouths.

Camo picked up the catalogue on his lap. He leafed through it till he came to the entry on the two fruit books. Their books. There was all the information that he hadn't bothered to find out before.

The Treatise on Fruit Trees dated from the mid-eighteenth century. There were over five hundred illustrations throughout the five volumes by the celebrated botanist Henri Louis Duhamel du Monceau.

It was a very similar auction process to the one Camo had been to before when he outbid Jem, phone-bidding from New York, for Dr Edge's gold disc. A dapper auctioneer came out from a back room. He stood at a lectern and introduced himself and his team. By his accent he was English not American. He took them through the catalogue, the bidding process – it was the same paddle waving system that Camo had seen before – and the Powerpoint display screen on the wall behind him.

They were formally welcomed to the auction house's bi-annual winter sale of rare books. And the whole extraordinary process began.

While he could see that Jane Shadwell was revelling in every minute of it Camo himself felt like sleeping through most of it, or nipping out for a pint. But he felt he owed it to her to stay for the whole show.

He was amazed at the kind of books people were bidding for and splashing out huge sums on. His main conclusion was that when it came to books people would collect and buy any old rubbish at extortionate cost. A Gutenberg Bible? Certainly. A First Folio of Shakespeare? Yes of course. But who cared about pictures of birds for example? Even if they were American? Or some drawings bound together with text of medieval mythical monsters?

He did perk up when the auctioneer announced an item which he described as a both a 'palimpsest' and a 'codex'. Camo had no idea what either of those words meant. But it seemed the item in question was a Byzantine prayer book in Greek dating from the mid 9th century. Was that really nice to have? Camo mentally discarded it. But he straightened in his chair when it was revealed that what was really being sold here was not the prayer book but the hidden writing on the underlying parchment leaves in the codex on which the prayers had been overwritten.

The auctioneer announced that on the parchment leaves under the later prayers original works by Archimedes had been revealed. Works which had been considered lost for centuries. Millennia. Works which were only known through reference, anecdote and note form by other later writers.

The auctioneer explained that during the 'Byzantine dark ages' after the Muslim conquest of Egypt, they no longer had a source of papyrus, the material the Romans and Byzantines used to make flat sheets out of to write on, like paper. They were thus forced to use vellum and parchment. And parchment was scarce, expensive and time-consuming to make. It also killed a lot of baby animals. So they resorted to breaking up old scrolls and codices and reusing the old parchment documents and putting them to new use.

The Archimedes documents had been broken up, the surface of the parchment scraped clean, the original writing erased, and prayers written in their place. The sheets were then bound into a new volume called a 'codex', which to Camo looked indistinguishable from a book.

But with the latest ultra violet and infra red techniques in the visible and the invisible across the entire optical spectrum, the original writing could still be read under the later additions. And so a series of original works by Archimedes had been discovered.

It went for over three million dollars.

Camo was amazed. Rox would love that, he thought. Archimedes has not left the building!

It made you think, Camo reflected. When the prayer book was written over a thousand years after Archimedes his works were considered worthless. Yet now over another thousand years later it was the prayers which were considered worthless, no more than advertising slogans for a non-existent product, and the Archimedes texts which were worth a fortune. Camo hoped fervently that in another thousand years that position would not be reversed again.

'Now we come to the star of today's proceedings,' the auctioneer announced.

It was their turn at last.

The auctioneer tapped a stylus on his lectern and an image of one of their wooden boxes flashed up on the screen behind him. He tapped again. The next image showed all five volumes of the fruit book laid out on a cloth covered table. The next image showed the title page of volume one.

An assistant came in from the back room carrying a box. He placed it on the table by the side of the lectern and brought the five books out one by one and laid them out on the table

There was a loud murmur of interest from the packed room. Camo heard some whispering close by speaking in French. The auctioneer tapped his wooden disc on the lectern for silence and attention.

'What we have here is an old book about fruit trees.'

Clearly the auctioneer had a sense of humour. There was an archipelago of laughter in groups across the crammed and buzzing floor.

Turning half round to his right and leaning his left elbow on the lectern he threw the bright red dot of a laser pointer onto the title page on the screen above and behind him.

'And for those of you who can't read what it says, it's in French,' he continued.

There was more laughter.

Camo was unused to this kind of preliminary banter. And he was not amused. Get on with it you clown, he thought.

After his little levity the auctioneer turned a shade more serious and business like.

'*The Traite des Arbres Fruitiers* by Henri Louis Duhamel du Monceau published in 1768 in five volumes is one of the most valuable books ever printed in French,' the auctioneer said warming to the task of bigging up the book to the potential buyers. 'Indeed it is possible that it is the most expensive French book ever to come to the market.

'Henri Louis Duhamel du Monceau – floreat 1700 to 1782 – was one of the world's leading botanists of his day. And perhaps the most important French writer on fruit, plant physiology and agriculture at any time. He was one of the outstanding botanists of the eighteenth century. There's no question that the *Traité des Arbres Fruitiers* is one of the finest books on fruit and fruit trees ever written.

'The first volume of the five alone deals with describing and illustrating different methods of pruning and grafting. This exhaustive description of techniques encouraged propagation of fruit trees throughout France. Monceau's intention was to promote the virtue and nutritional value of fruit-bearing trees. Many different genera of fruit and a number of their different species are described in the work – including almonds, apricots, barberry, cherries, quince, figs, strawberries, gooseberries, apples, mulberries, pears, peaches, plums, grapes and raspberries. Each plate illustrates the plant's seed, foliage, blossom, and fruit, all with a number of detailed cross sections.'

Camo had to admit he was both impressed and unimpressed with the whole book-collecting mentality. It didn't seem to matter if the text was utterly tedious, factually erroneous and unreadable as long as it was early and nice-looking and the workmanship was good. On the other hand there were works up for bids here where the workmanship was atrocious, where the text was actually faulty and full of mistakes and misprints and typographical errors, and they were going for big sums too. At least the fruit book was a pioneer and was factual and in its own small universe had changed the world.

'Now,' the auctioneer said, turning back from the screen behind him to face the room again. 'When the last five volume copy of this major work came to market in 2006, it was sold here in this very room for four and a half million dollars.'

There was a murmur and several audible gasps in the audience, then a sustained ripple of applause.

'I think we're going to do better than that today. I think there's every chance of that. Therefore without further ado let us begin.'

Camo was amazed again. This time the bidding started at five million dollars. The bid levels were increased by a hundred thousand dollars each time. Paddles were raised and flashed all round him. Several persons on the phone extensions along the side wall were so keen on waving their bats Camo wondered if there was a squadron of planes landing.

'This one is actually my copy,' Jane Shadwell said, looking intently at the code numbers in the catalogue. 'Yours is next.'

Bidding kept going on, up and up. Six million dollars was rapidly achieved, and passed. Then seven million. It kept climbing. Then eight.

It slowed down a little through the lower hundreds of thousands above eight million. But after a titanic struggle between a bidder in the middle of the floor and a phone bidder on the side wall, nine million was reached, then breached.

In the end the bidder in the middle bid highest.

The first copy of the Treatise on Fruit Trees was sold for nine million three hundred thousand dollars.

'Oh dearie me,' Jane Shadwell said.

The hubbub on the bidding floor had hardly settled down before the auctioneer flashed up another image of the same book on the screen behind him.

'This is completely unprecedented. Today we have not one but two copies of the most expensive book ever printed in French. Can we start the bidding please.'

As before the bidding began at five million dollars. This time nine million dollars was reached rapidly, and passed. Then the bidding climbed and carried on climbing.

Perhaps the bidding was higher for the second copy because buyers knew when they were bidding for the first copy there was always the second one to follow. That law no longer applied. Camo's copy of the Treatise on Fruit Trees would be the last known copy of the book to come to market. There might be no other copies out there.

The winning bid was eleven million one hundred thousand dollars.

It went to the phone bidder in the bank of phone bidders along the side wall. It was rumoured to be an agent representing the Louvre.

30. SPLIT

'You three take three million each and I'll take two million one hundred thousand plus the coins?' Camo said to them all the day he came back from New York.

They thought that was fair. Easier than dividing eleven point one by four and coming away with inelegant, impractical and ungainly numbers.

Then the various taxes, fees and commissions involved in the sale of the book would be deducted equally from their shares.

Prior to the auction, once Jane Shadwell had handed over the document giving Camo legal ownership of the second copy of the Treatise on Fruit Trees, Camo had immediately contacted his lawyer and had the document modified. The fruit book became owned jointly and equally by him, Rosie, Rox and Tyko.

Having one owner also solved the problem of splitting the coins up too.

The money from the sale of the fruit book had been deposited into their bank accounts. It was by no means wealth beyond their wildest dreams. But they were now extremely wealthy by any yardstick all the same.

What would they do with the money?

There were all the conventional ideas. Share it with their parents. Buy their parents a new house. Buy new cars. Go on luxury holidays? Buy other things for themselves?

But Camo did wonder what to do with the coins. Deposit them in a Swiss bank account? Sell them? Trade them in? In the end he decided to do nothing with them. He put them into a safety deposit box at his bank. Let them accrue, he thought.

Before doing that he gave a single coin each to the other three.

He asked them to keep it. 'Please hang on to it. Don't sell it or give it away. Keep it to remember.' He was sure over time they would drift apart and go their separate ways. The gold coin would always be there as a reminder of the extraordinary adventure they had all experienced.

It was interesting, Camo thought, that when they discussed what they were going to do with the money, and indicative of the ephemeral nature of wealth, that none of them thought they should now abandon their degree studies. And all of them bar one looked forward to starting jobs and having careers in their chosen fields.

The one who didn't was Camo.

He never knew what career to go into. He had chosen to study an English degree because he liked English and liked reading. He thought it was a good idea to study what you liked best. He had no idea what he wanted to do after he graduated.

So Rox would go on to become a municipal engineer; Tyko an electrical engineer; and Rosie would become a lawyer. But Camo? He didn't know.

Maybe he would find something. Maybe he would think of something.

Camo was a drifter. He always had been a drifter. He knew there was a danger he would always be a drifter.

He didn't know what to do, but at least now he didn't have to hurry.

He knew there was a real chance he would completely spend his two million one hundred thousand dollars rapidly, fritter it away; blow it until he had nothing left. He still had his trust fund of course. But he foresaw that he would blow that as well as soon as he came into it, when Laura and Sylvia and the others were no longer controlling his access to it. He saw himself throwing money away through a dim and deep alcoholic haze for the rest of his life till he had nothing at all. And then die young.

That was one strong reason why he put the coins in a deposit box and left them there. They would act as his lifetime reserve. They would keep on rising in value, he was sure. After all, the coins were now worth £1200 each. When Danny bought them in 1970 each one was worth £30. That was an increase in value by a factor of forty. Gold would fluctuate in value, he assumed, up and down over the short term; but over the long run he felt certain it would continue to rise.

So the coins would wait and wait. They would wait and wait until he needed them.

One thing he had which he kept for the rest of his life was the maroon coloured heavy jute plumber's bass. In a way it was more valuable to him than the coins. Without it he would be dead. Without it and the tools it contained they would have been trapped in their underwater tomb, under the drumming. Without it, when their skeletons were discovered perhaps decades later, as surely sooner or later they would have been, nothing would have been left to tell their story except some small surface scratches and indentations in the stone where they had desperately tried to use a spade to dig their way out through the solid stone wall.

Because Bayb Azmoun and Lurch had never seen a bass before, and had no idea what it was, they had left it. Their immense self-satisfaction at retrieving and successfully making off with nearly fifteen million dollars in gold overwhelmed any residual curiosity they may have had.

Vinyl Strat Lyly would have been immensely pleased and gratified that his strange lifelong obsession with collecting the right tools for the right job in the right bag – but never to be used – had saved his son's life.

Camo had it framed and mounted behind glass and it had pride of place on the wall in every flat and house he ever lived in.

31. DREDGE

Jim – Dredge – Lyly died in the spring.

The funeral was a big deal. There were news items on the main news channels. There were obituaries in the newspapers. There were analytical radio and TV programmes and retrospectives. It seemed a watershed had come and gone.

For many the passing of Dredge Lyly marked the end of an epoch. He was one of the last direct links to the golden age of British music. That golden age of creativity and the laying-down of classics; an unsurpassed age, perhaps unsurpassable, perhaps never to be reached again, that had changed the world and put Britain firmly at the top of the world's cultural map.

All Camo's family and friends were there of course. But there was a mass of celebrities and cultural figureheads all come to remember and pay their respects. Chris Sentinel was there, naturally.

After the service when the crowds and media had gone Camo sat with his mother Laura and his grandmother Sylvia on a bench in the crematorium garden.

'This sadness comes from the side,' Sylvia said. 'Not the front.'

Camo knew what she meant. This time it was a kind of sideways grief. Dredge's time in the nursing home had been the worst time. Whereas when his dad died that had been a kind of devastating blasting buffeting full-frontal grief for Camo. But this was a kind of relief in a way. Because the Dredge they knew had gone a long time before he died. All he had left was the music. That was still sublime. But it was one-way traffic stuck in a one-way street. It all came out from Dredge and you couldn't send anything back in return. Life and living is a two-way process and Dredge had been a single vector for a long time.

They would miss him. They all would. But it was the Dredge from the past they would always remember, not the present.

A few days later Camo's mother Laura asked him if he would go through Dredge's room at the nursing home and see if there was anything they should retrieve.

He had a good look. But all he came away with was Dredge's guitars and the small twin Marshall amps.

And the two gold discs on the wall.

At the turn of the year, while Dredge was still alive, Camo wondered if he should tell his grandad about the discovery of Felix Fairfax and the probable truth about her fate. And if he were to, then how and what to tell him?

He had realised a while ago how precious to Dredge Fairfax was. She was the one that Dredge mistook him for more than any other. And the greeting was always accompanied by the heartfelt 'Are you coming back?' Meaning are you rejoining the band? It was a yearning. He couldn't tell whether it was for professional reasons or for emotional reasons that Dredge fifty years on constantly sought Felix's return to the band. Perhaps it was both. Every critic said that while Dr Edge remained the best of the best even after the disappearance of Felix and her replacement by Pram Johnson, they all also agreed that the band was better when Felix Fairfax was in it. Marginally perhaps, but still better. Camo could see that Dredge felt that too.

And perhaps too there had been an emotional relationship between the two guitarists? Jane had said that Danny had broken her heart, many times. Maybe each time he did so Dredge was there to help put back the pieces.

Camo also knew that whatever he told his grandad there was the strong probability he wouldn't remember it anyway.

But he thought he had to do it.

It was an afternoon when Dredge had finished the gig that Camo gently as he could told Dredge that Felix Fairfax was dead and that her remains had been found in Fort Madeline.

Tears welled in his grandad's eyes and Camo knew that he understood.

Then Dredge said something that really shook Camo.

'Danny did it, didn't he?'

Camo said that it was very likely.

They never talked about it again. But for the rest of his life on his arrival Dredge never greeted Camo as if he were Felix, nor ever asked if she was returning to the band.

And again earlier, shortly after the new year, when they returned from New York, Camo asked Jane Shadwell if she would like to go with him to visit Jim Lyly?

She said yes of course.

They went in the afternoon. Camo thought Dredge might be under the beech tree – the music tree he thought of it now – at the end of the nursing home grounds. He hoped he was making music. Even though it was January, Camo thought making music under the beech tree was the most important thing in Dredge's life. He would do it even in the cold of winter.

They went to the nursing home. It turned out that Dredge was in the garden setting up his guitar and the two small Marshall amps under the beech tree. It was cold but clear and sunny. Dredge was wearing his habitual blue jeans, maroon Texas-cowboy steel-heel-and-toe-tipped snake boots and a faded black denim shirt. He had an olive-green US Army M65 field jacket over the top. And over that he wore a blue heavy-duty down-filled sleeveless vest. He was wearing tight leather gloves. The black woolly hat perched on his head made his long grey white hair stick out in sideways bulges either side of his head like Roger Rabbit's ears before dropping down to his shoulders.

Camo and Jane approached the beech tree and the stool on which Dredge sat tuning his guitar. He hadn't yet plugged the amp lead in.

'Arch?' Dredge said looking up from his guitar as Camo's shadow fell on him. 'Come for the gig?'

That was good, Camo thought. It didn't often go like that.

'Yes. Of course.'

'You've got the best seats.'

There was only one seat. A wooden bench. This was a piece of garden furniture by the bird bath on a piece of hard standing set at an angle to the beech tree.

'Jim?' Jane Shadwell said. She approached Dredge on his stool.

Dredge seemed to notice her for the first time. He looked up. A wave seemed to pass across his face. It was a physiological tsunami.

'Ja—' he said as though he could start the name but couldn't finish it.

But he got it. 'Oh Jane,' he said. 'Jane.' He stood up. They embraced and hugged each other laughing and giggling.

He really did seem to recognise her, Camo could see. He was amazed.

There was no gig that day. Dredge and Jane sat side by side on the wooden bench under the beech tree. They talked and talked. For a short time Jim Lyly seemed to know where he was and what was going on. He was Dredge again.

Camo watched them. His heart was lifted. He listened to them.

He left them there holding hands under the beech tree.

She came every day after that. Every day until he died.

32. FORT

Camo kept his speed down on the autoroutes, the French motorways, to not much more than a hundred and five miles an hour. That speed really seemed to suit the 911.

He was heading south. The late summer heat reflected off the road surface.

It was three and a half years since the sale of his copy of the Treatise on Fruit Trees had enabled Camo to come back from New York an extremely wealthy man.

For over three years Camo had done not much at all. He had graduated, they all had. But he never found a job. But something that did surprise him was he hadn't just explosively and comprehensively burnt through all his money. He had been relatively frugal. He'd bought things, of course he had. The Porsche 911 was evidence of that. But the bulk of his money remained. And he hadn't even come into the trust fund yet.

But there remained a gap in his life. He felt directionless. He was drifting still. Rosie had moved on. She had left him. She found it difficult to live with someone who sometimes stayed up all night blitzing on streamed box sets and who sometimes couldn't be bothered to get up in the morning.

He needed something to do. He knew it. His friends knew it. But the solution never arrived.

Then one night he caught the end of a documentary on The Great Stink of 1858 and how municipal engineer Joseph Bazalgette created the great network of intercepting sewers under London to cleanse the river and prevent further outbreaks of cholera.

It all came back to him. Engineering. Knowledge of how and why things didn't fall down. But primarily it was Rox and her knowledge. Without her knowledge they would have got nowhere in their search for the gold. More importantly it was Rox and her knowledge that got them out of the pit.

And though Jane Shadwell always said to him that he should never forget that he had found the fruit books, not her, Camo knew it was actually Rox who had found the books. Rox with her surveys and plans and scale drawings.

Next day he signed up for a university degree course in civil engineering. Then he enlisted in a cramming school to gain the necessary maths and science A levels. A little to his immediate surprise he passed them easily. He would be back at university in the autumn as a mature student.

Now the temperature rose up another notch as he hit the motorway hard and hammered southwards down the Rhone valley beyond Lyon.

Further south, but north of Marseille, he turned east through Aix-en-Provence and ran parallel to the Mediterranean coast on the autoroute behind the line of arid red-baked heat-shattered tree-spotted coastal hills. Later he turned off the motorway at the exit for Cannes and Grasse. He ignored the road south to Cannes and the coast and chose the northern option to Grasse. He put his foot down on the curving mountain road.

He was heading up the mountain to the perfume town of Grasse. Nearly all the world's perfumiers were born near Grasse or did their training there. The best 'noses' – those who designed and made perfumes – had all at some point in their careers worked or studied in Grasse. It was the surrounding lavender fields that had caused Grasse to be the centre of the perfume industry. The extract from the plant historically formed the base of most perfumes. That was still the case.

Camo wasn't seeking perfumes. He headed through and past the town perched on its hillside. He headed for a new big modern building stuck on the top of the mountain shoulder overlooking the town.

He was heading for Grasse penitentiary.

He was meeting Jem.

At some point well over a year ago, Camo had wondered privately without talking about it with the other three if there was anything they could still do about Bayb Azmoun.

She had after all got away with attempted murder. She must

have been surprised when there were no repercussions when the news of Felix Fairfax's discovery was announced. She must have wondered why "the kids" were keeping quiet. Camo was a little surprised she hadn't already come calling to find out exactly why they weren't talking and hadn't said anything to the police about her. And for Bayb Azmoun the fear would always be they hadn't said anything to the police *yet*. There was the continual risk that they might. Could she continue to function with that proviso imperilling her new life of luxury? It might be that at some point she would decide that she couldn't. And what would she do then? Would she finish the job she thought she'd already completed?

The condition of dissatisfaction and unrest worked both ways. For all the time that Camo and Rosie had lived together after they came back from Fort Madeline, Rosie could never relax. She often reported to Camo that she was convinced she had seen Azmoun in the street, or had seen a blacked-out SUV acting suspiciously by driving slowly along the street, as though searching for their whereabouts. Twice she demanded that they move address because she thought she had seen Azmoun in the neighbourhood.

Of course she wasn't there. Or was she?

That was the worrying thing. It was a problem that needed solving. And Camo thought it must be down to him to solve it. He was the one that had brought Bayb Azmoun shadowing after them. It was indirectly his fault that Bayb Azmoun and Lurch had sealed them in the pit.

He began to have the beginnings of an idea.

He didn't tell any of the others what he had in mind. Not even Rosie who was still with him at the time.

He hired a private detective.

The detective reported back a few weeks later.

Bayb Azmoun was living in a luxury apartment overlooking Central Park in New York.

Jem had been sentenced to four years gaol time for assaulting, shooting at and wounding a French police officer. With good behaviour he would be out in three years.

Then all Camo could do was wait. He waited for over a year.

Later the private detective reported to Camo again. This time it itemised Jem's actual release date.

But this wasn't the nasty sexually aggressive Jem that Camo had known. He had changed. He had been badly hurt in a knife fight in prison, the report said. His spinal cord had been badly damaged and had nearly been completely severed. He could barely walk.

Camo had the car serviced for a long journey.

He also removed a number of the gold Krugerrands from the box in the safety deposit vault at the bank. He cashed them in. He had them changed into dollars.

He bought a broad leather money belt from a camping and outdoor shop.

He set off for France.

Camo parked the 911 on the wide gravel expanse outside the tall steel double doors of Grasse penitentiary.

There was no one else waiting.

At exactly midday the port in one of the big steel doors opened and a stooped thin figure in a black suit hobbled out through the gate. He was walking slowly and painfully with the aid of two long aluminium crutches.

Camo emerged from the car and walked towards the figure in the black suit. He could see that the suit hung loosely on the man like a poncho.

'Hello Jem,'

Jem stopped and looked up. He leaned on his elbows on the crutches.

'Son,' he said. 'Didn' think it'd be you here.'

'Can I buy you a drink?'

Jem said he couldn't see why not.

He was a pitiful shrunken figure. Camo had to lift Jem's legs into the passenger seat well of the 911.

'Nice,' Jem said, peering round at the inside of the car. 'Real nice.'

Camo drove to a bar he'd noticed down the mountain on the outskirts of Grasse. It was quiet.

He helped lift Jem's feet out of the car then waited at the door to the bar as Jem struggled out and then hobbled and limped from the car on his crutches. They took their beers to a corner table and sat down.

Jem took a deep draught.

'How do you feel about Bayb Azmoun?' Camo said. 'Do you know she took nineteen boxes of gold coins from the fort? She took exactly nine thousand five hundred coins. They're worth roughly fourteen or fifteen million dollars. Did you ever see any of that money?'

Jem's shoulders seemed to sag. He clenched a fist and sucked air through tight front teeth.

'Bitch. Bitch left me to rot.' It was an unconscious echo of Bayb's own words about him, Camo noted. 'Didn' pay for legal. No smart Paree attorney like she got. I only got a local dude. No feckin' good. She done me over. No son I never saw no money. I never saw no gold. Three years. I was just doin' my job. What she paid me to do.' He coughed. 'Three years.'

Camo unbuckled the money belt from around his waist. The belt was thickly padded with the wads of dollar notes in the zipped compartment lining the whole inside length of its perimeter. He laid it heavily on the surface of the table in the corner of the bar. No one else was watching.

'There are fifty thousand dollars in that belt.'

Jem cocked his head to one side. Then he sipped his beer. He didn't smile, but his eyes gleamed at the sight and the prospect. Then his eyes became black seeds, dull and lifeless. He looked very very serious.

'Where is she living now, son?' was all he said.

Camo drove Jem down to Cannes railway station and dropped him off there. He hoped he would never see him again.

There was one more place he wanted to go to in France

before heading home.

He headed west, then south.

The next day he made his way slowly – much more slowly than the times in the Land Rover – up the packhorse trail up through the trees to Fort Madeline.

As always he stopped the car where the road crested out and looked across the lake to the fort.

It was hot up here in the summer sun, he thought.

He drove over the steel decking of the modern drawbridge and stopped in front of the double wooden doors of the archway. He opened the doors and parked the car in the courtyard beyond. He closed the doors behind him again. He didn't want to be disturbed. He unloaded the sleeping bag and the large amount of provisions he'd bought from the supermarket down the valley.

He sat in the kitchen and ate a sandwich. He checked the mobile signal on his phone was good and strong. He didn't want to miss anything at this stage.

He sent an encrypted text via WhatsApp to the private detective.

<Make your way there now> it said.

Two days later he began to receive regular updates from the private detective. He was installed in New York. He was watching the building and monitoring the news channels.

Camo spent ten days alone in Fort Madeline while he waited for news. He walked the long corridors at night and sometimes in the dawn. He kicked a football against the courtyard wall. He hiked along the trails in the woods. Occasionally he ventured further, up above the treeline into the high ground among the surrounding mountain peaks and cols. He followed the lake's incoming stream back along its course as far as he could, all the way to its source in a patch of swampy ground in a high and treeless corrie. He skimmed flat stones across the surface of the lake and counted the skips, and threw others far out into the depths until his arm ached. He waited.

This was his first trip back to the fort since they'd all been there together, on their second trip looking for the gold under the mill race. None of them had been back since. None of them wanted to go back.

Jane Shadwell had decided not to sell the fort. She had started coming down to the place herself. She had even begun to enjoy the place, she told Camo. 'Now I know Danny's gold is not hidden there, I can relax. I can appreciate the place. It really is a beautiful and dramatic place. I see now why Danny felt at home there.'

She'd had the stones replaced in the holes they made, he noted.

He didn't reverse the sluice gates to lower the water in the mill race and try to enter the inspection pit. He never wanted to go in there again.

After ten days Camo's phone pinged.

He opened up WhatsApp. There was no message. Only a link to the website of an American news channel.

He followed the link. A piece of video ran on the screen.

The anchor woman said the bodies of three people had been found dead in a particular exclusive thirteen-storey apartment block overlooking Central Park in New York. One of the bodies had been found in the street at the foot of the building. It was the working assumption by the police that this body had fallen or had been pushed off the balcony of the penthouse apartment on the thirteenth and topmost floor. The other two bodies had been found shot dead inside the apartment.

The body on the sidewalk was that of Bayb Azmoun, the daughter and only child of renowned rock-group manager Lionel 'The Lion' Azmoun.

One of the bodies inside the apartment belonged to a minor criminal by the name of Jeremiah Clay, a one-time associate of Bayb Azmoun's who was known to have formerly worked as her bodyguard. He had been shot dead. Clay was reported to have been recently released from gaol in Europe.

The other body inside the apartment was that of Jodee-Maree 'Lurch' Rozamund, a former professional bodybuilder and associate of Bayb Azmoun who was known to have been working as her current bodyguard. She had also been shot dead. The bullets recovered from both bodies had been fired by the same gun.

Why the daughter of a famous music manager and impresario needed a bodyguard was unknown.

The police were currently working on the theory that the deaths were the result of some kind of falling out between the three people.

It was faintly possible the death of Bayb Azmoun, presumed to have fallen from the top floor, was accidental, if unlikely, the news anchor said. Although suicide had not yet been ruled out.

There were two crutches alongside the body of Jeremiah Clay. They were assumed to be his. Reports said he had been badly injured in a series of fights while in gaol.

It was assumed by some that Jeremiah Clay had arrived at his former boss's home looking for his old job back, only to find the position had another incumbent. This had led to a deadly argument between them, followed by gunshots.

How Rozamund came to be shot was currently pure speculation. Two guns were found in the apartment. The weapon that had fired the shots that had killed both Clay and Rozamund was her own gun, registered to her.

The most popular theory, rife in the newspapers Camo had the detective send him the online links to over the next few days, said that none of the deaths was accidental. It was as the result of some kind of deadly rivalry between the two bodyguards, one current, one former. It was seen as obvious that Lurch Rozamund certainly had the physique and the strength to throw her employer over the safety guard rail on the thirteenth floor balcony. If she had done so, for whatever reason, perhaps because despite the crutches Azmoun was intending to give Clay his old job back. Then in a fit of intense anger perhaps, after such a rejection, she had thrown her boss over the rail, returned inside, shot Clay, then had then shot herself. It was speculated that remorse over what she had just done might have been an issue.

Detectives were working on the case. Further bulletins from

the police were expected at any time.

It all seemed very unlikely to Camo. The Jem he had seen wasn't capable of looking after his own body let alone guarding anyone else's. So why would Bayb Azmoun even contemplate offering him his job back?

He would continue to monitor the news media for a while to see if a more likely and plausible scenario emerged over the coming weeks. It was possible that the truth might never emerge. Perhaps no one would ever now what happened between the three of them that night on the thirteenth floor of the Central Park apartment block.

Camo didn't mind if the truth never came out.

It was time to go home, Camo knew.

He closed down all that needed to be closed down in the fort. He locked up. He headed down the packhorse trail one last time. He didn't look back. Then he headed north.

What would he do next?

He didn't know.

Would he complete the engineering degree course?

He didn't know.

What would he do after that?

He didn't know. But he would think of something.

Mark Moore
90,600 words
Casita Galgo
2020

Printed in Poland
by Amazon Fulfillment
Poland Sp. z o.o., Wrocław

53042263R00161